Clara knew that look on Tyree's face, and it spelled nothing but trouble.

Now she understood why he'd been so good at his chosen profession. It wasn't just tight breeches and a billowy shirt that made a man a pirate. It was his actions. A pirate didn't follow rules. He simply took what he wanted. And though Tyree denied it, she had the distinct feeling that what he wanted was her.

"What kind of bargain?" she asked.

One black brow arched. "Would it matter?"

"That depends on what you have in mind."

She was also beginning to realize that her own pirate fantasy ran deeper than she'd ever imagined.

Dear Reader,

It's fall and the kids are going back to school, which means more time for you to read. And you'll need all of it, because you won't want to miss a single one of this month's Silhouette Intimate Moments, starting with *In Broad Daylight*. This latest CAVANAUGH JUSTICE title from award winner Marie Ferrarella matches a badge-on-his-sleeve detective with a heart-on-her-sleeve teacher as they search for a missing student, along with something even rarer: love.

Don't Close Your Eyes as you read Sara Orwig's newest. This latest in her STALLION PASS: TEXAS KNIGHT miniseries features the kind of page-turning suspense no reader will want to resist as Colin Garrick returns to town with danger on his tail—and romance in his future. FAMILY SECRETS: THE NEXT GENERATION continues with *A Touch of the Beast*, by Linda Winstead Jones. Hawk Donovan and Sheryl Eldanis need to solve the mystery of the past or they'll have no shot at all at a future...together. Award-winning Justine Davis's hero has the heroine *In His Sights* in her newest REDSTONE, INCORPORATED title. Suspicion brings this couple together, but it's honesty and passion that will keep them there. A cursed pirate and a modern-day researcher are the unlikely—but perfect—lovers in Nina Bruhns's *Ghost of a Chance*, a book as wonderful as it is unexpected. Finally, welcome new author Lauren Giordano, whose debut novel, *For Her Protection*, tells an opposites-attract story with humor, suspense and plenty of irresistible emotion.

Enjoy them all—then come back next month for more of the best and most exciting romance reading around, only in Silhouette Intimate Moments.

Yours,

Leslie J. Wainger
Executive Editor

Please address questions and book requests to:
Silhouette Reader Service
U.S.: 3010 Walden Ave., P.O. Box 1325, Buffalo, NY 14269
Canadian: P.O. Box 609, Fort Erie, Ont. L2A 5X3

GHOST *of a* CHANCE
NINA BRUHNS

Silhouette®

INTIMATE MOMENTS™

Published by Silhouette Books

America's Publisher of Contemporary Romance

SILHOUETTE BOOKS

ISBN 0-373-27389-4

GHOST OF A CHANCE

This edition published by arrangement with Harlequin Books S.A.

® and TM are trademarks of Harlequin Books S.A., used under license.
Trademarks indicated with ® are registered in the United States Patent
and Trademark Office, the Canadian Trade Marks Office and in other
countries.

Visit Silhouette Books at www.eHarlequin.com

Printed in U.S.A.

Books by Nina Bruhns

Silhouette Intimate Moments

Catch Me If You Can #990
Warrior's Bride #1080
Sweet Revenge #1163
Sins of the Father #1209
Sweet Suspicion #1277
Ghost of a Chance #1319

NINA BRUHNS

credits her Gypsy great-grandfather for her great love of adventure. She has lived and traveled all over the world, including a six-year stint in Sweden. She has been on scientific expeditions from California to Spain to Egypt and The Sudan, and has two graduate degrees in archeology (with a specialty in Egyptology). She speaks four languages and writes a mean hieroglyphics!

But Nina's first love has always been writing. For her, writing for Silhouette Books is the ultimate adventure. Drawing on her many experiences gives her stories a colorful dimension, and allows her to create settings and characters out of the ordinary. Two of her books have won the prestigious Romance Writers of America Golden Heart Award for writing excellence.

A native of Canada, Nina grew up in California and currently resides in Charleston, South Carolina, with her husband and three children.

She loves to hear from her readers, and can be reached at P.O. Box 746, Ladson, SC 29456-0746 or by e-mail via the Harlequin Web site at www.eHarlequin.com.

For the members of the Charleston Author Society, especially Tamar Myers and Mary Alice Monroe, whose faithful friendship and steadfast loyalty mean the world to me. I would be lost without you amazing ladies!

For the members of the Summerville Writers' Guild, who bring liveliness and perspective to the craziness of the writing biz. Thanks for the inspirational hours spent in your company!

For the members of the Lowcountry RWA, bastion of romance fiction, wonderful camaraderie and killer lunches. Y'all rock!

Prologue

Magnolia Cove, Frenchman's Island, South Carolina
One week shy of 200 years ago...

Captain Sullivan Fouquet stared in horror as the woman he loved sank to the tavern floor in a pool of blood.

"God's Bones, St. James! What have you done?"

"'Twas not a'purpose! You saw what happened, Fouquet. She put herself in front of my pistol! Damned wench, what was she thinking?"

Throwing himself onto his knees beside his beloved Elizabeth, Sully gathered her to his breast, grasping her sweet, bloodied hand between his. "I swear on her eyes, St. James, if she dies, friend or no, I'll see you to your grave."

His heart wrenched as those self-same eyes fluttered open, her gaze upon him liquid and apologetic. "I'm sorry, my love," she whispered. Her body gave a little shudder, and then the light went out of her forever.

"No!" he cried, anguish sweeping through him like a cruel northern wind.

"My God, what have I done?" St. James murmured.

Sully turned to the man who had joined him on his knees on the other side of Elizabeth's body.

"Damn you," he swore, fury mounting. He sprang to his feet, whipping his sword from the sheath hanging at his chair. "You've killed her!"

"Calm yourself. It was not my intention, as well you know."

"Not true!" He lunged at the friend who was friend no more, aiming his blade at the blackguard's heart. "You loved her. You wanted her for yourself!"

"Don't be an ass, Fouquet."

St. James swiftly sidestepped his thrust. Sully drew back and thrust again, missing by a narrow margin. His rage doubled.

St. James snatched his weapon from the table. "Stop this before you come to harm. You are mad with grief."

"And you are a dead man!"

"Tomorrow you may pound me to your heart's content—till I am bloodied and blue if it will help. But stay your hand now, when it will only lead to misfortune. Think of the spoils of our last voyage, waiting for us on the island. It takes both of us to find it!" He parried Sully's lightning fast attack.

"The only fortune I seek now is your soul cursed to eternal hell on earth!"

"If so, I'll see you when the flames burn hottest, my friend," his betrayer muttered, furiously repelling his blade's assault. "Christ's Tears, Sully. Give it up, man!"

They danced across the tavern floor, sword a' sword, onlookers astonished to see the two fast friends in mortal combat. Suddenly, a blinding pain seared Sully's side. His blade dropped from his hand and he grabbed at the blood that bloomed from the gaping slash.

"And now you've killed me, too."

"God forgive me, you gave no choice."

As his limbs grew weak, the awful unfairness of this ignoble end to life settled over Sully like a gossamer shroud. He should have met his fate on the sea he loved so much, forcing the surrender of an enemy merchantman. Or in bed where he'd spent his happiest hours, coaxing the surrender of his ladylove. Now he'd know none of those things ever again.

He sank to his knees, looking up into the face of the man he'd loved as a brother. "Tyree," he whispered, beckoning.

"Save your breath, my friend. I'll fetch the leech."

"To the devil I curse you…"

"Lie down, now," St. James urged him. "'Tis not so bad as you think." But the anguished sheen in his comrade's eyes belied the soothing words.

He felt a sudden pang of sympathy for his murderer. Perhaps the man didn't deserve damnation for quite eternity. They had kept faith for half a lifetime, after all.

"May you haunt this earth for two hundred years, St. James—" Sully gasped, his breath coming short, his mind swimming in a thick, black fog "—or until you find a love so strong the lady is willing to die in your place, as did my Elizabeth."

But as he spoke, his gaze fell upon the lifeless body of his own true love. Nay! He reached for his fallen sword. With his last breath, he swung the blade true, piercing the heart of the man who had killed her.

"The devil I curse you, Tyree St. James."

And then he died.

Chapter 1

Magnolia Cove, Frenchman's Island, South Carolina
Sunday, mid-May, present day

God's Teeth, there was a woman in his bedroom!

Well, not actually a woman, but a woman's *things*. Which was bad enough.

What the hell was going on?

Tyree St. James barely stifled the urge to bellow at the top of his lungs for Mrs. Yates. Barely, for even after two centuries on dry land, the instincts of a sea captain still ran strong in his blood. Rose Cottage was *his*, and it was *his* bedroom and *his* bed the small pile of pink tapestry suitcases lay upon. Mrs. Yates had no business letting a perfect stranger intrude on the sacrosanct privacy Tyree had worked so hard for so long to maintain.

With a quick turn of his bucket-top boot, he stalked straight for the main house to have it out with the meddling old crone. How dare she? They had an arrangement.

No women on the property. None. Ever.

Preventing that circumstance was at the very foundation

of Mrs. Yates's caretaker duties. The one inviolable law between the two of them. The reason he'd originally selected her, a matronly widow, to continue the old tradition as the earthly steward of all he possessed.

And why she knew damned well that installing a woman—*any* woman—in his bed was completely, unremittingly unacceptable.

The fact that he hadn't actually slept since the night he'd run his best friend through, and therefore had little practical use for a bed, was irrelevant. Sleep had been the last thing on his mind when establishing the No Women Rule.

The real problem was, of course, sex.

Tyree streaked through the solid oak backdoor to the kitchen without bothering to open it—one of the handier abilities he'd acquired since being cursed with his present condition—and stopped dead in his tracks.

Mrs. Yates was sitting, cozy as could be, drinking tea at his kitchen table with the woman he assumed was the intruder.

He gritted his teeth at the sight of her. *Perfect stranger, indeed.* Young. Vibrant. Beautiful. Everything he'd been avoiding for so long he thought he'd forgotten what the painful slam of sexual attraction felt like.

What was Mrs. Yates trying to do? Kill him? He couldn't even manage a humorless smile at the irony.

Sliding silently through the wall into the large butler's pantry, he carefully cracked the door, snapped up his eye patch and peered through the opening. He knew the interloper almost surely would not see him even if he sat upon the chair directly across from her, but he didn't want Mrs. Yates to know he was about. He'd discover what nefarious scheme the old biddy had in her devious mind before confronting her. And then he'd let her know in no uncertain terms it wasn't going to work.

He had only one week left to endure this accursed state, and then he'd be well and truly quit of the bedevilment he'd suffered under for nearly two hundred years. He wasn't about to risk messing up his reprieve. God knew what strings were attached to that ridiculous love provision Sully had tacked on to his dying curse, but Tyree had no intention of finding out.

He'd come close once, and his heart was still smarting from the experience.

"Just imagine," Mrs. Yates was saying, "having such good luck on your first day!"

First day of what?

The village of Magnolia Cove on tiny Frenchman's Island, South Carolina, didn't have a hell of a lot to offer a visitor, and nothing at all that involved luck of any kind. A small, white sand beach, a dilapidated charter fishing boat, a couple of shabby antique shops, a few reportedly haunted houses—he did manage a smile at that—a restaurant of questionable culinary regard and…oh, God, *the Magnolia Cove Pirate Museum*.

Tyree almost groaned out loud. He should have known.

He was sick to death of hearing about his best friend and arch rival, Captain Sullivan Fouquet—or would be, if he wasn't already dead. For too many years, he'd had to suffer the hordes of euphoria-waxing historians and romance-swooning tourist ladies who invaded his remote coastal hideaway—all seeking to worship his benighted friend Sully and vilify Tyree himself.

Hell, just because he'd run the bugger through and shot the man's light-skirted wench didn't make Tyree a bad fellow. Both had been terrible accidents, after all. But everyone shed crocodile tears over the romantic, untimely demise of Captain Sullivan and the comely Elizabeth, giving the evil Captain Tyree St. James the moniker "Blackbeard of Magnolia Cove."

Damn it, he didn't even *have* a beard.

Next weekend, the village was hosting the annual Magnolia Cove Pirate Festival, where Tyree would no doubt be forced to endure yet more indignities to his already black reputation.

Obviously, the female now sitting in his kitchen must be another Sullivan Fouquet fanatic. Tyree clamped his jaw hard. Even from the blasted grave, the man wouldn't leave him in peace. Would he ever be quit the irksome bastard?

He parried a sudden stab of unreasonable pique. What could a pretty young thing like that possibly see in Sully, anyway, especially now that he was dead? Had the infamous Cajun captain still been alive, well, Tyree had no doubt as to the answer. But he wasn't. That left only one possibility. She had to be after the treasure of their last voyage, like everyone else.

"Yes, it was pretty amazing," the intruder replied to Mrs. Yates in a low, throaty voice that sent flames scorching through Tyree's loins. He could just imagine that voice murmuring words of encouragement in his ear as he moved in and out—

Christ's Bones! This was exactly what he'd feared. It had been so long…. He'd hoped he'd forgotten how much he loved the feel of lying between a woman's thighs.

Swallowing hard, he tried to block the woman's enticing voice and only hear her words.

"The sailor's diary is just what I was looking for," she said. "I'm sure I'll find the information I need to retrace Captain Fouquet's last voyage and find the lost gold."

Tyree rolled his eyes. Just *once* he'd like to be wrong.

Sullivan Fouquet was a damned menace, and he'd have thought so even if the man hadn't cursed him to wander the earth for two centuries seeking something he could never hope to find—not that he'd allowed himself to try. For how could any honorable man, even one in Tyree's present predicament, ask a mortal woman to die just to release him from his curse? It was a dilemma with no good solution, other than to wait it out.

Only one week left….

"I still can't believe nobody ever found the diary in your library before this," the young woman remarked.

What diary?

Mrs. Yates sipped her tea, and said in a much-too-innocent tone, "It *is* rather miraculous. It must have been fate, my dear."

Fate, schmate. Tyree knew her all too well to believe any such thing. No, he thought, and tossed his eye patch onto a pantry shelf. Mrs. Yates with her mysterious diary had something up her Belgian lace sleeve. He'd bet another century of purgatory on it.

Clara Fergussen yawned and glanced up from her reading to check the brass ship's clock on the mantle. It was after midnight. Mrs. Yates had retired a while ago and Clara should be getting to bed, too. Tomorrow would be a full day.

She looked down longingly at the old handwritten diary she'd checked out of the library, wanting nothing more than to dive back into the curled, faded pages and continue her reading. Even though the seaman had not sailed with Fouquet but his disreputable partner, the insights were still fascinating. She was so excited about her precious find she probably wouldn't sleep anyway.

Her first day in Magnolia Cove and already she was well on the way to fulfilling her lifelong dream. She could scarcely believe it!

Her friends and family back in Kansas all thought she was out of her mind to want to travel the world in search of new, exciting experiences. But Clara's dream was to win a berth on *Adventure Magazine*'s year-long, round-the-world yacht trip. The voyage, plus a generous freelance contract, was first prize in the magazine's annual contest to find new writing talent.

With a sleepy smile, she closed the diary in her hands and stowed it carefully on the top shelf of the bookcase along with her notes. An aspiring travel writer, she'd already made it to the final round of the contest by penning a poignant article about finding adventure in one's own backyard.

But for her finalist story, she'd ventured a little farther afield. Scraping together her meager savings from her job as copy editor for her hometown newspaper, she'd come all the way to this remote village on the coast of South Carolina to write the winning story about her lifelong passion.

Pirates.

Clara had always loved pirates. Ever since discovering black-and-white movies on TV at the tender age of four, she'd drooled over Errol Flynn and Douglas Fairbanks Jr., and had taken up collecting swords and ships-in-a-bottle shortly there-after. Of course, the fact that her great-great-great-great-granduncle on her mother's side was the famous Louisiana swashbuckler, Sullivan Fouquet, may have had something to do with her unusual obsession. But for whatever reason, she'd always found the sight of a handsome rogue with an eye patch totally irresistible.

Surely, the scandalous exploits of her distant ancestor would prove just as compelling to *Adventure Magazine*'s judging panel as to her. And now that she'd discovered this unknown sailor's diary, first prize was as good as hers.

After quietly closing the backdoor of the main house be-hind her, Clara started down the brick path leading to the tiny bungalow Mrs. Yates was letting her stay in during her six days on Frenchman's Island. Yet another miracle.

She'd met the delightful Mrs. Yates within minutes of ar-riving in the quaint historical village where the Pirate Museum was located. Because of the big Pirate Festival this coming Saturday, the few hotel rooms in Magnolia Cove had long ago been reserved, and Clara had expected to have to stay at a tacky motel about ten miles inland in the bigger city of Old Fort Mystic. But after hearing about her project, Mrs. Yates had insisted she stay at Rose Cottage. The gardener's bunga-low had no one living in it, and she'd be grateful for the com-pany.

Clara took in a deep lungful of the unfamiliar and, to a Midwestern girl, slightly exotic Carolina air. The night was warm and pleasantly sultry, filled with the flowery scents of the lush English garden, the fecund aroma of springtime on the salt marsh, and a tangy hint of the nearby sea. A brumming of frogs and chirping of insects filled the stillness as she wound her way through the tangle of climbing roses and flowers surrounding Rose Cottage and the gardener's bungalow.

Softly humming to herself, she looked up at the black night sky, spangled with a swath of twinkling stars. The whole place was magical. If ever the urge to settle down hit her, it would only be somewhere exactly like this which might have the power to quell the unrequited wanderlust in her blood.

Not that anything ever could. Her yen was for travel, excitement and passion. If she succeeded in her quest to get to the heart of the elusive Captain Fouquet and capture his excitement on paper, the resulting article had a great chance to win her the year-long yacht trip, the freelance contract and launch her exciting new career as a travel writer. And finally gain her the respect of her doubting family and friends.

Anticipation bubbled through her. Hugging herself, she spun dizzily in a full circle on the brick path. She wanted this so badly she could taste it.

Nothing would stop her now. Finally, finally, her real life would begin!

And on top of all that, she had six more days to spend researching her very favorite obsession, along with enjoying a day-long festival dedicated to the memory of her sexy, handsome, pirate ancestor.

How could it get any better?

Taking the front steps two at a time, she flung open the door and let herself into the two-room bungalow. Inside, it was cool and quiet, a soft breeze blowing through French doors off her bedroom. Following the breeze, she went through the living room into the bedroom and then walked past the billowing curtains out onto a postage-stamp-size veranda.

A few feet below, pink foxgloves winked up at her. Beyond a white picket fence, the spartina grass of the salt marsh swayed gently in the moonlight. Compared to the endless cornfields and prairies of Kansas, the sight seemed straight out of an old movie. Any second now, she expected to see the pirate Lafitte's sloop or Sullivan Fouquet's two-rigger sail up to anchor at Mrs. Yates's stiltlike dock.

What an unbelievable thrill that would be!

Clara had always harbored a secret fantasy of being swept away, captured by a devilishly handsome man in thigh-high boots and a lacy white shirt. Unfortunately, despite many a steamy daydream, she'd never actually met a man who came close—other than in the pages of her favorite romance novels.

She yawned. Perhaps tonight Sullivan Fouquet would come to her in her dreams. The atmosphere at the cottage certainly lent itself to flights of imagination. She'd be his ladylove, Elizabeth, and he'd make love to her as no man had ever done before. She sighed at the thought.

Her body thrumming pleasantly and her mind filled with delightful visions of olive skin and tight breeches, Clara wandered back into the bedroom. Too bad she hadn't brought any of those romance novels along. Yawning again sleepily, she flipped off her shoes and slid off her shorts. She turned on the muted Tiffany-style lamp, then went to the antique armoire that served as a closet and pulled her nightshirt from the drawer.

Catching sight of her dim reflection in the mirrored door, she sat down on the mattress. Even in the near darkness, she could see a glow about her that was unmistakable. Her whole future lay before her like a beckoning smorgasbord. It was amazing the difference a little expectation could make on a woman's face.

With yet another deep yawn, she leaned back on her elbows and let her heavy eyelids drift shut. Most men wouldn't kick her out of bed, but she didn't ever have to worry about being mistaken for a sex symbol. The very idea made her chuckle. Still, tonight she felt...attractive.

She lifted her lids for a moment and watched a flirtatious smile spread across her face in the mirror. Hmm. Maybe there was a cute bartender in the village who'd invite her to dinner and a movie, or a hunky docent at the museum, or—

Suddenly she was staring right into the reflection of a pair of black, seductive eyes. Well, one eye—the other being covered by a black leather patch. But all the more alluring for that.

It was also an eye that knew exactly what she was thinking.

With a loud gasp, she whirled.

A man lounged against the bed's headboard, watching her.

A really, really handsome man.

Dressed as a pirate.

Oh, Lord. Did fantasies actually come true?

She blinked once, then again for good measure. *Yeah, right.* Stuff like this didn't happen. Not to her.

"Who are you?" she demanded, leaping to her feet. "And what the hell are you doing in my bed?"

She could see him.

Tyree froze where he lay propped against the bed pillows. *She wasn't supposed to be able to see him.*

"Well?" the woman demanded, taking a step backward.

Hardly anyone could see him—one of the few real blessings of his benighted state. It was a one-in-ten-thousand occurrence. Not unheard of, but very rare.

Devil take it. Once again his unruly hormones had landed him in an indefensible situation. He should have known better, spying on the woman just because she made his head spin with lust. He *should* be doing his best to scare the bejeezus out of her, not enjoying the sight of her stripping off her clothes.

He had to get out of this. Fast.

"If you don't tell me who you are and what you're doing in my bedroom, I'll call the police!"

Tyree happened to know there was no phone in the bungalow. But maybe she had one of those cellular jobs. He grimaced. Police would be a disaster.

He rolled off the bed, his mind reeling. And said the first thing that popped into it.

"A dream."

Her brows snapped together. "Excuse me?"

"I'm a dream. More precisely, *your* dream."

The woman's bow-shaped lips parted and her Caribbean-blue eyes widened.

Speechless, thank God.

He pressed his advantage by levitating several feet off the floor and allowing himself to drift through the solid mahogany bedpost. It took a bit of concentration under the circumstances, but achieved the desired effect. Her eyes widened even farther.

"You see? A dream. A real person couldn't possibly do that, could they?"

He drifted back. She just gaped.

More than grateful for the undeserved reprieve, he touched down and eased toward the French doors. "But as you don't seem to be in the mood for a pirate dream, I'll just be—"

"No!" she exclaimed, her voice cracking on the word. "I, um… You're really a dream?"

Damn.

"Aye, but I really mustn't—"

She took a halting step toward him. "Please, stay."

His mouth opened and shut like a beached halibut.

Dear God, do not do this to me. Not again.

"I *am* in the mood. Honest." She looked at him hopefully, her expression a portrait of virginal skittishness. "For a pirate dream," she added, as though assuring herself that's what this really was.

Pure temptation of the sweetest variety warred with a century and a half of dogged determination. *Lord have mercy on his wicked nature.* This could only end badly. Especially for her.

"I—I—I shouldn't," he finally forced himself to stammer.

She took another step, bringing her tantalizing body to within inches of his. She was no classic beauty, but everything about her appealed to him. Long, shapely legs, a willowy form with enough generous curves to drive a man mad. Pretty face, soft, rosy lips just made for kissing. An impish sparkle in intelligent eyes. *Just like Rosalind.*

He felt his resolve slip a notch.

"Why not?" she asked.

He backed away from the alluring scent of her, struggling to remember the thousands of reasons why not. But all he could think of was the desire swelling painfully in his—

"Blast it, because…well—"

"This is *my* dream. You said so, right?"

Several more notches slipped away. "I, um, aye, I suppose I did—" *Witless idea. What a blunder.*

"So, *I* get to decide what happens next, right?"

"Ah. Not necessarily."

She moved closer. Put her hand on his sleeve. "Just a kiss. That's all I ask of you."

It was his turn to swallow. *Damnation.* How could he resist such an innocent appeal? He was only human. "Just one?"

Her lips parted slightly and she gave a nod.

He lost the battle and reached up to touch her cheek. "What is your name, sweeting?"

"Clara. Clara Fergussen," she whispered, then closed her eyes and tipped her face up to his expectantly.

He should have run. Sprinted out the French doors and up to the main house, awakened Mrs. Yates and demanded she evict this tempting young morsel from his bed, from his property and from what was left of his pathetic existence on earth.

Instead, with a sinking sense of awaiting fate, he took a deep breath, leaned down and pressed his lips softly to hers.

As they came together, his whole body sighed in pleasure. *So good.* With a low groan, he gathered her to him, tunneled his fingers through her hair and put his arm around her waist.

More than good. He'd forgotten how incredible a woman felt with her curves fitted to his.

"Open," he murmured, and she did.

The taste of her exploded through him, saturating his senses, filling him with a need that nearly brought him to his knees. Her soft breasts pillowed up against his chest; her hips leaned into his. His traitorous arousal gave a lurch of alacrity at the intimate contact. She moaned, and her body shuddered beneath his fingers.

It had been so long. So very long.

He couldn't help himself. He deepened the kiss. Pulled her tight. Reveled in the feel of the living, breathing woman cradled in his arms. She wound her wrists about his neck, clinging to him with a fervor that equaled his own. She returned his kisses, tangling her tongue with his, sweetly yielding to his growing ardor with soft mewls of surrender.

This was too much to resist. Far too much.

He growled and ripped her T-shirt over her head, tossing it aside. She gasped.

He paused in his task of ridding himself of his own shirt. "I frighten you?"

"No," she whispered, looking delectably terrified.

"Shall I stop?"

She shook her head. "No. I've always dreamed about, um, kissing a pirate."

He dropped his shirt on a chair and gently drew her back into his arms. "Have you now."

She nibbled on her lower lip. "Mm-hmm. It's been a sort of…fantasy of mine. For as long as I can remember."

"A pirate fantasy, eh?"

"Mm-hmm." Her eyes sparkled up at him, innocent and guileless.

"And what happens in this fantasy?" he murmured, wanting to know every single detail so he could fulfill them all, and give her a dream she'd remember for the rest of her life.

"I've always wondered what it would be like," she said in

a low whisper that sent hot quivers up and down his body, "to be captured and ravished by Sullivan Fouquet."

Tyree's head snapped back as though she'd smacked him. Indignation swept through his veins and he jerked away from her.

Did the man have to steal *everything*? Every damned scrap? He drilled his fingers through his hair and swore roundly.

Her jaw dropped at the virulence of his reaction. "What's wrong? What did I say?"

"I am not," he ground out, "nor will I ever be, Sullivan Fouquet."

She reached for his hand. "Okay. That's fine. Who would you like to be instead?"

His mouth compressed into a thin line. This had gone far enough. "Nobody. I'm afraid it's time for you to wake up."

Before he had a chance to pull away, she wrapped her arms around him. "Not yet. Please?" She raised her lips so they were within a hair's breadth of his. "Don't you like kissing me?"

She came closer. His arousal pressed into her and he saw stars. A rumbling moan squeezed from his throat. *Not fair.*

"Aye," he murmured, hopelessly captured by her innocent seduction. "You know I do."

Her cheeks reddened and she whispered, "Then don't go."

He held her shivering body, buried his face in her hair, breathing deeply of her warm woman's scent.

This was wrong. He knew it well. He was no dream, and though he knew no harm would come to her physically, if she were to find out the truth about him, what emotional toll would she pay?

"Do you have any idea what you've gotten yourself into, Clara Fergussen?"

Her head shook minutely. "No."

He held her for a long moment, savoring the silken slide of her bare skin on his, the mingling moistness between their bodies, the thunder of her heart hammering his chest as she nestled against it. Giving her the chance to change her mind.

But then her mouth found his, kissing away any thought of playing the gentleman. He was a pirate through and through, and God help this innocent maiden, for he would not stop save she begged him with her own tongue.

She kissed him again and he let her. Encouraged her. Made sure her tongue was too busy to protest anything his hands might do.

Her nipples tightened as he brushed his palms hungrily over her breasts, fingering the delicate lace edges of her bra. He'd seen such garments in advertisements, of course, but had never touched a real one before. Now was not the time to learn its art. He needed her under him.

"Take it off," he softly ordered, tugging at the wisp of fabric. "I want you naked."

Her fingers fumbled badly on the tiny hooks as he slid off her panties. But finally her body was bare.

"Beautiful," he whispered, and for a second couldn't move.

Neither a thousand pictures in a magazine nor a million images on film could ever capture the beauty of a living woman in the flesh. And it had been a century and a half since he'd beheld such a vision.

She smiled shyly, and the figure that hovered at the fringes of his memory vanished.

He kicked off his boots, peeled off his breeches and held out his arms.

"Come to me, my sweet."

She came into his embrace, warm and willing and all woman. He put his lips to hers, flicked his tongue across them and tasted her.

He groaned and lifted her onto the bed, needing more. Much more. He laid her down, drinking in the sight of her. Letting the anticipation build within him that soon he would possess her, possess every part of her. He wanted it all. Every luscious inch and every wanton thought. He crawled above her and ran his hands over every enticing dip and curve of her satin body, until she moaned with need for him.

"What shall I call you?" she whispered when he moved to cover her body with his. "If not Captain Fouquet, then who are you?"

"The name's St. James," he answered, spreading her legs with a knee, holding himself just above her as he watched her reaction. Suddenly wanting her to understand exactly who she was giving herself to. "Captain Tyree St. James."

Her eyes grew as big as saucers and she sucked in a breath of shock. "Tyree St. James? The Blackbeard of Magnolia Cove?"

"One and the same."

Slowly he trailed his fingers up her trembling body. When he found her wrists, he grasped them and brought them above her head. She whimpered but offered no resistance.

"This is just a dream," she whispered. "It's not real."

He slid a hand onto her breast, pinning her with his one-eyed gaze. "Dream or nightmare? Would you like me to leave, Clara Fergussen? Or shall I stay and play out this fantasy of yours?"

"What will you do to me?" she timorously asked, her naked body burning under his.

He caressed her breast, rubbing the pad of his thumb over the pebbled tip so her breath caught. And answered with a lazy wink, "Anything I want."

She swallowed heavily, and met his steady gaze. "In that case," she said breathily, "I'd like to finish the dream."

Chapter 2

Clara woke the next morning with a smile on her lips and a blush on her cheeks.

What an incredible dream! Lord, have mercy. For being her own creation, it had certainly had been imaginative....

She glanced over her shoulder, half expecting to see her dream pirate's indigo eyes glittering at her in sensual invitation. He was, of course, not there. But she'd swear she could still smell him on the sheets, on her skin. The bed was rumpled beyond repair, evidence of how embarrassingly realistic her dream had been. A wave of searing heat burned across her face just remembering the things she'd done last night with her amazing pirate captain.

Tyree St. James!

She couldn't believe it. What sort of dark, forbidden desires lurked in the hidden recesses of her subconscious, that when she finally dared to conjure up an erotic dream, it starred a demon like Tyree St. James instead of her own charming, romantic and comfortably distant ancestor? Best to blame it on the influence of the diary and not think about its meaning too closely.

Though it felt like she hadn't slept more than an hour, she made herself slide out of bed, then let out a yelp when her thigh muscles protested—along with a few other muscles she'd never felt before. Must have been all the bending and stooping she'd done at the library yesterday afternoon. Surely it couldn't have been last night's dream that had produced such aches. That would be taking the fantasy a bit too far.

But wasn't that exactly where St. James had taken her? Miles too far. Leagues too far. Light-years too far.

And she had enjoyed every last millimeter of the journey. For once in her life, she'd lived out a dangerous fantasy, more foolish than anything she'd ever done—or ever in a million years *would* do—in real life.

Lord, if a woman could have a dream like that every so often, she'd have little use for a real man. With any luck, this was the beginning of a long relationship with the sexy Captain St. James.

Most people would be aghast at the thought of having a relationship with a dream. But for Clara, it made perfect sense. She had no time or inclination for the complications of getting involved with a flesh-and-blood man.

She'd tried it a few times back in Kansas—having a real relationship—but she'd always felt pressured to conform to what her boyfriends and others perceived as the "proper" way for a woman to act in a couple—domestic, obedient, interested only in making her man's life easy and happy.

There was nothing at all wrong with living like that, if one truly wanted to. Most of her friends did, and were happy as clams. But it wasn't for her.

Clara wanted something different from her life. At least for the next few years. Which meant no ties or guilt trips imposed on her by a jealous or disapproving boyfriend. Later, when the time was right, she wanted starstruck, earthmoving romance—not to be a trophy on the arm of some underappreciative man.

What she wanted was breathtaking, passionate love. Someday.

But for now, she simply craved adventure, excitement and the freedom to experience the world to its fullest extent, in all its wonderful variety. Her hometown didn't grow men who'd go along with *that* kind of behavior from their women, at least not in her circle of acquaintances. Wives gallivanting off to Timbuktu was generally frowned upon, as were jobs that expected them to. Therefore, she'd avoided getting involved with any of the men she knew.

But Captain Dreamboat might just be the perfect solution to the occasional loneliness she experienced living life solo. She only hoped he'd follow her home to Kansas when she had to leave Magnolia Cove.

She headed for the shower, ready to start her first full day of research for her article. In her mind, she tried to organize the day's activities, but the sensual caress of the warm water sliding over her body just reminded her of Tyree's melting touch.

Suddenly, reading about Sullivan Fouquet lost some of its appeal. How had she ever thought him more interesting than the dark, mysterious Tyree St. James?

What an enigma that man was. His evil reputation as a greedy, womanizing, murdering traitor just didn't mesh with the generous man who'd held her and loved her all through the night, making her feel as though she were the only woman in the world.

Maybe she should write her article about *him* instead.

It was completely insane and irrational, but she couldn't shake the idea that perhaps Tyree had gotten a bad rap in all the publicity against him.

Of course, at this moment she was probably badly biased. Lord knew, she'd woken up half in love with the man.

Get a grip, she told herself firmly. *Totally* irrational. He was just a dream. A manifestation of her own excessively romantic imagination—not based on any kind of sound research or historical investigation other than a few references in a diary. Naturally, she couldn't admit the object of her nocturnal indiscretions was a bad guy.

A bad boy, yes. But not a bad man.

Still, her conjured version of St. James had to be based on some deep inner instinct or unconscious knowledge about the real man and not purely fantasy.

Didn't it?

She knew she'd gone over the deep end when, instead of continuing with her work on the diary, she decided to return to the library and look into the legends about St. James. Especially those concerning his alleged betrayal of his partner and best friend, Sullivan Fouquet. It was the least she could do. Besides, if she found out something really interesting, it could only improve her article.

At least that was what she told herself.

After dressing, she headed for the main house and breakfast with Mrs. Yates. She smoothed her hands down her shorts and tried to look normal as she walked into the kitchen, but after one glance at her, Mrs. Yates paused in her preparations at the stove and remarked, "You look positively glowing, my dear! What happened to you last night?"

"Um…" Clara considered evasion, but before she could come up with a suitable diversion, Mrs. Yates broke out in a wide grin.

"That sailor's diary must have been quite something. You'll have to let me read it. I could use a little…entertainment."

Clara giggled at the irrepressible twinkle in the older woman's eyes. "It wasn't the diary," she admitted with an answering grin. "It was a dream."

"Well, aren't you the lucky one! My husband's been gone for nearly ten years now, and not once have I awoken with such a sublime expression on my face."

Clara chuckled. "Trust me, this is a first for me, too."

"So, tell me about this dream. I need the vicarious thrill." Mrs. Yates turned off the burners and slid ham and eggs onto two plates, along with a scoop of grits for each.

Clara cleared her throat. "I'm not sure—"

"Oh, do tell. You may not believe it, but I was quite a handful in my day."

"Oh, I do believe it," Clara said, then dug into the savory breakfast, as ravenous as if the exhausting events of the night had really happened. "All right, I dreamed I met a pirate."

Mrs. Yates glanced up from her plate. "A pirate?" A sudden frown creased her forehead. "I suppose that's natural," she said slowly, "considering where you are and what you're doing here. What happened with this…pirate?"

Clara felt her blush return with a vengeance. "What didn't?" she muttered. "He was unbelievable." And from the tight, barely leashed desire in his expression to the musky, slightly mysterious scent that floated to her senses on his body heat, the man had seemed vividly, scintillatingly alive. "Handsome, sexy as hell and a body to die for. He literally swept me off my feet."

"Indeed."

She blew out a breath. "Oh, Mrs. Yates, you just wouldn't believe how incredible he was! He made me feel like an enchanted princess being awakened by her true prince. We spent the entire night in the bungalow—" She caught sight of the older woman's expression. "What?"

Not curiosity, suspicion. "The bungalow was in your dream? Rose Cottage?"

Clara nodded. "And it was so realistic," she said with a sigh. "I could even smell the roses and the salt marsh."

Mrs. Yates looked at her sharply. "Clara, dear, did this pirate have a name, by any chance?"

Clara brushed aside a spurt of unease at the unexpected change in her demeanor. Her hostess appeared almost…upset.

"As a matter of fact, it was Tyree St. James."

A crash resounded through the kitchen as Mrs. Yates's knife and fork clattered onto her fine china plate.

"Tyree St.—" Her brows beetled in consternation. "He didn't! He simply couldn't! Oh, dear, this is all my fault."

"What is? Mrs. Yates, is something wrong?"

"Why, the old scamp! I would never have believed it of him!"

"Who?"

With a rattle of dishes, Mrs. Yates rose from the table and paced the uneven kitchen floor, clearly distraught. "This is unforgivable!"

Clara stared in astonishment as her hostess suddenly called out in a reedy, but surprisingly loud voice, "Captain! Captain St. James, you come here this minute!"

Okay, this was now officially weird. Had the old lady completely lost her marbles?

"At *once*, do you hear me?"

Maybe she had a thing for St. James and didn't want anyone else dreaming about him. "Look, um—"

"What did you expect me to do when you install a sweet young thing like Miz Fergussen in my bedroom?" drawled a deep, honeyed voice directly behind her.

At the all-too-familiar accent, Clara whipped around in her chair.

No! It wasn't possible!

"What the—" She froze at the sight of her dream pirate lounging against the kitchen door frame as though that were perfectly plausible and possible.

Which it wasn't. Because the man wasn't real.

She had to be hallucinating.

"Hello, sweeting. I trust you slept well after I left?" His gaze prowled over her like a wolf sizing up his prey.

Her chair crashed to the floor as she rocketed to her feet. "You!"

He bowed slightly. "As you see."

Omigod.

"You can't be here!"

One black eyebrow rose in that knowing way that had been so arousing last night, but now set her teeth on edge. There was something very, very wrong here.

He *was* real.

But…how?

Clara clenched her fists at her sides, anger coursing through her. She'd obviously been played for a royal sucker. "Very clever. How did you do it? Smoke and mirrors?"

"Do what?"

"Don't even try." She raised an accusing finger. "Just who the hell are you, anyway, and what's with that ridiculous outfit?"

Blandly, he glanced down at the pirate getup from the night before, which he was still wearing—except for the hokey eye patch.

"I gotta say, it loses its effect the morning after." She grimaced at a sudden thought. "God, don't tell me, you work at the museum, right? What was the plan? Thought you'd get a big laugh playing dress up for the gullible Midwestern hick?"

"Oh, dear," Mrs. Yates mumbled from the corner, wringing her hands.

"I assure you, I do not work at the museum, and was not—"

Clara held up a palm. "Never mind. I really don't want to know. Just get out of here. Now."

The pirate leaned back on his heels, folding his arms over his broad chest. The broad chest she'd collapsed on in exhaustion more than once the night before…

"That could be a problem," he said in those smooth-as-molasses tones, thankfully interrupting the memory. "Since this is *my* house."

"What?" Clara sliced a disbelieving glance at Mrs. Yates. "This guy *lives* here?"

"Well, in a m-manner of s-speaking," the old woman stammered.

Great. Just great. "And you didn't think to tell me about him?"

"Or me about her?" the faux pirate chimed in.

Mrs. Yates looked thoroughly flustered, but Clara was too

embarrassed to feel sorry for her. She wanted to sink straight
through the kitchen floorboards and never come up again.
How could she possibly face this man after the scandalous
way she'd behaved with him last night? After the things they'd
done together?

Damn.

"This isn't happening." She covered her face with her
hands and groaned. "You told me you were a dream."

"It was the only thing I could think of."

She heard him take a step toward her and she jumped
away, tearing her hands from her eyes. "How about the truth?"

A peculiar expression came over his face and his mouth
quirked. "The truth?"

"Oh, dear," Mrs. Yates echoed again, wringing her hands
even harder.

"Well?"

He assessed Clara with narrowed eyes. But his words were
obviously for the older woman. "Shall we tell her the truth,
then? It seems you had that in mind all along, or you would
never have invited her to stay here. Isn't that so, Mrs. Yates?"

"I just thought…you only have a week left, and she seemed
so nice." Mrs. Yates drew herself up. "But frankly, Captain,
I expected you to act like a gentleman, not a—"

"Pirate?" His expression was mocking, but Clara thought
she detected an odd sadness to it. Then he sighed, the sound
spiced with weariness like salty air from the sea.

"Captain?" Clara questioned, picking up on Mrs. Yates's
words. "You're a captain? Of what?" She'd absolutely die if
he was a cop.

He leveled his near-black eyes on her. "Believe me, you
don't want to know."

A tingle of foreboding trickled down her spine. "Oh, but
I do," she said, despite the growing certainty that she really,
really didn't. Mrs. Yates looked like she was about to expire,
and the pirate's expression was growing more stormy by the
second. "Just who *are* you?"

"You know who I am," he said quietly. "I'm the man you spent the night—"

"Captain!" Mrs. Yates exclaimed.

"Captain *who?*" Clara asked with dawning dread.

"I told you before. My name is St. James. Captain Tyree St. James."

She just stared. First at him, then at Mrs. Yates, praying a rational explanation was forthcoming.

It wasn't.

Her heart sank. *Oh. My. God.*

Not only had she slept with him, but the man was a certifiable fruit loop.

And evidently Mrs. Yates was just as batty as he was.

Clara started backing toward the door, and let out a nervous chuckle. "Don't be silly. Tyree St. James died two hundred years ago."

"That's right."

She laughed again, sounding just the slightest bit hysterical, even to herself. She took another step backward, remembering the story she'd read in her travel guide about Magnolia Cove's several haunted houses. "Ha ha. And I suppose you're going to tell me you're his ghost."

"Nay." A muscle ticked in his cheek. "I am *not* a ghost."

What a relief. Not completely delusional.

"I am a cursed soul, caught between mortal life and heaven."

Ho-kay, then. Not delusional. Totally out of his mind.

"Sure you are. Well, it's been swell running into you, Captain, but I have a lot of work to do today. Research, you know. At the library." She pointed at him and forced a smile. "About *you* as a matter of fact. Isn't that a coincidence?"

Damn. She was babbling. If only she could make it out of the house before—

Before what? Jeez! What were they planning to do to her?

Her butt hit the screen door. Whirling, she hurled herself through it. And ran smack into a solid barrier. *St. James.*

Or whoever the hell he was. She screamed and leaped away. He grasped her arm, preventing her from running down the steps.

"Let go of me!" she cried, trying to break free. But he was strong. Unnaturally strong.

"I'm afraid that won't be possible."

Suddenly, it struck her. He'd been in the kitchen... *No way.* "How'd you do that?"

"Do what?"

"Get out here on the porch before me."

Setting his jaw, he turned to Mrs. Yates, who was now standing next to the open door. "This was your bright idea. *You* explain it."

"Come back inside, Clara dear," Mrs. Yates said. "I know it all sounds crazy. But please. Before you do anything rash, give us a chance to explain."

The pirate released her arm but didn't move away from the stairs. She wasn't frightened exactly; neither of them struck her as the serial killer type. She was more mortified that last night she'd actually fallen hook, line and sinker for this handsome nut ball. But if she listened to another word either of these Looney Tunes said, she'd be as crazy as they were.

She closed her eyes. What should she do?

He was standing close. Way too close to think clearly.

God, he smelled good. Last night, she'd loved being surrounded by his distinctive, musky male scent. And by him. Her breasts ached remembering how he'd lavished them with his lips and tongue, suckling them like a babe starving to be nurtured. Touching them like a man who desperately needed to be loved back. And not just physically. The emotions that had poured from those hands and lips had taken her breath away.

But it had all been a sham. Hell, an outright lie. He'd told her he was a dream, and she'd actually believed him.

Was she really so desperate that she'd fall for a setup so transparently absurd? How could she have been so stupid?

Because…because he'd proven it. With her own eyes she'd seen him do things, things no living person could do.

So how had he managed his little demonstration of levitation and gliding through the bedpost? And how had he gotten through the kitchen door, just now, before she did?

A cursed soul, caught between mortal life and heaven.

No. Not a ghost of a chance. There had to be a logical explanation. One that didn't involve cursed souls. He must be some kind of performer. A magician. Or…

"It was hard for me to believe at first, too," Mrs. Yates said kindly, interrupting Clara's desperate thoughts. "Took me almost a week to acknowledge with my mind what my eyes were clearly showing me."

"This is insane," Clara murmured, appalled she would even consider such a preposterous assertion. This was not the kind of excitement or adventure she'd had in mind when she came to Magnolia Cove. Definitely not.

"Go inside," the pirate ordered softly. His midnight eyes, accented by a thin blue scar running just below the left one, commanded her from a face sculpted with severe planes and rugged angles. A face that was used to being obeyed.

Last night, she had. Willingly. Her knees went liquid, remembering. Truth was, she'd been thrilled to obey his every whispered demand.

Reluctantly, she acceded now, too. "All right. But just for a minute. Then I really must get to the library."

"We'll see," he said.

She stepped into the kitchen, rubbing her arms. Had it suddenly grown chilly?

"Close the door," he said, still standing on the porch outside.

"But—"

"Do it."

She had a bad feeling about this. Nevertheless, she closed the door, leaving him on the other side.

"What's going on?" she asked Mrs. Yates.

"Look." The old lady indicated the door.

"Wha—" The word congealed in Clara's throat as she watched in disbelief. The shimmering image of St. James filtered through the closed door like a bad special effect from an episode of *Star Trek*, then came to a halt right in front of her. The door hadn't budged. Not even a fraction.

All thought drained from her head like blood from a corpse.

Bad analogy. She resisted the urge to laugh hysterically. Or run like hell. Oh, Lord. What was going on? She knew darn good and well there were no such things as ghosts.

Absolutely not.

"That was very impressive," she said, pulling herself together and inching toward escape. "But the library calls."

She'd think about this later. When the two of them weren't standing right there. In the same room. Staring at her like she was actually supposed to believe all this. Crazy old Mrs. Yates and Tyree St. James.

Captain Tyree St. James, Blackbeard of Magnolia Cove. *Cursed soul, caught between mortal life and heaven.*

Lord almighty. *She'd slept with a ghost.*

What could possibly happen next?

Chapter 3

Tyree watched Clara hurry down the garden path toward the road to the village and the pirate museum library.

"I should have kept her here," he said crossly.

"Captive, you mean? Like in *Beauty and the Beast*?"

"Thank you very much, Mrs. Yates," he muttered, and turned on a heel, heading back into the kitchen. Without thinking, he grabbed half a bagel from the table and ripped off a piece with his teeth.

"Hungry?" she asked with irritating amusement. She was well aware he only ate when agitated. Or thinking about female companionship.

"Perhaps I'll even have jam," he retorted, and slathered on a thick layer of blueberry preserve, daring her to comment.

"My, we did get up on the wrong side of the bed today."

He glared at her. "What the devil were you thinking, bringing an innocent girl here? A week before I'm to leave!"

"She's not a girl, she's a grown woman. And obviously a

lot less innocent this morning than yesterday afternoon when I met her," Mrs. Yates intoned, clucking at him disapprovingly.

He ripped off another bite. "Aye, well. That was a huge mistake. She took me by surprise."

Mrs. Yates harrumphed.

"I didn't count on her seeing me. Or asking me to kiss her." That widened the old bird's eyes. "Anyway, it won't happen again, I can assure you." He glanced out the window at the oyster-shell path down which Clara had disappeared at a fast clip. "I just hope she doesn't start asking questions about me in the village."

"You asked her not to," Mrs. Yates stated in a practical tone. She could be so naive. "Besides, even if she does, you'll be gone before anything unpleasant can come of it."

"I don't want any trouble, for your sake. If anyone should question your ownership of this estate, or the trusts and charities I've set up…"

He let the thought trail off. He'd arranged for the final disposition of his vast accumulated fortune as carefully as he could, drawing on two centuries of experience with the sticky legal dealings inherent in his situation. But one curious reporter or prying cop could spoil everything for Mrs. Yates and the other beneficiaries.

Not to mention potentially making his last week on earth a hellish media circus rather than the peaceful, contemplative ending to physical existence he'd envisioned.

Mrs. Yates's expression turned tender. "I'm going to miss you terribly, you know."

He put down his bagel, which suddenly tasted like sawdust. "I'll miss you, too," he said, heart tugging. Lord, he hated goodbyes. Over the years there had been far too many.

"You've been like a son to me. The son I never had," she said, getting misty.

He walked over and gave her a hug. "And you've been a wonderful friend and a great help."

She fished in her pocket for a hankie. "I'm sorry about Clara—"

"Don't worry about Miz Fergussen," he interrupted. He still hadn't decided exactly what to do about her, so it was best to avoid the topic. "She can stay for now and do her research and I'll steer well clear of the gardener's bungalow." That much he *had* decided.

Mrs. Yates tucked away her hankie and straightened. "If that's what you think is best."

"I just pray she keeps her mouth shut," he said, casting an uneasy gaze back out the window. "I don't suppose you'd want to…"

"Go to the museum and check up on her?"

He immediately thought better of it. Mrs. Yates didn't drive, and he didn't want her walking all that way unnecessarily. "No, I'm just being foolish."

He pulled out his pocket watch and consulted it. "And now you must excuse me. I have to get to my office. I want to check on a bid I put in on an Internet auction."

Mrs. Yates peered over her glasses. "Now what? Another new toaster?" She swept her hand toward the kitchen counter, where two four-slicers already occupied a corner. "Or a coffeemaker?" Three of those were lined up next to the toasters. In his defense, they all had different features and one was actually a cappuccino maker that steamed milk, too.

"Not this time. It's a new MP3 player with— Never mind," he said, grinning at her long-suffering mien.

"You already have three of those!"

Gadgets of any kind, especially kitchen and electronic gadgets, were his weakness, but they were the bane of Mrs. Yates's existence since she had to find room for them all in the cottage. She liked to run a tight ship.

"One can never have too many MP3 players, Mrs. Yates."

"If you say so, Captain," she said with a sigh.

"Why don't you send a box of things over to the women's

shelter?" he suggested as he bounded up the stairs. "I'm sure they can use another toaster or two."

"We sent them three boxes last month," she called after him.

"The retirement home, then," he shouted back, closing his office door behind him. She'd work out where the donations could best be used. She always did.

He took a seat in front of the computer and turned it on. As he waited for it to boot up, his gaze once again traveled through the bank of mullioned windows overlooking the path to the village. From the second floor, he could see much more of it, winding its way through the estate toward the small hamlet of Magnolia Cove.

Clara would have reached the village by now. It wasn't far, maybe a mile or two, and she was in good shape. Very good shape. His body tightened recalling just how good her shape was. Trim and fit, yet soft and curvy in all the right places.

Staring out over the palmettos, oaks and saw grass, he tried to pin down a rising sense of discomfort—besides the obvious. And realized it stemmed from a sudden gnawing desire to go to the museum library and check on her.

Which was ridiculous. He hardly ever left the estate. Certainly not to go to the village. He hadn't gone there for years. Decades.

He folded his arms over his chest. What could she be doing now?

She'd come to the island to find his and Sully's lost treasure, so she was probably cuddled up in the pirate museum library with some obscure dusty volume she'd excavated from deep in its bowels, searching for clues to the gold's location. A harmless enough task.

Or was she instead drinking coffee with the docent, asking questions about the crazy recluse at Rose Cottage who dressed as a pirate and walked through walls?

He set his jaw. Who was on duty at the museum today? Mrs. Yates volunteered on Thursdays, but today was Monday.

Clara had thought Tyree worked there, because of his clothes. He frowned. Why would she think that?

She'd spent yesterday afternoon at the museum. Maybe they'd hired someone new. Maybe some young stud who liked to dress as a pirate to amuse the tourists. His frown turned to a scowl. Or to attract the attention of pretty, inquisitive women....

He rose, stalked out of his office to the top of the stairs and bellowed, "Mrs. Yates! Have they hired anyone new at the museum lately?"

She appeared at the foot of the staircase looking puzzled. "Why, no, not since Miss Dalrymple."

"Good," he muttered.

He stalked back to his office, clapped the door shut and strode back to the windows. Still, maybe he should—

What in blazes was wrong with him? He couldn't believe he was actually considering going to the village to spy on her.

Shaking his head, Tyree returned to his desk and logged on to the Internet auction site. He'd been outbid on the MP3 player, so he registered a new bid. Then he logged off. Usually, he surfed the other auctions for a while to see if there was anything interesting, or checked in at the various online news services to find out what was happening in the world. There was one story in particular he'd been following, about an arsonist who had burned down two historic houses in the area. But today he couldn't concentrate.

The only thing on his mind was the image of Clara rushing down the path to escape him, her embarrassment over their night together and his fantastical story about being dead.

Suddenly he came to his feet. What a fool he was!

She was after treasure, and what better treasure existed in this day and age than a story you could sell to the ever-gossip-hungry media? A tale of ghosts and pirates and curses and treasure? A sharp woman like Clara would know exactly what to do to cash in on a story like that. Even now, she was probably on the phone to the *National Stargazer* or another one of those tabloid papers pitching it.

The last thing Tyree wanted or needed was for Rose Cottage to be invaded by reporters, curiosity seekers and ghost hunters. He had to put a stop to it. Now, before she could bring a disaster down on their heads.

He strode to the upstairs bedroom where he kept his small collection of street clothes. Except for ridding himself of the annoying eye patch, these days he seldom bothered changing out of his pirate gear. Even if he did, he always ended up right back in them somewhere in the wee hours just before dawn, when his consciousness was at low ebb and drifting. The garments never aged, as he didn't, his physical manifestation always reverting back each day to the precise moment of Sully's curse.

Rosalind had made him change clothes during those years they were together. She'd buy him the latest fashions and dress him up like a proper dandy, even though she was the only one who ever saw the fruits of her labors. Once in the beginning, he'd tried to stay alert for several days straight to see if he could avoid the reversion. He'd lasted about seventy-two hours. They'd laughed about that. Young, carefree and in love, clothes had been the last thing on their minds.

When she died, he'd stopped changing again.

But he always maintained a small wardrobe of current menswear along with an up-to-date driver's license and passport in the name of James Tyler. Just in case. Thank goodness jeans and T-shirts never went out of style.

Quickly, he pulled on a pair of blue ones, still a little stiff despite their age, along with a white T-shirt and boots, and checked his reflection in the cheval mirror. If anyone in the village actually saw him, he'd blend right in, even with his overly long hair caught in a queue at his neck. Those who weren't able to see him wouldn't see the clothes, either. Anything he wore or carried on his body disappeared into the same dimension that he himself occupied.

"I'm going out for a while," he called to Mrs. Yates, taking the stairs two at a time. He ignored her astonished face when she saw what he was wearing, and her even more shocked expression when he added, "To the village."

But he could have sworn he saw the beginnings of a smile as he headed out the door.

Whatever that was supposed to mean.

Tyree made it to the pirate museum in record time, not running but striding at that double-time pace he and Sully had used for evading the odd French or Spanish militia who didn't take kindly to American privateers relieving their Caribbean merchantmen of their cargoes. Sully always was a cocky devil; after a job, he could never resist putting ashore for a pint or two before pushing off for home. Tyree grinned at the memory. His own weakness had been the ladies, so naturally he hadn't objected too strenuously to a tavern visit before a long voyage. But it did tend to land them in the kettle.

He puffed out a breath. It seemed his weakness had struck again. Would he never learn?

Nobody noticed him as he swiftly made his way down Fouquet Street—it still made him grit his teeth when he saw the street sign—past the quaint village antique shops, the lone filling station and the coin-op Laundromat. He rounded the corner at the historic Moon and Palmetto, the very tavern where he'd received his fateful blow. Miraculously, the inn was still in business. He hurried along the short block to the pirate museum.

Slipping in the front door, he prepared to duck right out again if anyone spotted him.

Behind the reception desk the bespectacled, blue-haired Miss Dalrymple looked up expectantly when the bell over the door jangled. He winced, but she just adjusted her glasses when nobody came through it before it closed again.

The museum was housed in a stylish Georgian town house which had been renovated and refurbished years ago by an enterprising city council looking for ways to attract the trickle of tourists who'd begun to discover the delights of South

Carolina's sea islands. Using the romantic legend of Sullivan Fouquet as a hook, they'd achieved moderate success with day-trippers heading for the more popular beach and golf resorts. Today, however, none of them were in evidence.

Tyree did a quick glance through the lobby, tearoom and small museum shop on the first level. No Clara. He glided up the main stairway to the second floor, where the library was situated. He didn't see her there, either. She wasn't sitting at the old wooden library table, or in either of the leather armchairs flanking the fireplace. Where the hell was she?

With growing panic that his fears would prove correct, he ran down the hall and searched one by one through the several small rooms that had been fitted with floor-to-ceiling bookcases. In the last one, at the very back of the building overlooking a manicured French-style garden, he found her. Folded into the window seat, she held an open, oversized folio on her bent knees and was staring at one of its pages with an odd expression.

He halted, a peculiar feeling zinging through his insides. She looked angelic. Lit by the yellow sunshine pouring through the window framing her, hair a tangle of spun gold against the cerulean blue of the sky, she reminded him of a painting he'd once seen on the ceiling of a chapel in Italy. All she lacked was a pair of wings.

He shook off the feeling. He knew better. Last night, she'd been no angel. And today she might very well be plotting to upend everything he'd worked so hard to achieve before going to his own reward. He'd be damned if he'd let her.

He stepped forward. "What are you doing?"

She gasped. "Jeez, you scared—" She caught sight of his face and gasped again, jumping to her feet. "You!"

The large folio landed on the floor, open. To a portrait of him. It had been painted a few years before his demise, for ale money, by Thom Bowden, a friend who fancied himself an artist. A fair likeness, though by no means perfect. He'd been in his cups at the time, and he appeared angry and brooding.

"I never liked that painting," he remarked, studying it with distaste. He'd forgotten about it. Some collector had bought the actual oil from the owner of the Moon and Palmetto sometime in the beginning of the century, along with another of him and Sully together, and it had disappeared from public view.

"You look just like him," Clara said, pulling his attention from the portrait. She looked wary.

"Fancy that."

"You're his descendant, aren't you," she stated. "That would explain your remarkable resemblance. That's cool," she continued, speaking a little too fast. "I'm a descendant of Sullivan Fouquet. Well, more of a distant relative, really." She stooped to pick up the book. "He's my great-great-great-great-granduncle on my mother's side."

Taken aback for a split second, Tyree decided he couldn't deal with the irony of having unknowingly seduced Sully's great-great-great-great-grandniece; he'd save that one for later.

"I died with no offspring," he informed her instead. "There are no descendants."

She paused, then carefully put the folio down on a piecrust table flanking the window. "What do you want?" she asked evenly.

"I want to know what you are up to."

Her brows lifted. "Not that it's any of your business, but I already told you. I'm researching."

He regarded her. "So I gather. Well, save yourself the trouble, because you'll never find it."

"Find what?"

He had to credit her—she looked innocent enough to fool a clergyman. But not him. Suddenly, her being Sully's descendant made perfect sense. "I know why you're here. I heard you talking to Mrs. Yates yesterday. But I'm telling you there is no hidden treasure, so it doesn't matter if you are Fouquet's heir."

"Heir? What are you talking about?"

"And if you're thinking of cashing in on any *other* circumstance—" he gave her a piercing glare "—you can forget about that, too."

She stared at him and her lips parted.

Her pretty, berry-red lips.

Lips still plump from his own kisses.

He dragged his gaze away from them, up to her eyes, which widened with sudden awareness.

He took a step forward and her eyes grew bigger still. He crushed the impulse to do what she so obviously expected, and said, "Only three people on earth know about…my condition. I intend to keep it that way. Using any means I must."

"I—" She cleared her throat. "Don't worry. I won't breathe a word. I swear. And I'm not after your treasure. That was a joke. Honest."

"Then what, exactly, are you here for?"

Her tongue peeked out from between her lips, swiped over the bottom one. "Please, just tell me you're not an ax murderer."

"Why would you—?" He puffed out a chuckle. "Oh, I get it. You think I'm an escapee from some mental institution."

She peered up at him uncertainly. "Are you?"

"Nay. I really am dead."

She closed her eyes. "Sure you are. Silly me."

Poor thing. She was having a hard time with this. He turned and stepped away from her, making a decision. "Look, let's call a truce. I really don't care if you believe me. If you can ignore what you've seen and think I'm just some guy with paranoid delusions, that's fine. It matters not either way."

"Then why the threats?"

He raised his hands, palms out. "No threats. I simply want your word that you will not mention my existence to a living soul. There are things at stake that I don't want jeopardized. Important things. Do we understand one another?"

After a second, she gave a reluctant nod, and said, "All right. Who you are is none of my business, anyway. Just swear I'm not living with an ax murderer and you have a deal."

He breathed a sigh of relief. "I promise I've never killed anyone. Well, except during the war, of course. That was inevitable."

"The war?"

"The War of Independence. And your obnoxious great-whatever-uncle and his blundering wench. But you already knew about them."

"Yeah," she said, and sighed. "So I did."

"And that wasn't with an ax."

"No." She tilted her head. "You never killed anyone else?"

"No one." He was very proud of that accomplishment.

"And yet you say you were a pirate," she said casually.

She looked so damn cute thinking she'd caught him out. Pirates were supposed to be bloodthirsty. But he knew a thing or two she didn't. He strolled back over and leaned in close. "I'll tell you a secret."

She tried to step backward, but hit up against the window seat. "No, that's—"

"I wasn't a pirate," he whispered in her ear.

"Oh!" She was obviously surprised by the admission. "There's no shame in admitting it," she whispered back.

He so hated to disappoint her. "Sully and I were privateers. We had fully legal letters of marque. All that pirate stuff is misinformation perpetuated by Sully. He'd started out as a pirate in Louisiana and saw no reason to correct his ruffian image when he made the switch."

"Oh," she said again, this time deflated. Then suddenly she recovered. "Can you prove they were privateers? Have you found the letters of marque?"

The two of them were standing practically nose to nose and he could almost smell her eagerness. He could certainly smell her perfume. Sweet, flowery. He remembered well being enveloped in that scent last night as they— Blast.

"Aye, I have the letters. Mine at least."

"Can I see them?" she asked hopefully.

He couldn't help reaching out and sliding a hand around

the nape of her neck, combing his fingers up into her silky hair. "Maybe. But first you have to answer my question."

She made a little noise. Just like the ones she'd made last night, right before he'd touched her in some pleasurable new way.

"Wh-what question?"

He caressed her nape. "Tell me what you're here for."

"I—" She swallowed heavily and met his gaze head-on. "I'm *not* here for an affair," she said, her voice shaking slightly.

"No?"

"No. I'm not blaming you for last night. I was as much at fault as you. But I want you to know, that's not how I am. I'm not…interested. In that sort of thing."

Oh, she was so wrong. She was interested, all right. He could feel it in the slackness of her muscles, hear it in the breathy way she spoke, smell it in the musky response of her body to his nearness. He could see it in the depths of her soft, glittering eyes. If he kissed her now, she wouldn't even murmur a protest.

"Good," he said. "Because I'm not, either."

But he didn't move. Not a millimeter. If he did, he'd be proven a liar.

"Good," she echoed.

"Then tell me why you are here."

She blinked, and said, "I'm writing a story. For a travel magazine."

"You're a journalist?" He controlled his alarm. Barely.

"Trying to be."

"And you're writing a story about the treasure?" Okay. That wouldn't be so bad. They popped up every so often. No one ever got close, though. Because it wasn't there anymore.

"No, not the treasure. Well, I may mention it, but the article is for a contest. Sponsored by *Adventure Magazine*."

"And you're writing about pirates."

She nodded up at him and their noses brushed. He tightened his grip.

"Actually, just one."

It hit him like the business end of a yardarm. "Let me guess. Your illustrious ancestor, Captain Fouquet."

He spun away from her, getting his unreasonable reaction under control.

This was a *good* thing. All of it. She didn't want to get involved, and the article had nothing to do with him. Perfect.

"Ideal subject," he heard himself say, gesturing around at the rows of bookcases. "Lots of material available."

He felt her hand on his arm and his skin jolted with electricity. "Yes, but this morning I got to thinking," she said. "I'd rather write about you." She faltered when he turned and speared her with a look. "I mean Tyree St. James. The original one."

For a moment a battle of ego raged within him. The idea of someone writing a sympathetic article about him—the *real* Captain St. James, not the usual penny dreadful villain—was seductive.

Too seductive.

"No," he said firmly, and escaped her hand. "Your first idea was far better. Sully's your relative. Write about him."

He felt her gaze on his back as he went to the small stack of books she'd collected on the piecrust table and examined the spines. He extracted one and set it aside. "Don't use this one. The author's an illiterate idiot. I don't think there's a single accurate fact in the whole book."

"Nothing's accurate about you, is it?" she said softly.

"Not Sully, either."

"No, I don't mean in the book. I mean out there. What everyone in the world thinks." He looked up and she was searching him with dreamlike eyes. "I was right, wasn't I? You're not who everyone thinks you are. You've gotten a bad rap."

"I?" he queried, attempting to turn the subject. Wondering how the hell she'd come to that conclusion after knowing him only a few hours, most of those spent in pursuits that didn't involve talking.

"You." Her head gave a little shake. "Tyree St. James."

"You're wrong. Everyone knows I'm the bad guy. I killed my best friend."

"He killed you, too."

"Out of grief. You know these hot-blooded Cajuns. I'd just shot his woman. What else could he do?"

He felt as though she looked right through him, through all the years that came before, right back to the moment of truth.

"You tell me."

A chill of premonition ran down his spine. "Nothing. He killed me and that was that."

"Was it?"

"Aye. It was."

"Oh, I don't think so," she said. "I happen to know quite a bit about my ancestor. Including the fact that he aided the Haitian slave revolt in 1791 by offering transport to one of its leaders, and as a reward was initiated into the leader's voodoo cult."

Tyree folded his arms across his chest. Naturally, no book mentioned that *he'd* been right by Sully's side during the whole episode. "That has nothing to do with me," he said testily.

"Possibly. But in your own words you are a cursed soul, condemned to walk the earth between life and death."

How did she do that? He couldn't believe it had taken her less than a day to figure out what no one else had for two hundred years. He pressed his lips together silently, unwilling to aid in his own unraveling.

She walked over and stood before him. "Why are you still here, Tyree?"

"It just happened."

"Things like that don't just happen." Reaching up, she laid her hand on his cheek. "Tell me."

He shook his head. "Don't go there, Clara. Don't get involved."

"I already am involved," she murmured. "You saw to that last night."

"And I'm deeply sorry."

"I have a right to know."

He shook his head. He couldn't give in. "Too dangerous." Especially for her.

"Dangerous how? Spill, Tyree. Did Sullivan Fouquet put the curse on you?"

Chapter 4

"So you believe me, then?"

Clara stared up at Tyree and slowly returned from her flight into full-fledged temporary insanity. Oh, Lord. For a few minutes there, she had actually believed the man was a cursed soul. She snatched her hand from his cheek. Good grief. Magician *and* hypnotist. Aside from being crazy. He was building up quite a curriculum vitae.

She suppressed the urge to laugh. Could you have a vitae if you were dead?

Of course, he wasn't dead, so the question was moot.

This was getting way too weird.

"Let's say I believe you," she hedged. Regardless of his mental state, he seemed to possess a lot of interesting and pertinent information on the original St. James. Pertinent to her article. "Will you tell me about the curse?"

He smiled. "No."

With difficulty, she held her exasperation in check. "Why not?"

He sighed, looking suddenly tired. "I don't want anything to happen to you."

"Like what?"

He lifted a shoulder. "I don't know. But I'm not taking any chances. I wouldn't want my worst enemy to go through what I've had to for the past two hundred years."

"Even Sully?"

"Sully wasn't my enemy. But no, not even him."

"Even though he put you in this position?"

"You," he said, tapping the end of her nose with a finger, "are fishing."

"But—"

"No dice. I told you, it's too dangerous."

"I don't see how."

He grimaced. "Look, I may be in the middle of whatever this is, but that doesn't mean I understand it. Nobody ever came to enlighten me. I've never met any other wandering souls, I've never talked with God, or even the devil. I have no idea how this whole thing happened, and I'm only going on faith that it'll end when it's supposed to."

Here was something new. "And when's that?"

He halted in the pacing he'd started and planted his hands on his hips. "I'm not sure I should tell you."

"Oh, for crying out loud." Every time he got to something good, he refused to tell her. "What do you think's going to happen if I know? When your time runs out, the curse is going to switch from you to me, so I'm stuck here instead?"

His gaze snapped to her, filled with horror. "This is no joke! Don't even say that!"

Whoa. "Seriously? Is that what'll happen?"

"Nay, that's not what will happen. At least—" He turned away again. "No. That's not what will happen."

She wondered. He was obviously hiding something. The question was, what?

Uh, no. The question was, was she losing her mind? The man's sensual aura and skill with magic tricks had clouded her thinking big-time. He was *not* cursed—other than maybe with a bad experience that had made him this way—and she certainly wasn't going to be, either.

"Have you ever thought about getting help?"

"You mean like an exorcist?" he asked, and she almost choked. She was about to tell him, no, like a psychiatrist, when he said, "Aye, I tried that once."

This time she did choke. "Excuse me?" His back was still to her so she couldn't tell if he was kidding.

"Mrs. Gaylord, my fourth caretaker, was a devout Catholic. She found a priest who performed exorcisms and invited him down from New England."

"What happened?"

"Obviously it didn't work. He couldn't even see me."

"He couldn't *see* you?"

Tyree faced her. "Most people don't. You're an exception. Didn't I mention that?"

"Must have slipped your mind."

"Guess I've had other things on it," he said. His mouth curved with a roguish tilt. She wished he wouldn't do that. When he smiled like that, her insides turned all funny and she couldn't think straight.

"Why do you think you caught me lounging on your bed last night? You weren't supposed to see me. And when you did, I was shocked into telling that fib about being a dream. I thought I could escape. But then you…well…"

Oh, God. He *had* been trying to leave. But she'd gone and— "Asked you to kiss me." She groaned. *All her fault.*

His smile widened. "And how could I refuse?"

She didn't want to think about that kiss. Or what followed. "So let me get this straight. Not only are you cursed, but you're also *invisible*?"

"A few people can see me. You, and Mrs. Yates, of course. I've run across a handful of others."

"Why us?" she pressed. Maybe it would give her a clue as to why he persisted in this delusion.

He shook his head. "I've never figured it out exactly. Something to do with believing in elves and the tooth fairy, or some such nonsense."

Maybe not.

"But you know, it's actually a blessing," he said.

The man obviously had serious people issues. This was taking antisocial tendencies to the extreme. Someone must have hurt him badly to make him so wary of human interaction.

"How can it be a blessing?"

"If people can't see you, you aren't tempted to get close to them."

Make that *very* badly. She knew it was the wrong thing to do, but her heart went out to him so much she just couldn't help herself. She reached out to give him a hug.

"I'm sorry," she whispered. "You must be very lonely."

At first he was tentative, but then his arms went around her, and he sighed. "Damn. This is what I've missed most. Just holding someone and being held."

Her, too. The downside of avoiding relationships, for everyone, it seemed. Thank goodness for her dog. It wasn't exactly the same, but he was always warm and fuzzy when needed.

"I used to keep hounds," Tyree said, as if reading her thoughts. "But I'd miss them too badly when they passed on, so I stopped."

She felt him kiss the top of her head and adjust his arms, shifting her slightly against his body so they fit perfectly together, curve to curve, soft to hard, heart to heart.

She loved the way he smelled—spicy, exotic and male. His large body surrounded her, so strong and powerful, yet gentle in the way he held her. She could hear his heartbeat, steady and sure. Tucked against him, she felt safe, secure, like nothing bad could ever happen as long as she remained in his arms.

Which was madness. Because she wasn't going to remain

in his arms. She'd be leaving in six short days. She didn't do holiday romances. But even if she did, was this the kind of man to get involved with?

Sure, he was sexy as hell, made love like a god and was a real gentleman when he wanted to be. But could she really consider a relationship with a man convinced he was a 200-year-old pirate?

No. She didn't think so.

As if to drive home the point, Tyree said, "How long are you here? In Magnolia Cove?"

"Till Sunday morning. I only got a week off work."

His throat hummed against her temple. "Sunday. By then, I'll be gone."

She drew out of his embrace. "You'll be gone?" She couldn't fathom why the thought of him leaving Rose Cottage before she did suddenly distressed her. But there it was. "Where are you going? When?"

His smile went charmingly lopsided. "*Where* is a matter of some debate. I'm counting on heaven, myself. When? Saturday."

"Huh?" She could make neither head nor tail of what he was saying.

"I'll be dead, Clara. For real, this time."

"Dead?" She felt a sudden stinging in her eyes and a pool of dread in her stomach. *He was dying?* "What are you talking about?"

"On Saturday. The curse is up at midnight this Saturday."

She had to get hold of herself.

Clara settled back into the window seat and gazed out over the beautiful formal garden behind the museum.

Before Tyree left half an hour ago, she'd grilled him over and over until she was satisfied he didn't have some awful, fatal disease with only a week left to live.

"It's impossible," he'd informed her. "Technically, my body is already dead so nothing can live in it. I can't get infections or cancer or even tooth decay. I also can't get you pregnant," he'd added quietly, "in case you were worried," and she'd blanched. That possible complication of their night together hadn't even occurred to her—it had been a dream, after all. One didn't bother about such practicalities in dreams.

She didn't know what to think. About that, about anything. He seemed so calm and serene at the thought of ending his existence. And yet, he was anything but suicidal. His attitude was closer to cheerful.

Something wasn't right. Maybe she should keep an eye on him. Just in case.

No. This was ridiculous. She'd come here to write an article on pirates and adventure, not nursemaid a man with serious problems, regardless of how much she liked him. She had her own problems to deal with.

She reached for the top book in her to-be-read pile on the piecrust table and opened it resolutely.

This contest was her ticket out of Kansas and into the big, wide world she so craved to see. She had just a few days to do the research for her winning article. And that was exactly what she intended to do. No way would she blow her chances by getting distracted.

No matter how much her heart seemed determined to do so.

Tyree waited anxiously for the rest of the morning and half the afternoon for Clara to return. Mrs. Yates kept clucking at him for being underfoot, but he couldn't seem to involve his interest in anything except watching her putter about.

Finally, he heaved a sigh, flung himself into his favorite armchair and snapped on the TV. Maybe there was something good on the History Channel. He enjoyed shows about archaeology. They reminded him there were things on this planet even older than him. Unfortunately, the show playing was about World War II. He flipped stations for fifteen minutes; then, with a bored huff, he switched it to the news and threw aside the remote.

"What on earth has you so restless?" asked Mrs. Yates.

"Where is she?" he demanded for about the dozenth time.

"Right where you left her, I wager. At the library, doing what she came here to do."

No doubt true. So why was he so on edge?

The weather was on the news, so he cast around for something else to occupy himself and spotted some papers sticking out from the top shelf of the bookcase. Odd. He strode over to investigate. Pulling them down, he discovered an old handwritten diary, along with some modern papers which appeared to be notations. Was this the diary Clara discovered yesterday?

Curious, he opened it at random and began to read.

What the devil!

He knew that chicken scratch and lame wit! This had been written by none other than Davey Scraggs, his book-learned second mate from the *Sea Sprite*!

Tyree endured a hearty stab of wistfulness at the thought of his old ship. He'd commanded her for eight good years before being banished from her decks by Sully's fatal wound. A sad smile came to his lips. He'd missed her so much he'd even haunted her for one memorable voyage.

The smile faded. Until a new cabin boy came aboard and spotted the ship's dead captain walking her decks at night. Tyree had tried to restrict his movements to times the lad wasn't abroad, but one night he'd run smack into him. The boy had jumped overboard in terror and Tyree was forced to go in after him, holding him afloat until the crew turned the *Sea Sprite* about and was able to fish him out. The lad was never quite the same. And Tyree had decided, as much as it pained him, he'd best give up the sea forever.

Davey Scraggs was one of the men he remembered with most fondness. Skinny and with bad teeth, he was nevertheless sharp as a ray's sting and interested in everything under the sun. Many a day, Tyree would see him with his bottom perched on a barrel, scratching lengthy paragraphs into the small journal he always kept in the breast pocket of his tunic. Each year at Christmas, Mrs. Scraggs would present him with a new one and take charge of the old. Tyree had often wondered what became of the books.

"Mrs. Yates!" he bellowed.

"Yes, Captain?" she answered from the kitchen.

"Where did this journal come from?"

She peered around the corner. "Oh, the diary."

"Well?"

"You remember old Miss Jane Wiggs on Angel Island, don't you? The last time I visited her in the retirement home she gave it to me for the pirate museum library."

"Why haven't I seen it before?"

"Careful with that!" came the sound of Clara's voice from the back hall. "It's fragile."

He turned and demanded, "Where have you been?"

"Worried about me?" she asked as she came up and slid the diary from his fingers.

Loaded question. He ignored it and took the diary back. Carefully. "What are you doing with this?"

"And you accuse *me* of being nosy."

He gritted his teeth. "Just answer the question, Clara."

She held out her hand expectantly.

"You are the most stubborn wench...." Nevertheless, he gave her the book.

"I'm reading it," she said. "It's pretty amazing stuff. I wish I knew who wrote it."

"Davey Scraggs," he said with no small amount of satisfaction at her start of surprise. "Second mate on the *Sea Sprite*."

"How did—" She stopped. "Of course. The *Sea Sprite* was St. James's ship."

"Aye." He told her about Davey and his bent for writing everything down.

"Wow, that's fascinating." She weighed the volume in her hand. "Especially since this one was written the year you—

St. James died." A sudden worried frown creased her brow. "Um, Mrs. Yates, I need to speak with you. Privately," she added, and tucked her free hand under the woman's elbow. "Can I help you with dinner?"

He could just imagine what she had to discuss with the plotting old busybody. "May I borrow that in the meantime?" he asked, reaching for the diary.

She snatched it away. "In your dreams, baby."

"Or maybe in yours?" he said with a wink to mask his irritation. He needed to find out if Scraggs had written anything about his death or Sully's curse. It would be just like Davey to root out every detail and record it all in his damn journal. Clara finding out the details of the curse would be a complication he didn't need.

Never mind. He'd get hold of the diary while she was sleeping.

Just then, his attention was snagged by a voice from the TV. He'd left the news on, and the anchor was talking about the arsonist case he'd been following.

"Another historic Lowcountry home has been badly damaged by fire, this time on Frenchman's Island," the anchor reported. "Investigators believe the fire at the Pryce-Simmons house, built by Harold Simmons in 1784, was deliberately set in order to cover up a robbery."

The Pryce-Simmons house? Why, he knew it well! He and Sully'd spent many a pleasant afternoon sipping ale with old Harold, a wealthy merchant to whom they'd sold portions of the goods they'd been awarded from their privateering voyages. In fact, Tyree had spent time in both of the other houses that had burned down, too. A strange coincidence.

He frowned at the video of firefighters dragging dirty hoses through the smoking interior of the historic house. It made his stomach churn, though he knew the firemen had no choice; they were only doing their job spraying down the room so nothing would reignite.

Something else about the picture bothered him, though, besides the unfortunate and unnecessary destruction of the beautiful and familiar house. If the fire had been set to cover up a robbery, what had the thief taken? Valuable things were strewn everywhere the camera pointed. Antique vases, silver, figurines and fixtures had all been left behind, all portable and easily sold for a small fortune.

Why hadn't the thief taken them?

Tyree quickly popped in a tape and set up the VCR to record the news at 11:00 p.m. They'd no doubt repeat the story, and he could examine the scene more closely. Looking for what, he wasn't sure.

But one thing he was sure of. He didn't care for coincidences.

Clara sliced okra at the kitchen table, deep in thought.

Mrs. Yates had given her exactly the same story as Tyree. He had no health problems. The curse was up on Saturday.

Mrs. Yates was mildly surprised that Tyree had divulged that bit of information, but she hadn't seemed worried. And had confirmed it all. Back in Psych 101, Clara had learned about shared hallucinations. She wondered if there was such a thing as shared delusions.

In any case, there was another thing Clara had learned over the past thirty years: if you can't beat 'em, join 'em.

Obviously, her two hosts were harmless, so from now on she would just go along with their little eccentricities. She'd call Tyree by the name he insisted was his, nod politely when he talked about being cursed and copy his attitude about whatever was happening on Saturday at midnight. Next time he tried one of his little magical illusions, she'd find the strings and mirrors he used to fool her.

Sooner or later he'd let the truth slip. She'd pump him for all the information she could for her article. And hopefully he'd reveal where he'd found all his interesting tidbits, as well as show her whatever historic documents he'd managed to collect.

Such as the letters of marque. If that was really true, if Fouquet and St. James were actually privateers and not pirates, she was about to change local history. No small achievement.

The two professions were nearly identical, but with one huge difference. Pirates were criminals, working beyond the law. Piracy was a hanging offense. Privateers, on the other hand, were officially sanctioned by the war department of the day to prey on enemy vessels during times of war. If Fouquet and St. James possessed legal letters of marque, they would be patriotic heroes, not outlaws.

And by changing history with her article, Clara would be a shoo-in for first prize in the *Adventure Magazine* contest.

When supper was ready, she set the table for three, wondering why Mrs. Yates pursed her lips at the sight.

"Won't Tyree be joining us?" Clara asked.

"The captain doesn't really eat," was the reply.

"His loss," Clara said, unperturbed. "Your chicken gumbo smells wonderful."

As it turned out, Tyree did join them. But his place setting remained pristine as they chatted of this and that. Clara studiously avoided any controversial topic, including why Tyree didn't touch so much as a morsel of food. He did have a sip or two of wine, but then he set his glass aside and ignored it for the rest of the meal. If this was a regular thing, it was a miracle he held on to his magnificent physique.

His arms were sinewy and muscular, nothing slight about them; his torso was lean but solid—no ribs poking through those six-pack abs. And his thighs, she vividly recalled, had been hard as iron.

Her face flooded with warmth as she realized he'd caught her staring at his body. A little smile curled the corners of his mouth.

"Finished?" he asked. When she fumbled for a response, he pointed at her empty plate. "With your supper?"

"Oh. Yes," she managed.

"Let's go watch the sunset," he suggested.

"The dishes—"

"Oh, no, I'll take care of those," Mrs. Yates said.

"But I should—"

"I happen to know Mrs. Yates has a top-of-the-line dishwasher," he said. "I bought it for her myself. Come." He pulled out Clara's chair. "The sunsets here are quite breathtaking."

Clara found herself following Tyree down a crushed oyster-shell path toward the salt marsh. The temperature had cooled a few degrees from the heat of the day, but it was still sultry and warm. Once they'd passed the white picket fence and left behind the jumble of pinks, marigolds and daisies of Mrs. Yates's English garden, they entered the unique forest of oaks, palms and tall grasses that seemed to define the sea island environment. It was a combination Clara had never seen anywhere else. Lushly green, yet sparse enough to allow a generous view of the darkening sky, sharply fragrant with a kaleidoscope of scents from sweetgrass to rotting plough mud, and the sounds of the humming insects and rattling sedges filling her senses.

Tyree took her hand and they walked out onto an old wooden pier that extended far into the waving brown-green sea of marsh grasses. It was like walking the plank into another world, linked to this one only by his hand holding hers, silent except for the sigh of grass and the soft groan of the shifting boards underfoot.

"This is one of my favorite places," he said as they came to a small, square fishing platform about halfway down the pier. "I like to come here and just lie on my back and listen to the lap of the water. Especially on a clear night. I can watch the stars for hours. It's almost like—"

He stopped, but somehow she knew. "Like being at sea?"

"Aye." He dropped her hand and went to the silver weathered rail, leaning his elbows against it as though it were the rail of a ship. "When the wind's died and we're stuck in some godforsaken place and the men are all passed out from drink and there isn't a sound to be heard and the ship's barely rocking. And I should be mad as hell 'cause I've got my orders and there's plunder to be taken, but it's like God's lain down for a nap and everything around us is holding its breath for Him to awaken." He turned to her and smiled. "How can a man be angry when God's sleeping all about him?"

And how could a woman be doubtful of a man who could say something so lovely? She swallowed the lump in her throat and smiled back. "Impossible," she said.

He held out his hand to her, and she took it, expecting to be pulled into his embrace. But instead he continued walking down the pier.

Near the end, it emerged from its cocoon of marsh grass into the open water of the inlet. Clara's breath caught.

"It's so beautiful!"

Slate-green water rippled below gnarled gray planks, reflecting the bright oranges and reds of the setting sun. Across the inlet, black silhouettes of stately Spanish moss-draped oaks mingled with tall, elegant palms along the blazing horizon.

"You were right about the sunsets here."

"Nothing like them in the whole world," Tyree agreed.

She sighed. "I suppose you've been around the world, so you'd know." She turned to find him watching her.

"I suppose," he said, his fingers toying with hers, not quite letting go, not quite holding on.

Awareness zinged through her. She took a step back.

"Watch yourself," he warned, and grasped her hand harder. She was right on the edge. "There are no guardrails this far out."

Didn't she know it. She made a quick effort to shore up the ones around her heart. The man had an uncanny way of slipping past them.

She felt a tug and suddenly she was right in front of him, looking up into his soulful eyes. *Oh, Lord.* He was going to kiss her. She tried to resist, she really did. But for some reason, when he reached out and touched a strand of her hair, she couldn't move.

And when his mouth began to descend to hers, all she could do was close her eyes. And pray she had the will to say no.

Chapter 5

Damnation.

Tyree caught himself just in time. His lips were within inches of Clara's. *Folly and a fool's errand.*

Ignoring the ache in his arms to hold her and the tightness in his throat to taste her, he veered up at the last second and kissed her softly on the forehead.

Her eyes popped open. Was it relief he spied in their depths, just beyond the disappointment?

He motioned to a lone wooden Adirondack chair that perched at the end of the pier. "Make yourself comfortable."

"What about you?"

He answered by stretching out on the wooden deck next to the chair and stacking his hands under his head. "I'm fine down here." Far less temptation. "Tell me about Clara Fergussen," he said, partly as a diversion, partly because he really wanted to know. "Why is it so important to win this magazine contest?"

And so, he heard all about how she'd grown up on a small farm in Kansas, a place where adventure was a bad word and travel something to be avoided at all cost. Clara, in whose veins the blood and spirit of an outlaw pirate flowed so generously, and whose dearest dream was to sail around the world on a yacht, living life to the extreme.

She sounded so much like Tyree at age fifteen, he had to remind himself she was Fouquet's relation, not his own.

"You'll do it," he said. "I'll help with your research, if you like."

"Will you?" she asked, and he could hear her smile. "I was hoping you'd say that. Come with me to the museum tomorrow and help pick out books?"

"Can't."

"Oh." That was definitely disappointment.

"It's Tuesday. Museum's closed."

It was dark by now, the horizon a thin, ragged ribbon of flame against an indigo sky. He heard her shift in the wooden chair, and felt, more than saw, her look down at him.

"In that case, is there something else you can show me?"

A good time came to mind.

"Maybe his favorite places?"

Like that spot on Tyree's inner thigh that had begun to itch madly for her touch. She'd found it last night, clever girl.

His already uncomfortable arousal pitched. This was not good. How was he to avoid her bed tonight, let alone for the whole week?

"There has to be somewhere open," she mused.

He couldn't sleep with her again. It wouldn't be fair to her when he disappeared. Besides, he couldn't risk it.

May you haunt this earth for two hundred years, St. James—or until you find a love so strong the lady is willing to die in your place….

What if she fell in love with him and somehow found out about that provision in the curse? Too dangerous.

"What about the Moon and Palmetto?"

"No," he said emphatically. Sleeping with Clara was the absolute worst thing he could do. Going to the Moon and Palmetto was a close second. "I've only been there once since I died, and that was once too many."

He must simply suffer through this last week and hold out against the overwhelming temptation.

"Where shall we go, then?" she asked.

He got to his feet and helped her from the chair. "How would you like to see where the treasure used to be hidden?"

"The lost treasure? You're kidding!"

"It's not lost. I recovered it a few years after my death. I needed something to live on."

She stared at him wide-eyed in the moonlight. "You have a huge stash of gold at Rose Cottage? No wonder you're afraid to let anyone near it."

"I am not—"

"Ever hear of a thing called the bank?"

"Don't be silly. There's no gold. I invested it ages ago." Most of it, anyway. There was still a small stash of bullion at the Federal Reserve Bank in New York. Maybe he'd transfer ownership of it to Clara. She was Sully's descendant, after all, and as such deserved a share of the spoils.

She chuckled. "So you're a millionaire, I suppose?"

"Millionaire? Heavens, no," he said with a wink.

He had far more than a mere million.

But what was the use of having all that money if you couldn't share it? Tomorrow, he'd have Mrs. Yates speak to his broker. Clara would have her yacht trip, and the yacht, too, if she wished, after he was gone.

"Thank God," she said. "I'd hate you to think I only like you for your money."

He grinned. "Nay, I know exactly what you like about me, and it's not the size of my wallet."

She blushed charmingly and poked him in the chest with her finger. "You're obnoxious, you know that?"

His grin widened as he started humming an old tune from the radio. Something about wanting you in my arms, with all your charms, in a dream.

Her mouth dropped open, scandalized. After half the chorus she turned and started marching down the pier toward shore. But he hadn't missed the laughter in her eyes, or the slight hesitation before she'd turned. Like she was deciding between running away or throwing her arms around him and making all those dreams come true again.

He sauntered after her, whistling. Wishing like hell it was just lust he was feeling. That he didn't like her quite so much, along with wanting her so badly he could barely walk straight.

He caught up with her effortlessly and took hold of her hand just as she reached the fishing platform.

"Clara, sweeting, wait."

She turned, her eyes sparkling in the glow of the moon, her lips parted in breathless anticipation. He could so easily have taken her then. Pulled her body to his and lowered them both to the swaying floor of the pier. Rocked himself into the cradle of her embrace until she cried out like the sea birds swooping and diving around the inlet. It would have been so easy.

And so wrong.

She was alive and vibrant. She deserved to stay that way, and be with a man who could spend a whole lifetime with her, laughing and sharing love and adventures along with his body.

Tyree could offer her nothing but death.

"What is it?" She looked up at him and the lure of her was almost too much to bear. So luscious and soft.

"I need your help," he heard himself say.

She nibbled on her lower lip, obviously suspecting he would do exactly what he was trying so hard not to. He couldn't decide if she'd welcome it, or was getting ready to flee again.

"Help with what, Tyree?"

"You know those fires that are being set?"

For a second she looked confused. "The historic houses, you mean? To cover up the robberies?"

He nodded. "Exactly. I want to find out what is being stolen."

She looked even more puzzled. "Why?"

"I'm getting a bad feeling about that whole thing. I think the guy is after something specific."

"Well, of course he is. Why else would he be doing it?"

Tyree decided to tell her what was really bothering him. "I'm worried the robberies might have something to do with Sully and me."

"Huh? How could they possibly have anything to do with you and Sully?"

He jetted out a breath. "We knew the owners of all three of those houses that were set on fire. We did a lot of business with them."

"You mean the original owners?" she asked incredulously. "Two hundred years ago?"

He spread his hands. "I know it sounds unlikely, but…I'd feel better if I knew exactly what the guy was stealing. Will you help me?"

"How?"

"You're a reporter. Nose around."

"Tyree, I'm not a reporter. I'm not even an official travel writer yet. Why don't *you* nose around?"

He gave her his best social-misfit-agoraphobic-hermit smile. "I'm shy."

She rolled her eyes. "My aunt Bessie."

"C'mon, please?"

He could see she was reluctant to get involved with any of his flights of fancy, but couldn't help being curious. Luckily, Sully's lingering spirit tipped the scales.

"Oh, all right," she relented, and started walking down the pier again. "But you'll have to show me those letters of marque first."

"You drive a hard bargain," he said with some relief, and followed after her. He'd planned to show her the letters in any case.

He wasn't sure why this fire thing bothered him so much. He had to admit, his theory sounded preposterous even to himself. Still, better to relieve his mind and feel foolish than to find out too late it was something he should have dealt with. He didn't have much time left to waste.

How was it he could be bored to tears for two centuries and now suddenly have ten things nipping at his heels to be done before Saturday? Nothing made sense anymore.

Not since Clara had come into his life.

Reaching shore, Clara and Tyree strolled back through the gardens to the main house, where they found Mrs. Yates knitting in the living room. It wasn't late, and Clara decided to do a little work before retiring, so while Tyree stretched out in an oversized leather armchair in front of some TV reality show, Clara fetched Davey Scraggs's diary.

After lighting a vanilla-scented candle on the mantelpiece, she curled up at the end of the cushy velvet sofa and started to read. It was so peaceful, time flew by before she realized she'd finished over five pages of notes.

She smiled inwardly. Strange how it worked sometimes. Here she was on the biggest adventure of her life, yet the only thing that could possibly make the evening feel any homier or cozier would be a plate of her mom's oatmeal-chocolate-chip cookies.

She stole a glance at Tyree. Okay, maybe one other thing might make it cozier. Too bad he'd chosen the armchair instead of the sofa by her. Even if she wasn't interested in pursuing a romantic entanglement, it would be nice just to sit next to him. Close enough to feel the warmth of his body, maybe catch a drift of his scent now and then. Brush shoulders.

He glanced up and their gazes met. They both smiled. She looked away first, heat creeping up her neck. He'd been a perfect gentleman all day. Hadn't so much as tried to kiss her, despite his mild flirting. He'd apologized for last night, and both of them agreed it had been a mistake not to be repeated. Neither was interested in that sort of involvement.

And she wasn't. Honestly.

She squirmed. So why was her body relentlessly reminding her of all the pleasure she could experience with him? Of his slow hands and skillful mouth, his commanding weight on her and his consummately sensitive touch?

Maybe…

Good grief. What was wrong with her? Could she really consider inviting him to her bed, knowing it would be nothing more than physical gratification? Was she capable of sleeping with a man with whom she had no intention of pursuing a relationship?

She really liked Tyree. It was so tempting to sweep away her qualms and for once allow herself to indulge in a passionate affair. But she knew by doing so she would only end up hurt. Because she did like Tyree. Far too much to risk getting any closer.

No way would she be able to change him and his fantasy world—nor was it her place to try. He was who he was. But she had other plans for her life than to spend it cosseted away on some remote island estate with an eccentric, if captivating, recluse. No matter how heavenly his naked body felt joined with hers.

Their eyes met again and she felt herself weaken. Damn him for being so sexy.

She looked away and closed the diary. Rising, she deliberately yawned, and said, "I can barely stay awake. Think I'll have an early night."

His brow rose a fraction and she was careful to keep her face neutral so as not to send him any "follow me" signals or a look that could be interpreted as encouraging.

"Are you sure, my dear?" asked Mrs. Yates. "I've baked some oatmeal-chocolate-chip cookies for our evening tea."

Clara groaned appreciatively. "Save me one for tomorrow, Mrs. Yates." She made for the door before the two of them completely broke her resolve.

"I'll try to locate those letters of marque before morning," Tyree said, his eyes darting to the diary in her hands.

"Great."

"Do we still have a date, then?" he asked as she walked past his chair. "For treasure hunting?"

She couldn't resist trailing her forefinger over his. *Playing with fire.* "Wouldn't miss it."

Four hours later Tyree rubbed the spot where Clara had lightly touched his fingers. It still tingled down a path as clear as if she'd drawn it with a black marker.

The letters of marque lay before him on his desk, a yellowed parchment bearing a neat black scrawl, affixed with the distinctive wax imprint of the U.S. Department of War seal.

He wondered if he was doing the right thing giving them to her. It went without saying he didn't want ghost hunters swarming over Rose Cottage testing for otherworldly presences, nor did he want cops investigating reports of strange sightings on the property. Either could lead to an investigation into Mrs. Yates's real estate and financial holdings. Something he wanted to avoid.

But what about historians coming at him from the other end of the spectrum, from his own life and demise? The letters would undoubtedly trigger investigations into their authenticity. Could that scrutiny also lead to someone uncovering irregularities in the title to Rose Cottage and the myriad other trusts and accounts Mrs. Yates oversaw for Tyree?

He didn't think so. He prayed not. For he had given his word to Clara.

But he'd do anything to avoid jeopardizing his legacy. Too many deserving people depended on the income.

He rose and gathered up the document, glancing at the clock. 2:15 a.m. Now was as good a time as any to drop it off in Clara's bungalow. And he hadn't forgotten about the diary. He must find out if he could allow Clara to continue her reading. He feared old Scraggs might have weaseled the whole curse from eyewitnesses that fatal night. If Davey'd recorded it, Tyree might just have to rip out that page. Or at least hide the diary until it wouldn't be a danger to anyone.

If he took the diary from her, she'd surely be mad as that Spanish captain whose cargo of French brandy Sully had purloined back in '96. Tyree had relieved the captain of his wild Irish mistress on the same occasion, but he hadn't taken that nearly as badly. Now, there had been an interesting voyage home. And cause to avoid brandy and wild Irish females ever since.

Tyree chuckled at the memory. Come to think of it, was Fergussen an Irish name? He tried the knob on the gardener's bungalow door. Locked. How sweet. She thought she could keep him out. Silly wench. He concentrated his thoughts and let himself drift through the door.

Holding the parchment close to his chest, he passed through the solid wood. Even after all this time, it still confounded him how this spirit thing worked. It seemed impossible that a material could be firm and substantial sitting on a desk, but as soon as he picked it up its molecules changed so dramatically as to be able to pass through any solid barrier along with him.

To be sure, his whole state of being seemed impossible, so what was one more mystery? But whatever it was, he was grateful for it. Otherwise, staying clothed might have proved a thorny task.

Tyree arranged the parchment on the small kitchen table so she would be sure to see it. Then he quietly turned on a light to look around for Davey's journal. It was nowhere to be found in the main room of the bungalow. *Devil take it.*

He stood and gazed at the closed door to Clara's bedroom, battling his compulsion to enter. This would not be a good idea.

But he must find that diary.

He'd simply go in and search for the book. Nothing more. He wouldn't even look at her. Lying there in his big four-poster bed. Asleep. Perhaps wearing one of those pretty, frilly diaphanous things women wore at night.

Nay. He'd go straight to the journal, grab it and depart without so much as a glance at her.

But what if she'd hidden it?

What if she'd hidden it under her pillow?

Or had it in bed with her, clutched to her bosom?

He silently groaned, wrenched out a chair at the table and sank into it, clutching his head in his hands. *God in heaven.*

Maybe the curse had already lifted; maybe he'd left the world behind and this was hell.

This particular agony was far worse than any mere fire and brimstone he could imagine. Wanting her. Having her within reach, but not being able to take her.

Or maybe it was a test. Another in a long line of earthly trials designed to see if he was worthy of a place in heaven, despite having killed his best friend.

The thought quelled the fire in his blood sufficiently to bring him to his feet and turn them toward Clara's room. He'd pass this one, too, as he'd passed all the others.

Taking a fortifying breath, he went through the door and stood for a moment getting his bearings. Despite the few peculiarities and special powers of his state, his physical abilities remained largely the same as before he died. He wasn't able to leap tall buildings in a single bound, or stop speeding bullets with his bare hand—they went right through it—or see any better in the dark. A damned nuisance.

Luckily, he'd brought a penlight. Which he took out of his pocket and had a look around. The journal was not on the dresser, not in the armoire, not on the vanity, or table or chair by the window, not on the floor or the nightstands. He let out a silent curse. And shone the light onto the bed.

His angel. The one he'd seen in the library window earlier today. She lay ensconced in a cloud of lace that was the coverlet, the tresses of her pale hair curling over his pillow and about her head like a nimbus. Perhaps this was heaven, after all.

But alas, he was not meant to share her cloud.

He spotted the journal on the bed by her hand, papers strewn around as though she'd fallen asleep working. Leaning over the mattress, he gingerly collected the papers and deposited them in a neat pile on the nightstand, then slipped the diary from the bed. Hesitating, he was unable to stop himself from reaching up and caressing her cheek. So warm, so smooth and peaceful. In her sleep she made a little noise and turned her face, placing a tiny kiss on his fingers.

His heart melted. He slammed his eyes shut for a second, then leaned over and softly, gently kissed her lips. Then before he could do anything they'd both regret, he twisted away and swept from the room.

Taking a seat at the table in the kitchen area, he pored through Davey's journal, searching for the entry about the night he died. He couldn't help but stop and read many another passage, though, so many memories did it bring back for him of that last year on the *Sea Sprite*. He laughed again over the antics of his unorthodox crew, once more felt the adrenaline rush of taking an enemy ship captive and emptying her hold, shed a sad tear over two friends they'd lost to fever. Davey had left out nothing.

He knew before he reached them that the pages he sought would contain everything he feared. And sure enough, they did. Everything, down to the last drop of blood and each word of the curse.

Suddenly the door opened behind him and he heard a feminine gasp.

"What are you doing here?" Clara asked.

He looked up and saw hazy sunlight peering through the windowpanes. How could it already be morning?

Clara stared at him from the doorway, one finger unconsciously touching her lips as she took in his attire. "How did you get in?"

He hadn't even noticed when he'd reverted to his pirate togs. Letting out a swift sigh, he rose to his feet and snapped the book shut.

"I'm sorry, I can't let you continue reading this." She frowned, but he headed her off before she could speak. "I brought the letters of marque, though."

Her gaze dropped to the parchment lying on the table. Then she swiped a hand over her eyes. "I can't deal with this without coffee," she said, and walked to the kitchen.

He shooed her away. "I'll do it. You get dressed. Or something." Best to have this conversation with everyone fully clothed. Her sleep shirt wasn't frilly or diaphanous, but it was short enough to be far too diverting.

He flipped off his aggravating eye patch and threw it on the table on his way to the counter, knowing no matter what he did with it, it would miraculously reappear upon his eye on the morrow. As for the modern clothes he'd been wearing last night, they could now be found exactly where he'd pulled them out of the drawer to don yesterday. He batted down the high bucket tops of his boots to knee level. What a pain they were. Footwear had come far in two hundred years.

He filled the coffeemaker with water, ground the beans from the cupboard and dumped them into the basket. After a quick survey of its various buttons and LCD screens, he pressed a combination and left it to drip.

Still no Clara, he discerned, and heard the sound of the shower running. This time he groaned aloud, and forced himself to take a seat at the table and not move until the sound ceased. Honor was a hard taskmaster.

When she reemerged toweling her hair, dressed in a short, tight jean skirt and skimpy tank top, he jumped to his feet.

"Are you *trying* to kill me?" he asked with exasperation.

She halted and her eyes flashed to his before her lips twitched and she asked, with a shade too much curiosity, "What would happen if I did?"

He folded his arms over his tunic. "Nothing. You've seen the movie *Groundhog Day*?" She nodded, her grin widening. "Well, my life is like one long, bad, two-hundred-year-old version of *Groundhog Day*. So you can forget about your little plan to make me die of frustration. It won't work."

He poured a cup of coffee and handed it to her.

"No cream?" she asked.

"Don't push it, wench."

She blew on her coffee and took a long sip and he was supremely proud of himself for not watching her lips, and also for not trying to figure out whether she had on one of those sexy bras under her top.

She had no such disinclination about him. "You're dressed like a pirate again," she observed.

"Aye," he said. "Unfortunately it happens every morning."

"Like in the movie."

"Aye."

She took another sip and nodded. "Did you know *Groundhog Day* is my all-time favorite movie?"

He gave a moue of distaste. "I hate it."

She chuckled. "Why am I not surprised?" She put down her coffee cup. "Okay, I'm awake now," she said. "So what's all this about not letting me read the diary?"

"That's right. I can't let you."

"Why not?"

He exhaled. "Let's just say…there are circumstances about…about the curse and all, that could make it dangerous for you to know the details."

"That's crazy," she said.

He let out a short bark of laughter. "Tell me about it."

"Seriously. Why is it dangerous?"

"We've been through this before, Clara. I can't explain. You just have to trust me. You could get hurt."

"Does this have anything to do with the fires?"

He jerked her a look of surprise. "Of course not." Then he thought about it for a second. An intriguing possibility. But how could it? He shook his head. Now he really was going crazy. "Nay. The fires have nothing to do with the curse."

She gave the diary which he was holding in his hand a bleak look. "That was my best source, you know. For the article."

"I'm sorry."

"He has such great stories in it. Like the time you risked your life to rescue that three-legged dog from those hungry French soldiers." She gave a heartfelt sigh.

Christ. Thank God he'd skipped the first part of the journal. "The cur bit me for my trouble," he informed her gruffly. "I should have let them eat it."

She gasped. "Tyree!"

He waved his arm. "Enough. This won't work, either."

She made a face. "Fine. Okay, what if I promise not to read that part? The part about the curse?"

"Surely you jest."

"Hey, you expect me to trust you. Don't you trust me?"

"In a word—"

She raised a warning finger. "Careful."

He swallowed his knee-jerk response. Did he trust her? Well, he'd let her stay, hadn't he? Did he suspect her of some nefarious purpose in being here? Nay, he was sure she was who she professed to be, doing exactly what she'd said.

He weighed the diary between his fingers as if it were her heart. "Can I trust you to keep your word?"

"Only as far as I can trust you to keep yours."

"My word is my honor," he said.

"As is mine," she responded.

Fair enough. He'd ages ago outgrown his archaic chauvinist bent, having lived long enough to know that most women possessed far more honor than many men who purported to live by its rule.

His gaze swept over her tank top and snagged on a lacy strap peeking out at the shoulder. He followed it down to the mouthwatering outline of a bra pushing her breasts up like the most wanton of corsets.

God's Teeth.

Tyree always kept his word. But that didn't mean he was always virtuous.

"I'll tell you what," he said, and slowly smiled. "Perhaps we can strike a bargain."

Chapter 6

Clara knew that look on Tyree's face, and it spelled nothing but trouble.

Now she understood why he'd been so good at his chosen profession. It wasn't just tight breeches and a billowy shirt that made a man a pirate. It was his actions. A pirate didn't follow rules. He simply took what he wanted. And though Tyree denied it, she had the distinct feeling what he wanted was *her*.

"What kind of bargain?" she asked.

One black brow arched. "Would it matter?"

"That depends."

"On?"

"What you have in mind."

She was also beginning to realize that her own pirate fantasy ran deeper than she'd ever imagined. No wonder the men wearing eye patches at Halloween parties had never done it for her. But fantasy or no, this one was well on his way to stealing her very breath.

Whatever happened to not wanting to risk getting any closer?

Unfortunately, at the moment Tyree's fantasy world coincided a little too neatly with her own. She really had to get him to change those clothes.

"I want you to teach me something," he said. "Something I've wanted to learn for a long while, but never had the opportunity."

"What makes you think I'll know this thing?" she asked, vainly attempting to tame the squeak in her voice.

His smile turned devilish and her nipples twisted into tight knots. Damn, how did he do that with just a look?

"Aye, you know how."

"But you don't?"

"Nay."

How bad could it be? They both knew when it came to anything sexual, he had it all over her, hands down. As it were.

"Well?"

"What do you want to learn?"

He stood there smiling like the rogue he was. But didn't answer.

Her mouth dropped in disbelief. "You're not going to tell me?"

"How badly do you want to read Davey's journal?"

"Forget it, St. James," she said firmly. "No deal." She rinsed out her cup and headed for the front door. "Mrs. Yates will be making breakfast for us."

"It doesn't involve sex, if that's what concerns you," he said from behind her. There was something rough and seductive about his voice…like callused hands on soft skin.

She shook off a shiver. "You're not very convincing."

"Sweeting, I like my women willing, not obligated. Takes all the fun out of it."

She wasn't so sure, but she didn't need to tell him that. "No taking off any clothes?"

He held up two fingers in a pledge. As if he'd ever been a Boy Scout. "I swear I won't remove a single stitch."

"And me?"

He waggled his eyebrows. "Only if you want to."

She ground her jaw. "You're impossible, you know that?"

"And obnoxious," he reminded her.

She thought furiously. She really, really wanted to read that diary. And she figured she could handle anything as long as it didn't involve him being naked....

"Oh, all right. You have your bargain. So what is it?"

"You give me your word you won't read any of the section that I mark as off-limits? Nothing to do with the night of my death?"

"Yes, yes, I agree. And in return you want me to teach you to...?"

He gazed at her in that powerful, heart-stoppingly sexy way he had, his black lashes all thick around his dark, bedroom eyes. He let them drift slowly over her breasts down to the nipples that had tightened so hard they were almost painful.

He lied, she thought in desperation... *He's going to make me—*

"Unhook your bra," he said.

Her heart stopped. "I knew it! There is no way—"

"Nay, just *show* me how it unhooks," he said, calm as could be. "I've never touched a real one—" he coughed "—before yours."

She regarded him evenly. "You're kidding, right?"

"You needn't take it off. We do have an understanding." He added in that slow drawl, "Don't we?"

Oh, Lord.

"That's right," she blurted out and bolted for the door. "And this isn't part of it."

"Your choice," he said, ambling after. "Just let me know if you change your mind."

To his credit, he didn't stare at her breasts during breakfast. He didn't have to. Clara's own imagination was working overtime picturing Tyree's requested lesson. But in every scenario she came up with, she ended up naked under him.

Not good.

"Actually, I thought we'd take the Sea-Doo," Tyree was saying. "What do you think, Clara?"

She yanked herself out of another image of him removing her bra. "Hmm? I'm sorry, I was—" She cleared her throat. He must be talking about the day's planned excursion to the treasure's hiding place. "What's a Sea-Doo?"

"Sort of like a motorcycle that rides on water."

She remembered seeing those on TV. Far too cozy. "Can't we get there by car?"

He shook his head. "Only by water."

"Don't you have a regular boat?"

His lips curved up knowingly. "Scared?"

Of sharing a narrow seat, bodies pressed tightly together and clinging to his waist for dear life? Oh, yeah. "Let's just say I'd prefer a boat."

He leaned back in his chair and grinned. "No problem. I have a boat, too."

When they were ready, they walked to a dock where a sleek, arrow-shaped speedboat was tied up along with a Sea-Doo.

"For a guy who never leaves his property you have some pretty impressive horsepower here," she remarked.

"I'll admit to taking an occasional late night boat trip around the marshes. Can't keep an old sailor from the sea."

He said the last with such wistfulness that she asked, "Don't you ever go sailing?"

"Nay," he answered, but didn't elaborate.

From the dock, he lowered down her tote, the picnic basket Mrs. Yates had prepared for them, a life jacket and a pair of waders he had insisted on bringing for her. He still wore his ridiculous pirate boots and skintight breeches, but had shed his white tunic in favor of a sleeveless T-shirt. It was a strange combination, but on him it somehow worked.

She was trying to decide whether to risk climbing in by herself when she felt Tyree's hand on her waist.

"I'll go first," he said, and with a graceful move leapt into the boat, landing like a cat. He reached up for her. "Jump. I'll catch you."

She leaned down to grab his hands, took a deep breath and jumped. She found herself wrapped in his arms in a wildly rocking boat.

"Landlubber," he chided, holding her close as the motion underfoot slowed. "Never been on a boat before?"

"Not a lot of them in Kansas." She tried to take a step away but fell right back into his embrace. "At least where I grew up."

"What are you going to do for a whole year on that yacht without me to hold you?"

She gazed up at him and wondered the same thing. Two days and she'd already miss him.

She drew back. "Guess I'd better start practicing, huh?"

"Guess so." He steered her to the captain's chair behind the wheel and plopped her into it. "You drive."

"But—!"

"Just take it easy. You'll do fine." He smiled at her reassuringly.

And to her surprise, she did. First, he took her a few times around the inlet, to get her used to the feel of the big engine behind the simple controls. Then he took her out into the wide, shallow channels between the islands, where they scupped and scudded across the low waves, their hair streaming out behind them and their laughter echoing across the sparkling blue water.

She had no idea where they were. If for some reason Tyree abandoned her, she didn't have a clue how to get back to Frenchman's Island. But she didn't care. She knew he'd never do that. He'd never leave her alone.

"Ready to find some treasure?" he called above the noise of the rushing wind.

"I thought you said it wasn't there anymore," she yelled back.

He shrugged, grinning. "Never know, I might have missed a chest or two."

He was teasing her. She could tell by his eyes, all crinkled up in amusement. Still, the thought of finding a treasure chest brimming with gold and jewels and pieces of eight made her grin right back. Boy, wouldn't that be a story....

"Which way?" she shouted with a whoop.

She followed his directions and soon they were chugging through a maze of tall sea grass, forging a path through the watery wilderness like an icebreaker.

"Are you sure you know where you're going?"

"Hope so," he replied, and pointed in front of them. "Watch out for the alligators."

"Omigod!" she squealed, and bounced from her seat to clutch at him. "Are they real?"

He grabbed the wheel and steered around the nasty-looking creatures. "Never seen an alligator before, either?"

"I thought they only lived in Florida." She held him a little tighter.

"Hell, no. We've got tons of them. Here, I'll show you."

"No, thanks!" Before she could protest he'd switched seats and turned the speedboat, taking them back to where the pair of reptiles floated. "I really don't—"

"Look at those teeth."

"I'd rather not."

She had no idea how she'd ended up sitting on his lap behind the wheel with her arms around his neck. But when he pulled her a little closer, she suddenly noticed where she was. She looked up from the alligators into his eyes. And couldn't remember what they were talking about.

"I suppose it would be a bad idea for me to kiss you right now," he said softly.

"Yeah," she agreed. But for some reason her fingers didn't. They crept up and toyed with the strands of his long black hair. "A very bad idea."

"That's what I thought," he said, but his face moved a shade closer. Not touching, just enough so she could smell the salt on his skin mixed with the low note of musky spice he always carried. Enough to imagine the feel of his stubbled cheek on hers.

"Maybe just a little one?" she whispered, and let her lips skim his ear.

He shifted his legs and her breasts bumped up against his chest. "Think we can keep it little?" he murmured.

She eased out a breath, loving the feel of his hard body against hers, the tension of his muscles as he held her, the obviousness of the arousal he didn't try to hide.

"No, probably not."

He held her just like that for a long moment. "I don't want to hurt you," he said.

"Me, neither."

"Then I suppose we'd better not."

"No," she agreed again. And drew out of his arms.

It was the hardest thing she'd ever done in her life.

Somehow Tyree banked the urge to change Clara's mind about that kiss. They both knew it was better this way. His body would eventually learn to accept it.

He eased the speedboat up to the shore of the tiny, uninhabited island they were making for and handed her the waist-high waders. "Better put these on."

"So attractive," she mumbled, but put them on over her sneakers anyway. The only way from the boat to shore was to wade through a wide band of thick mud and rushes, crawling with fiddler crabs.

At the sight of the crabs, she balked. "There are millions of them!"

"Shall I carry you?" he asked with a wink. Cheap thrill, but he'd take what he could get.

For a second, she looked like she was actually considering the offer. "Do they bite?"

"Through those things?" He pointed to the wader boots, which were probably thick enough to stop an attacking dog.

She grimaced. "I guess this should go under the heading of Having An Adventure."

"That's what you're here for," he said. "Here, hold my hand so the mud doesn't suck you down."

"You're going to ruin your leather boots."

"Trust me, they'll be fine in the morning."

"Hmm."

He knew she still didn't believe his story, *Groundhog Day* or no. To be honest, it was nice just being a regular guy for a change, instead of some kind of cosmic freak. Well, sort of regular. But his eccentricities didn't seem to bother her overly much. Aye, it was very nice being normal again.

"How the heck did they carry big heavy treasure chests through this mud?"

"We used gangplanks. And it was just Sully and me, so we brought everything in small loads. Lots of trips."

She grinned. "Worried that helpers would come back and make off with the treasure if they knew the location?"

"You got it. Even Sully and I didn't know exactly where the cache was hidden. It took us both together to find it. He only knew half the route and I knew the other half."

Clara gave him a sardonic glance. "So how do you know where it is now?"

He chuckled. "Took me almost two years to find the right place, wandering around every coastal island and waterway within a hundred miles. Not that I had anything better to do. I needed funds to buy a place to live, so I didn't have to set up residency in some poor innocent's household."

She laughed. "As their resident ghost?"

"I told you I'm not a ghost. I'm a—"

"Yes, yes. A lost, wandering soul."

"Big difference."

"Which is?"

"A ghost is permanent, I assume. Not that I've ever met one. My tenure is temporary. I'll be gone soon."

"On Saturday."

"That's right."

After that, she was silent. And for the first time in memory, he didn't want to think about leaving. So he put it out of his mind.

They trudged down the twisting animal path he'd memorized almost two centuries before, and finally arrived at the correct spot.

Tyree halted and let his gaze wander over the meadow around the old gnarled oak where he and Sully had hidden their cache.

"This is it."

He'd never forget this patch of earth. It had been tough going digging those holes with nothing but a pick and shovel, and a rusty saw for the tree roots. Green grass was dotted with meadow flowers and crisscrossed by tangles of flowering creepers.

"So peaceful," Clara said. "You're sure this is the right place?"

"Aye."

"How did you *really* find it? Did you find a reference in a book? Or maybe a treasure map?"

He laughed out loud. "Nay. We made no map."

She waited for him to continue, but when he didn't she shuffled the toe of her wader in the dirt. "So, did you bring a spade today?"

He grinned. "Nay."

"So you didn't miss a chest or two."

"Actually, I did."

Gold from the first one had bought the estate where he'd built Rose Cottage. After that, he'd moved them one by one to his property, and over the next fifty years with Rosalind's help had sold or exchanged most of the treasure for land or other investments. He'd kept some bullion, now safely stored in the reserve bank, as well as one chest filled with odd coins and other things which hadn't been worth much at the time.

That he'd buried under Rose Cottage for emergencies. It had never been touched.

"Really?"

"Aye, there was one chest I never found. I dug everywhere." He shook his head. "We must have miscounted when we buried them. Ah, well. Let's have a look around."

They deposited their gear in a shady spot and took a walk around the whole island. It didn't take more than an hour.

"So you really think you miscounted?" Clara asked after they removed their boots, spread the blanket and broke out Mrs. Yates's lunch.

"We must have. Trust me, there were no other chests here."

"Hmm. Sandwich?" she asked, and he shook his head no.

"Even Bill Murray ate," she said in a mildly reproving tone.

"It was a movie, Clara. Bill Murray wasn't dead."

He could practically hear her bite her tongue against saying he wasn't, either.

"All right, if it pleases you." He smiled and accepted a ham and cheese sandwich, stretched out and nibbled, watching her as she speculated about possible reasons for the missing chest.

"Could St. James and Sully have been followed?"

"I can't see how. Though, I suppose anything's possible."

He and Sully had been very careful, but nothing was ever foolproof. The crews of both their ships knew they cached their shares of the spoils together. Every sailor received a generous portion, but there were inevitably those whose greed exceeded their good sense.

"Still," she said, "if someone had followed, he'd have come back and taken the whole lot, not just one chest. That makes no sense."

"Dead man's treasure," Tyree said solemnly.

"Huh?"

"Sailors are a superstitious lot. Taking a dead man's treasure is inviting his revenge from beyond the grave. In this case, there were two dead men."

"And that cabin boy's tale of the ghost of St. James rescuing him at sea," she murmured thoughtfully. "Adding to the superstition."

He glanced at her sharply. "How did you know about that?"

"From a book about local hauntings I found at the library yesterday. Okay, how 'bout this. Maybe whoever took the chest died before he could come back for the rest?"

He smiled and relaxed. Was she starting to believe him? Maybe. Regardless, she obviously had no idea how bad he used to be at math.

"And maybe he wrote down the location before he died."

He couldn't resist teasing her just a little. "Or she. It could have been a woman who followed us."

"True." Clara glanced at him, attempting to look nonchalant. "If it was a woman, perhaps she didn't even *have* to follow you."

With a grin, he crooked an elbow and propped his head on his hand. "You mean Sully and I may have indulged in a little pillow talk?" His grin broadened. "Do I detect a note of jealousy?"

"Don't be ridiculous," she said archly.

But he knew a jealous woman when he saw one. For the life of him he couldn't figure out why it pleased him so much.

"Aye, well, I don't think Sully's Elizabeth could even write, so I doubt it was her. And as for me—" he sent her a wink "—you know firsthand I don't do a lot of talking while sharing my pillow with a pretty wench. Leastwise not about treasure."

Her cheeks turned a delightful shade of crimson. "St. James might have talked in his sleep."

It was strange hearing himself constantly referred to in the third person. But in a sense, it gave him a distance from his past he hadn't experienced before. As though he were a new man, with a new life, talking about someone completely different.

"No woman ever complained of nocturnal discourse while I was alive."

"And after?"

"I don't sleep, and I've shared my pillow with only one other woman besides you. After dying, that is."

Shock skidded across her face. Then uncertainty. "Really? Why not?"

He rolled onto his back and gazed heavenward, watching the tall palms sway in the breeze. "As you may have noticed, I try to avoid human entanglements. Especially with young women."

"Why?" she repeated.

The words slipped out before he could stop them. "The price is far too high."

He could feel her eyes on him, gentle and sympathetic. "Who was she?" she softly asked.

"Who?"

"The other woman. The one you fell in love with."

Chapter 7

Clara didn't think Tyree would answer. He lay on his back staring up at the sky for so long she thought he might have fallen asleep. Except his eyes were open.

"Her name was Rosalind," he finally said. "Rosalind Winters. I'd traveled to Charleston to arrange for furnishings for Rose Cottage, which was newly built. I ran into her while having a look around a fabric merchant's warehouse. She could see me, just as you can." He turned his head and smiled. "She was beautiful like you, too. And it had been so long since I'd been close to a woman. At least, it seemed long at the time."

"What happened?"

"The merchant was busy with another customer, so I wandered with her among the fabric bolts. She had exquisite taste. I asked for her help in picking out materials and furnishings for the cottage. When she agreed, I gave her the bag of gold I'd brought, the drawings for Rose Cottage and the directions to Frenchman's Island."

"Weren't you afraid she'd take the money and run?"

His lips curved up, his eyes a million miles away. "Nay. I stole a kiss to seal the bargain and asked her to come help me set up the house when the things were delivered. She came and never left."

Clara fought a stab of irrational jealousy and anger at the woman who had so obviously hurt him. "Where is she now?"

"She's dead," he answered with a deep sigh. "But enough of this." He climbed to his feet. "We have work to do."

Clara winced at her insensitivity. "I'm sorry. I didn't mean to make you sad."

He waved a hand. "Ancient history."

Obviously not, if it still influenced the way he lived. He'd as much as admitted this Rosalind was the reason he avoided relationships. Could she also be the reason he was so obsessed with death? Clara thought about that as they packed up their picnic things and headed back to the boat. She'd have to ask Mrs. Yates about the woman.

"Are you up for a quick stop on the way home?" he asked as they slogged through the mud and he helped her over the side of the speedboat.

"Where did you have in mind?"

He revved up the engine. "The Pryce-Simmons house."

"The place that burned?"

"Aye. It's time for that nosing around you promised me."

She'd hoped he'd forgotten. Naturally, he hadn't, since he'd brought her the letters of marque that morning.

"But the cops might still be there," she shouted over the engine as they sped along a wide natural channel between two flat islands. "Doing forensics and such."

"That's what I'm hoping."

"What am I supposed to ask them?"

"What the guy was after."

"You don't think they'll get a little suspicious?"

He grinned over at her. "Don't worry, you were in Kansas when the other fires started. You won't turn into a suspect."

"Great."

"Just bat your eyelashes and say you're writing an article. That's true enough."

"Bat my eyelashes, eh?"

"Hey, it would work with me."

"What if the investigator is a woman?" she muttered.

As it turned out, it wasn't a woman. Or a cop. It was the arson inspector from the Old Fort Mystic Fire Department, according to the bright red emblem on a beat-up yellow truck parked in the driveway. She could see both it and the man as she hopped out of the boat and tied up at the Pryce-Simmons dock.

"Remember," Tyree said as the inspector looked up from the rubble. "Don't say anything about me or Rose Cottage."

"Right." She took off up the boardwalk toward the badly damaged house. Most of it was still intact, but the outer wall of one wing had burned, exposing the gaping innards of a study or library which she recognized from the video they'd shown on TV.

The arson inspector met her at the edge of the garden.

"You from the Historic Society?" he asked without preamble.

She stuck out her hand. "No. Clara Fergussen. I'm—"

"Where the hell is the Historic Society person? She was supposed to be here an hour ago."

"Can't help you there." Clara let her hand drop. "Listen, I was—"

"So who are you?" he asked, and scrutinized her as though it were the first time he'd really noticed her. His eyes were a clear, hard gray, like the color of a tornado cloud just before it mowed down some unsuspecting trailer park. Set in a tan, ruggedly good-looking face topped by thick, chestnut hair, he should have been handsome. Very handsome. But there was something about him, a menacing quality that sent a cold shiver up her spine. Any minute now, she expected lightning to strike around him.

Batting her eyelashes would probably not be a good idea.

She repeated her name.

"What are you doing on my crime scene?" he asked.

"I'm writing an article, and I was wondering if you could give me a little background on the fire."

"An article for who?" He gave her another one of those glaring stares.

"Ah." *Busted.* "Well, *Adventure Magazine*, actually."

He continued to glare. Silently.

"It's about pirates. Sullivan Fouquet and Tyree St. James. They were from Frenchman's Island, you know. In my research I ran across, um…"

He wasn't buying it. No doubt about it. The silent glare didn't budge. This guy probably had people confessing to setting fires who'd never lit a match in their lives. Heck, *she* wanted to confess, just to make him stop glaring at her like that.

He grunted and turned on a heel. "Get lost," he said, and strode back toward the house.

Drat. "Wait! Mr., um, wait a second! I noticed a connection between Sully and Tyree and the three houses that burned down. Something you may not be aware of."

He halted, slowly turning. His eyes sharpened. Like those of a bird of prey. "Sully and Tyree?"

She felt herself flush from head to toe. "Fouquet and St. James. Captain Fouquet was my great-great-great unc—anyway, I know it's probably not anything, but—"

"What kind of connection?"

She cleared her throat and stuck her hands under her armpits. This was definitely the last time she'd ever, *ever* do Tyree any kind of favor.

"According to my research, they did business with all three of the original owners."

"What kind of business?"

"Fencing their booty, from what I gather."

"Is that so."

"Yeah. So I wondered if the thefts had anything to do with

that. It would make a great angle for my article." She stopped talking to give him an opportunity to comment. Which he didn't. After a prickly silence, she asked with a bright smile, "So do they? Have a connection?"

A full ten seconds ticked by, then he said in a clipped voice, "Know anything about paintings?"

"Um, sorry, no."

He set his jaw. "In that case I'll have to ask the Historic Society lady." He grunted again, said, "Thanks for the tip," and once more turned on a heel and strode away toward the house, calling over his shoulder, "Call me in a couple of days and I'll tell you what I find out."

She blinked. "What's your name?" she called back.

"Jake Santee."

"Any luck?" Tyree asked when she got back in the speed-boat.

She relayed what had happened blow by blow as she settled behind the wheel and followed his directions through the maze of channels and inlets back to Frenchman's Island. She kept the speed low so they could talk without shouting.

"Paintings, eh?"

"It would seem so."

"In other words, nothing related to me or Sully."

"Nope."

"That's a relief. Now I can concentrate on other things for my last week on earth."

She darted him a look. "Don't say that. It's so morbid."

He gave her a half smile. "I know it must sound that way to you, sweeting. But I've been looking forward to Saturday for a long time. These years have been hard on me. Very hard."

"How so?"

"Being isolated, deprived of the things I love most in the world."

"Such as?"

He gave a lusty sigh. "Wine, women and sailing the high seas."

His eyes filled with merriment and she nearly fell for his attempt to divert her from the topic. Nearly. It just didn't follow. Despite his hang-ups, Tyree was so full of joie de vivre, the thought that he wanted to die was even less comprehensible than his hermit-like lifestyle at the estate.

"What's really happening on Saturday?" she asked.

"I've told you. The curse is up."

Lord, the man was stubborn about this creepy curse thing. "Just so you know, I'm not going to let you out of my sight the whole day."

"Wouldn't have it any other way." He took the wheel from her. "Hang on!" With a little-boy grin, he set the throttle to full and the boat skipped over the waves with a roar.

As she watched his face light up with pleasure at steering the speedboat among the sandbars and reeds, she resolved to find out more about Rosalind Winters. His unhappy love affair with Rosalind must be the key to whatever was going on.

Not that Clara wanted to pry into his love life. Just because she'd slept with the man once didn't give her license to meddle. Still, if she could somehow help him get past that painful memory, maybe he could move on with his life in a more normal way, giving up this crazy ghost obsession and getting out into the world.

That would be a good thing, wouldn't it?

Unfortunately, helping him would mean getting more involved with him. Something she should avoid. Despite everything, she already felt more drawn to Tyree than she wanted to admit. Getting any closer would only mean more pain when she left Sunday morning.

Five days were not long enough to fix his problems. It was just long enough to get herself into big trouble.

So what was she doing spending the whole day with him?

She should be avoiding his company like the plague! That would be the best thing for both of them.

She had to be strong. From now on, no more fun trips together. No more confidences. No more cozy evenings in front of the TV. No more hugs or near kisses. And definitely no more thinking about him naked.

If she avoided all those things, maybe, just maybe, she'd survive the next five days with her heart intact.

What was up with Clara?

Tyree sat brooding at his computer, watching the colorful fish swim by on his screen saver and listening to fake diver bubbles. He should put on a CD, but he wasn't in the mood.

He never should have told Clara about Rosalind. That's when everything had gone south.

Or was it when she'd brought up Saturday again? He would have to downplay the importance of Saturday in future conversations. Maybe he should just forget about the truth and tell her he's going on a business trip or something.

He exhaled heavily. Today had been so much fun and they'd gotten along so well. He loved how she jumped into things with both feet, unafraid. Aye, she was as yare as the *Sea Sprite*. If he'd met Clara while he was alive, he'd have swept her away and sailed her till sunrise every chance he got.

But that wasn't possible now. Not when there was so little time. And when it might put her in danger. Devil take Mrs. Yates for bringing her here!

He was getting in over his head. He needed to back off, as she had so obviously done since their return this afternoon. She'd barely spoken to him. Which was good, because Lord knew what could happen between now and Saturday. If she found out the particulars of the curse, about a woman in love being able to release him from it, she might take it into her head to do something foolish. Women could be so irrational when it came to love.

Not that she was in love with him, not by a long shot. Nor

would she ever be, if he had anything to say about it. He must preserve their distance, keep an aloof and businesslike manner in his dealings with her.

But God's Bones, how was he to do that when every time he looked at her he wanted to taste her?

He pounded a fist on the keyboard and the fish disappeared, replaced by his Internet sign-on screen. He pulled the keyboard toward him. Nothing like the endless blind passages of the Internet to distract a man. Besides, there was something he wanted to research.

Paintings.

He was still curious about the arson case, even though he'd given up the idea there might be a connection with him and Sully. The inspector had implied the thief was taking paintings from the houses he burned. Tyree wanted to know which paintings.

Surely somewhere on the Internet he could find out what was in the collections of those three houses. They were all on the historic register, and therefore had to have been carefully inventoried by the Historic Society. Not to mention insurance records. Shouldn't be too difficult to find the information he sought.

And with any luck the search would keep him occupied all night.

Hours later, Tyree sat back in his leather office chair and grabbed a small stack of color printouts from the printer tray. He passed a hand over his stubbled chin.

Unbelievable.

He'd been right all along.

Clara sighed in pleasure.

He was finally kissing her. Tyree had been practicing unhooking her bra for hours, but for some reason every time he almost had it off, suddenly it was back on and they had to start all over again. It was maddening. And frustrating. She wanted his hands on her. She wanted his lips on her. She wanted *him* on her.

She moaned and went to put her arms around his neck, to pull him closer, but found only air.

"Tyree," she whimpered softly.

"I'm here, sweeting."

Sweeting. She sighed. She loved when he called her that. So romantic.

"Where?" Reaching for him again, she opened her eyes. And realized she was in bed. Alone. In the bungalow, the misty light of dawn painting the gray night shadows with yellow.

"Here, in the chair by the window."

She bolted upright. Sure enough, there sat Tyree, the biggest shadow of all, a strange expression clouding his uncovered eye.

She grasped the coverlet to her breasts. "What are you doing?"

"Waiting for you to wake up," he said, tossing his eye patch onto the windowsill and unfolding his long, booted legs. "I have something to show you."

She glanced at the clock and groaned. "At 5:30 a.m.? I can't believe you woke me up this early."

"I didn't. You called out for me and I answered."

"Yes, well, I was dreaming," she said in as reproving a tone as she could muster under these conditions.

The shadows on his lips shifted. "Without me?"

Ho-boy. No way was she going there. "I could have sworn I bolted the door," she muttered.

He got to his feet and strode over to the bed, waving a small sheaf of papers in his hand. "Clara, look at these. I was right about the fires."

"Seriously?" She rubbed her eyes and peered at the papers. "What are they?"

"Inventories of the collections at the houses that burned. And photocopies of the paintings the families owned."

She took the papers and leafed through them. "There are several paintings of you and Sully, but I don't see—"

He sat on the edge of the bed. "Look at the lists of books."

Each of the arsonist's victims owned an assortment of books on the subjects of Tyree and Sully, and pirates in general.

"And check out the collections," he prompted, pulling three other papers to the top.

The owners also each had a respectable collection of pirate artifacts—knives, guns, pennants, coins and the like.

"Okay, I'll grant you they're all interested in pirates. But where's the connection with Sully and St. James?"

He spread out a dozen or more of the color printouts on the bed, surrounding her with them. "Thom Bowden."

"Who?"

"Remember the painting of me in the book at the museum? The one I didn't like?"

Definitely. He'd thought he looked angry in it, but she just thought he looked handsome as hell, all broody and Lord Byron-arrogant. She'd hang that portrait over her bed any day of the week.

She squirmed under the sheet and decided he was sitting a little too close in his sexy pirate outfit. "I remember," she said, and scooted out of bed, heading for the bathroom. "Keep talking."

"Thom Bowden painted it," he called over the running water. "Thom never had a coin to his name and was always hanging out at the Moon and Palmetto sketching portraits for ale and grocery money. Sully and I were frequently his subjects, along with our ships and crew. We all liked him and felt sorry for his wife, so we put up with his oils and canvas."

She tried fitting the pieces together as she freshened up and brushed her teeth. But it was still too early to think. She needed caffeine.

"You think those are the paintings the thief stole? Thom Bowden's?" she asked when she came out.

"I taped the news footage from the Pryce-Simmons House. I couldn't see any of the listed paintings among the debris."

"But even if they are the ones he stole, maybe he just likes that particular artist."

Tyree gathered up the papers and followed her into the main room, where she started a pot of coffee.

"Maybe. But then explain the fires."

She leaned her bottom against the counter. "To cover up the robbery, like the news report said?"

"I don't think so." He straddled a kitchen chair at the end of the table, stretching his already tight dun breeches even tighter. "The guy's not fooling anyone with those fires. Even the media knows he's robbing the places first."

His thighs looked really good in those breeches. Buff and muscular.

"So why, then?"

"The fires must be personal. My guess is he's angry about something."

His butt looked even better. Not an ounce of wasted flesh. She did her best to avert her gaze, but failed. "Angry?"

"It's like he's taking it out on the houses."

"Maybe he's looking for something and *not* finding it," she suggested, tipping her head for a better view.

There was a short pause, then he said, "What about you?"

"Hmm?"

He got up, ambled over to the coffee pot and poured them each a cup. "Keep lookin' at my butt like that 'n I guarantee you'll find something." He offered her a cup. "That what you want?"

She took the cup, feeling the heat from it radiate up her arms and neck. Or so she told herself. "Put it on display, you should expect a little attention," she rejoined. "May as well not be wearing pants at all."

He took a step closer. "That could be arranged."

The warmth reached her face. "I know you have jeans. Don't you think they'd be more appropriate for this century?"

He winked. "Nah. I like it when you look at me like that."

She marshaled her composure. This was not going well. It was not even 6:00 a.m., and already her plan was going down in flames. Obviously if she was going to make it work, she'd have to avoid him when he was dressed in his pirate gear.

"Anyway," he said, "I like your idea about the thief looking for something he can't find. That would explain the anger. And maybe why he's lighting the fires."

Grateful for Tyree's single-mindedness, she focused. "Okay, then what is he looking for?"

"That," he said, "is exactly what we're going to find out."

"Oh, no." She raised a palm. "*You* find out. I've got my own work to do today."

"Not necessary. I'm familiar with everything about Sullivan Fouquet. Just ask me what you need to know."

"Tyree, I'm writing a magazine article, not fiction," she explained patiently. "Who would I list as the source of my information? The ghost of his dead partner?"

She could tell he was about to correct her on the ghost thing, but for some reason changed his mind.

"I see your point," he conceded. "However, I can steer you in the right direction, show you the appropriate volumes in the library."

"It's very generous of you to offer—"

"Yesterday you seemed to want my help."

Yesterday she hadn't realized the danger in it. Yesterday she hadn't dreamed of him all night until she ached with the need to feel his arms around her and his lips on hers, and more.

Yesterday she hadn't been afraid she was falling for him.

"I have to do this myself, Tyree. If I win the *Adventure Magazine* contest, I want to know it was because of my own skills."

He nodded thoughtfully. "I can see that. A matter of honor."

She took his coffee cup and refilled it along with her own.

"I'm glad you understand. I wouldn't want you to think I'm ungrateful."

"Not at all," he said as he took it from her. "When does the museum open?"

"Ten o'clock."

He glanced at the brass clock on the mantel. "Four hours from now." He looked back at her with a slow smile. "How shall we fill the time?"

"Ah." A light panic trickled through her. Under no circumstances should she spend those hours with him. It was already hard enough to keep her distance. The man was like a magnet pulling her in with his power of attraction, even against her will. "I thought I'd get some work done here. Maybe on the diary."

His cup halted halfway to his lips. "The diary?"

Suddenly she realized her mistake. She'd forgotten all about— "Oh!" —*the bra lesson.*

Chapter 8

Tyree stared at Clara, never so torn as he was in just this moment. Unbidden, his gaze drifted downward. So tempting.

He shouldn't.

"You've decided to accept my bargain, then?"

"No!" she squeaked. "I mean, I forgot about that." She shook her head. "No lesson."

He licked his lips, remembering the taste of her dusky nipples on his tongue, the feel of their hard tips as he dragged it over them. It had been so long, and one night was not enough. *Not nearly enough.*

"Sure?"

A strained laugh. "I'm not even wearing a bra." Slapping her hand over her mouth, she let out a muffled curse.

She was still in her sleep shirt. Large and almost to her knees, it covered far more territory than her outfit had yesterday. But he could tell she was naked under it. Naked and his for the taking.

He definitely shouldn't.

"I suppose you have X-ray vision, too," she said, her voice oddly raspy. He must have looked confused, for she added, "Along with walking through walls and being invisible...."

He gave a wry half smile. "Alas, nay." Who needed X-ray vision? The memory of her lush, curvaceous body was still vivid in his mind.

"Thank the Lord for small mercies."

She looked terrified. Yet in her eyes burned a desire that was unmistakable. A desire for the same thing he wanted.

He'd never get through the rest of the week without tasting her again. Without feeling her silken body under his, without hearing the sound of his name pouring from her lips like a prayer.

So he would.

He took her cup before she dropped it, and set it with his on the counter. She backed away, but he followed her, pursuing her step by step until her bottom hit the kitchen table.

"Tyree," she said in a strangled whisper. "We shouldn't—"

He grasped the hem of her sleep shirt so she couldn't escape. "I'm a pirate, Clara. I take what I want."

"Privateer," she corrected. "And we're not at war."

He slid his hand up her silken thigh, wanting her too much to stop and think. "Men and women have been at war since the beginning of time. It's what makes life interesting."

His hand reached her bare hip. She let out a whimper. A small, throaty noise filled with trepidation. And longing.

Or was it he who had whimpered?

He pulled her to his chest, banding his arm behind her, and urged her closer with a hand to her sweet backside.

His.

He covered her mouth with his and kissed her.

Groaning long and low, he closed his eyes as the taste of her burst through him. Her hands kneaded his shoulders, alternately pushing him away and pulling him back.

"Tyree, please."

"Surrender," he urged softly. "Let me take you."

He deepened the kiss, claiming her mouth with his tongue as he wanted to do with the rest of her. His fingers reached her breast and claimed it, too, squeezing, caressing.

She moaned and her arms circled his neck, this time holding him fast.

She tasted so good. So young, so open, so vibrantly alive. Everything he wasn't. He wanted to suck it all in, swallow it, absorb the very essence of her being. So he'd remember for all eternity.

He tugged at her sleep shirt. "I want this off."

Suddenly a loud, high-pitched trilling ripped through the air. They tore apart, breathless. He searched for the source of the noise as she gazed at him, eyes wide and wild.

"Alarm clock," she finally said between gulps of air. "It must be six-thirty."

"Let's shut it off." He grasped her hand and started toward the bedroom.

She balked, tugging her hand from his. "N-No. Don't."

He stopped dead and stared at her, the buzz ringing in his ears like the aftermath of a cannon shot. She took a step backward. Away from him.

"Clara—"

"I can't."

"Sweeting—"

"I can't do just sex."

Anger flooded him. "This isn't just sex and you know it!"

At his words, her expression turned even more desperate. "But it can't be more. We'll never work. I'm leaving and…God knows what you're doing. My life has just started, and yours—" She halted, folding her arms over her abdomen.

"Is over?" he supplied.

Once again, his gut felt sliced through, but the pain was far worse than the first time Sully had dealt the blow.

She shook her head and her gaze dropped away. "I don't know. I don't pretend to understand a thing about you. All I know is—" she swallowed "—I like you too much to do this to myself, or to you."

He reached for her. "Clara—"

She jumped back. "Please, Tyree. I'm not strong enough for both of us."

He slammed his eyes shut, insides churning with need. And indecision.

She was right. He knew she was right. He'd told himself precisely the same thing after that first night, and again yesterday. Warned himself over and over to keep his distance or disaster would result.

The obnoxious buzzer stopped abruptly.

He opened his eyes and met her gaze. Frustration seared through him, but it broke his heart to see her so distraught.

"Don't worry," he said, his whole body a knot of aching disappointment, along with his heart. "It's all right. I'll—" He sighed and gave her a weak smile.

"Live?"

"That, or a fair imitation." He drilled a hand through his hair. "I better go."

Determined to forget about Clara and what had just happened, Tyree strode back to his office and went online to check his outstanding auction bids. He was winning one and losing two, so he upped them all to where he was sure to win.

That took all of fifteen minutes. And he was back to thinking about Clara.

How the devil was he to get through the rest of the week?

He waffled between the idea of storming back to the bungalow, crashing through the door and simply taking her, or packing up his truck and hitting the road to anywhere but here.

Of course, his present state precluded any sort of really good door-crashing. He'd just glide through it. Didn't make much of a statement. How could you ravish a woman after a wimpy entrance like that?

And as for the truck, he'd enjoy a road trip if it weren't for the cops. They tended to get a bit tetchy about vehicles on the freeway with no driver. He'd have to stick to the back roads and drive at night. Wouldn't see anything anyway. Why bother.

With a heavy sigh, he went back online and cancelled all his bids. He wouldn't be around to receive the items anyway. Mrs. Yates would just have to find homes for them, which annoyed her to no end.

He logged off and looked at the clock.

Seven-thirteen.

It was going to be a hell of a long day.

When Tyree left, Clara went back to the bathroom and took a marathon shower. A cold one.

She'd had to tell men no before. But never, ever, had it been as difficult as with Tyree. Never before had she so wanted to just let herself go and enjoy the moment, worrying about the future in the morning.

She wanted him beyond anything she'd ever experienced.

She groaned into the spray and turned the handle all the way to cold, gritting her teeth against the icy chill.

It didn't help. She still wanted him.

She felt like crying. Was she being stupid? Should sex be a part of her new adventurous spirit?

Uncertainty rained down on her along with every drop of water that hit her skin.

Maybe.

She was an adult. Single. Lonely. Would it really matter so much if she had a quick fling?

But could she really sleep with a man, then walk away after only a few days—and nights—without a backward glance? No feelings? No regrets? No pain?

Not a chance.

But was the pain perhaps worth being with him, if only for a short while?

Maybe not.

But then again, maybe it was.

She'd have to think about that one carefully.

In the meantime, her research had to be completed, which meant she had to forget Tyree and get to the museum. Try to be productive despite her chaotic mind.

Somehow she managed to get through breakfast without jumping out of her skin at every creak of a stair or brush of a branch against a windowpane, thinking it was him. On her walk to the museum, she passed the Moon and Palmetto and decided to eat lunch there later. In the window was taped a large, colorful poster for the big Pirate Festival on Saturday. There was also a brochure advertising an historic walking tour of Magnolia Cove, which included the graveyard where Sully and Tyree St. James were buried. The real, original Tyree St. James.

A shiver crawled down her spine. Could her Tyree really be…?

No.

She shook off the absurd thought. The man who'd touched her this morning had been very much alive, all parts in full working order.

She should go to the graveyard. Take some pictures. See for herself that Tyree St. James was dead and buried, not some wandering spirit. Maybe put flowers on the grave of her childhood obsession. And her new one.

Anyway. She had a lot of work to do before the weekend, between the museum and seeing everything she wanted to see. There would be no time for obsessions, other than her article.

Forget the man. Forget the situation. Forget the ache low in her belly. Concentrate on her research, nothing more.

Naturally, he wouldn't let her concentrate.

He was spying on her. Sort of.

The first time Clara spotted Tyree, she was looking through a book by the back window of the library and happened to glance outside. He was sitting there on a bench in the garden. Ripping petals off a flower. She dropped her book. After she bent to pick it up, he was gone.

She thought she was seeing things.

Until she saw him again, in the stacks between the rows of books. Watching her with such a fierce expression it made her gasp. Bolts of electricity shot through her whole body as she recognized his look. Hunger. Hunger for *her*.

She turned and fled.

This was so not fair. Why did *she* have to be the strong one? The one to put on the brakes and build the barrier?

Life had been so much easier when her dream pirate was still a fantasy that existed only in her mind.

Add to that her research was not going well. She was trying to find out why Fouquet had turned to a life of plundering on the high seas in the first place—be it as a pirate or a privateer—and not one book offered a reason. She needed something better than simply for the money. Something more romantic and compelling.

Early in the afternoon, she whacked her tenth source onto the stack of volumes she'd already searched through, and gathered her things. Lunch at the Moon and Palmetto sounded pretty good. Maybe she'd skip the sandwich and go straight for the beer.

It was late enough that the business crowd had thinned and she was seated right away by a waiter dressed as—what else?—a pirate. They were all dressed like pirates. Black-and-white striped calf-length pants, open black vests, and kerchiefs tied over their heads. Mercifully, no eye patches. She almost laughed. They looked like cartoons compared to Tyree. Enticing, sexy, handsome Tyree.

Who was now sitting at a table in the darkest corner of the cave-like pub, staring at her.

She puffed out a breath and ignored him, checking out the place instead. It certainly looked like something out of the distant past. Low-beamed ceilings topped walls that sloped like they'd been through a hurricane or two. The rough wooden floor was strewn with sawdust; plank tables and spindle chairs were set up in untidy rows, along with a few more private booths sectioned out along the side where she was sitting. Paintings, posters and memorabilia—all centered around pirates—occupied every available inch of wall space.

When her order came, she took a long sip of her beer and leaned her head against the back of the booth, letting her eyelids drift down.

What a day. And it was only half over.

"How's your research going?"

Her heart stopped, then restarted with a lurch.

"Why are you following me, Tyree?" she asked, trying to sound calm and reasonable when what she really wanted to do was first smack him silly and then rip his clothes off, throw him on the floor and—

"Am I bothering you?"

She cracked an eyelid. "Yes."

"Good," he said, and settled into the booth, sliding his beer along the table. "Then we're even."

She cracked the other lid, taking in his well-fitting jeans and snug white T-shirt. "You're making this very difficult."

"What?"

"Trying to pretend you don't exist."

He took a sip. "Sorry."

"Are you a glutton for punishment, or what?"

"Guess I must be. I can't seem to leave you alone."

She wanted to be mad. She really did. But he looked just as miserable as she felt.

"Listen," she began, but he held up a hand.

"Here." He slid one of those high-tech cell phone headset gadgets that looked like a black hair band with a mouthpiece, onto her head. "Now people won't think you're talking to yourself."

She squeezed the bridge of her nose between her fingers and counted silently. When she reached ten, she looked up. "Fine, Tyree. Whatever."

"So, you were saying?"

She shook her head. "Never mind. The moment passed."

"All right." He took another big sip from his beer. It was the most she'd ever seen him drink. Of anything.

"Are you going to get drunk?" she asked, only half joking.

His somber mien splintered slightly. "Cheeky wench."

"I'm sorry about this morning."

He waved a hand. "No apology necessary. I shouldn't have— Anyway, tell me how your research is going on the old baggage."

"Badly. I'm trying to flesh out his background, but no one seems to know why Fouquet started out on his piracy career," she said dejectedly. "Legal or not."

"Maybe you should switch topics," Tyree suggested. "Write about the arson case instead."

"You forget I'm doing this for *Adventure Magazine*. There's nothing adventurous about arson. So do you know?"

"Know what?"

"Why Sully became a privateer."

He pursed his lips belligerently. "Safer than being a pirate."

She glanced up. "Which you said he started out as in Louisiana."

He nodded. "Unlike me. I was never an outlaw."

She smiled. "And yet here you are, known far and wide as the Blackbeard of Magnolia Cove. Hardly seems fair."

"Tell me about it."

"So why did Sully become a pirate? Was it just for the money?"

"He was a Cajun," Tyree said, as though that explained everything. But everyone already knew he was Cajun.

"So all those Cajuns living down in Louisiana are really pirates, not hardworking citizens?"

"Funny." He drummed his fingers. "No, Sully was one of the original Cajuns. Or practically. His parents were among the seven thousand French Acadians forced to leave their homes in Nova Scotia in the mid-1700s."

"Forced?"

Tyree shrugged. "Nova Scotia ended up British and the Acadians were French. The British took their land, forced them to give up their religion and still wound up sending them to the American colonies as indentured servants, little better than criminals."

"I had no idea."

He pointed at her. "You're Acadian, too, if you're his sister's descendant."

"With a name like Fergussen?"

"Names don't matter. It's the culture that's important. You should know this stuff."

"Well, I'm from Kansas, not Louisiana like Sully."

"Sully was born in Connecticut, along with his sister Theresa, your ancestral grandmother, while their parents worked as unpaid labor on some British lord's farm."

"You mean like slaves?"

"Practically. That's one reason we always captured slave ships when we ran across one, regardless of its flag."

"And helped the slave rebellions down in the Caribbean."

Tyree nodded. "Many a freed slave sailed with both our crews."

"I still don't understand the piracy."

Tyree traced the edge of his beer with a finger. "Sully was nine when he witnessed his mother's rape and his father's hanging for defending her against that British lord. Sully was transported to Louisiana, to a distant relative, and Theresa was hired out to a middle-class family going west."

"My God! She couldn't have been more than eleven. Did they ever see each other again?"

"Only letters. Sully learned the pirate trade shortly thereafter in the swamps of south Louisiana. Then came the War of Independence and with it a way to go legit and get revenge for his parents, too. We met in '81 on a rebel schooner plying the New England coast. The rest is history."

Clara sat back and digested his information. "Wow."

"He didn't talk much about his past. I expect Theresa didn't even know the whole story. He would have protected her from the truth."

She tipped her head at Tyree. "What about you?"

"Me?"

"Why were you on that rebel schooner?"

He shifted uncomfortably on the wooden bench and took a sip of beer. "Nothing nearly as dramatic. Just bored."

"How old were you?"

"Fifteen."

Her brows shot up. "A little young for that much boredom."

"My daddy had one plantation, three sons and a whole collection of hickory canes." His eyes softened. "When my mama died, I decided to seek my fortune elsewhere."

"Since you were the baby of the family and not in line to inherit."

"More research?"

She smiled. "Lucky guess. You loved your mama a lot."

"Everyone loves their mama," he said gruffly. With a scowl, he pointed at the remains of her sandwich. "Are you finished?"

God, he was sweet.

"All done."

"Good. Let's get out of here. The place gives me the willies." He slapped a twenty on the table and jerked his head toward the entrance. "This way."

"Wait!" she said, jumping to her feet. "Show me where it happened."

He fisted his hands on his hips. "Right where you're standing," he said, and her jaw dropped.

She looked at the floor, suddenly seeing the dark, stained wood beneath the sawdust, imagining it covered with blood. Were there still traces? Of course not. It had been too long.

"We were all sitting over here." He pointed to a place across from the booth they'd shared. "A long table. I was at one end, and—"

"Is there anything you need, miss?" a passing waiter asked.

She started. "No, thanks. I'm just…looking at the spot where the duel took place."

"Ah, where the famous Captain Sullivan Fouquet died."

"And Captain St. James."

"I guess. Blackbeard killed Captain Fouquet. Ran him through in cold blood, the blackguard."

She glanced at Tyree, who was standing behind him, feet spread in the sawdust and a nasty glint in his eyes.

"St. James wasn't Blackbeard," she informed the waiter before Tyree decided to bean the kid. If he was going to work here, he should get his facts straight. "And it wasn't in cold blood. It was an accident. They were best friends."

The waiter gave her a doubting look. "Yeah, whatever. Have a nice day." With that, he took his tray of dirty dishes and walked off.

She shook her head and turned to the door, only to hear a large crash behind her and a chuckle from Tyree.

"Clumsy oaf," he offered in a tone of unrepentant satisfaction.

As they went out into the bright sunshine, she looked reprovingly at him. "You are so bad."

"The guy was an imbecile."

"You should go back and pay for those glasses and plates."

"I'll send them a check. Where to now? The museum?"

She stopped at the front window where all the brochures and advertisements were taped. "No, I was thinking—"

Tyree interrupted with a groan, pointing at the poster for the Pirate Festival. "I'd forgotten that farcical masquerade was this weekend."

"Yep, I can't wait. You'll be going, right?"

He muttered a curse. "Not on your life. Especially not if it's Saturday."

Lord, the ubiquitous Saturday. "Ah, but you'll have to. I vowed not to let you out of my sight that day, remember? And no way am I not attending the festivities. It's my last night and I plan to celebrate."

"Celebrate?" he asked with a knife-edge to his tone. "Your leaving, or mine?"

She frowned. "Neither. Finishing my research."

His jaw flexed. "Sorry. It's just that… Damn, this is a first."

"What?"

He sighed. "That I'm not looking so forward to…going away. I'm going to miss you."

A couple of tourists walked past and he moved out of the way, leaning back against the tavern's mullioned window.

"I'll miss you, too, Tyree."

They stood side by side in silence for several minutes, pretending to enjoy the sunshine and the quaint atmosphere, when in reality she was sure he was thinking just as hard about her as she was about him.

"Then don't go," she whispered. "You could come with me, if I win the trip. You love sailing, right?"

When the silence continued, she forced a laugh. "Never mind. I probably won't win anyway."

"You'll win," he said.

She turned to him. Her knees were suddenly, inexplicably shaking. "Will you come with me?" she asked again, every instinct of logic and survival screaming at her to keep her mouth shut.

He traced his fingers down her cheek, brushing a thumb over her quivering lower lip. "I'm sorry, sweeting. I cannot."

The sharp sting of rejection spun through her and she turned away before he could see how much it hurt. She'd known his answer all along, but hearing the actual words defied her attempts at calm reason. She started walking.

His footsteps followed. "Clara, honey—"

"No, it's okay," she told the sidewalk as it sped up beneath her. "I understand."

"You *don't* understand. Not really." His steps quickened.

"I do." She was practically running now.

He was a recluse. He'd had a bad love affair. He was afraid to feel anything again. Afraid to live to the point he imagined he was dead. She'd been forced to stay home all her life when she wanted nothing more than to get out into the world. She'd never had a love affair, not a real one. She wanted to feel everything, experience everything this beautiful world had to offer.

Everything, she suddenly realized. Even if it meant getting hurt.

But not if it was one-sided.

He wasn't willing to take a chance on her, and that was that. Experience was one thing. Stupidity was quite another.

"Clara!" His hand wrapped around her arm and pulled her to a stop. "Where are you going?"

She lifted her chin, squaring off against the allure of him. "The cemetery," she said, and looked him in the eye. "I want to put flowers on your grave."

And with them, lay to rest the ridiculous notion that anything at all could come of the crazy emotions she was feeling for this helplessly confused and complicated man.

Then hope like hell they didn't come back to haunt her.

Chapter 9

"Clara!"

Tyree wanted to rush after her retreating back, but his feet wouldn't move.

Flowers on his grave? Why the hell would she want to do that?

He didn't like visiting his own grave with its crooked headstone, stuck way in the back of the cemetery where no one ventured except to knock down tent caterpillars and spray for poison ivy. He liked looking upon his own grave even less than seeing the place he'd died.

"Clara!" he called again, and took off after her. She was kidding about the grave. She must be. She didn't even have any flowers.

But she was angry. Understandably. Had she really asked him to go with her? This was not good. It meant he was failing miserably to put emotional distance between them. Only a woman with feelings for a man asked him to run away with her. Feelings that could lead to disaster if she found out the details of the curse.

At all costs he must protect her.

He looked up just in time to see her disappear into one of the dozen or so small boutiques that crowded the main street of the village. A flower shop.

Blast. He waited outside until she emerged with an armful of calla lilies tied up with vines of fragrant white jasmine.

"For God's sake, why are you doing this?" he demanded.

"To convince myself you're dead. Maybe do a little spell of my own."

He frowned. "What kind of spell?"

"Something to get rid of unwanted apparitions."

"Very amusing."

At least she still had her sense of humor. He took the flowers from her and hooked his arm through hers, steering her to the shop next door—Sweet Secrets Lingerie.

"I've got a better idea. Why don't you go in here and pick out something nice. We'll spend the afternoon in bed instead."

She stared at him like he'd suddenly grown horns. "Are you nuts?" She slapped her forehead. "No, wait, I already know the answer to that."

She grabbed the flowers back and marched down the street.

Well, it had been worth a shot. And if he didn't miss his mark, it had also made him look like a royal jerk. How could she have feelings for a royal jerk?

He walked after her, catching up at the gate to the cemetery.

She aimed a glare at him. "Are you still here?"

He smiled. "In spirit only."

Her eyes rolled heavenward. "Show me where Sully's grave is."

He frowned. "I thought you wanted to put flowers on *my* grave."

"Changed my mind." Her foot tapped impatiently on the cobblestones. "Will you show me or shall I find it myself?"

He resisted grabbing the flowers from her again. Just. "Very well. It's not like you could miss the thing."

He led her to a large enclosure surrounded by an ornate wrought-iron fence. Black, of course. In it stood two giant windswept marble headstones, one for Sully and one for his Elizabeth, engraved with names and dates. Below the lettering sailed a pair of carved ships, the hulls of which contained two insipid poems.

No vow to God or girl or friend
Could keep this gallant from his fate
For Death leaves port without a sail
Its driving breeze a cruel betrayal

The second one read:

Ne'er a chance to be a bride
For swiftly came life's changing tide
Beauty and charm, her virtues exalted
In the arms of her love her voyage was halted

Nauseating. Tyree's only consolation was that surely Sully lay spinning in his grave with equal revulsion. Or up on his cloud, or wherever the hell he was.

Clara stood perfectly still.

"Moving, aren't they?" he asked, his voice deliberately neutral.

"They're awful. Did you put them up?"

"Hardly. The first director of the pirate museum did. Maybelle Chadbourn. She was obsessed with Sully and Elizabeth."

Clara looked at him for the first time. "Maybelle Chadbourn? The one who wrote the infamous penny dreadful?"

"*The Pirate's Lady.* One and the same."

"I must have read it a hundred times as a girl."

"Figures," he muttered.

"So scandalous. And the original source of St. James's dire nickname and black reputation, if I'm not mistaken."

He lifted a shoulder. "The nickname, anyway. Don't give her all the credit for my reputation. I had something to do with that, too."

"You mean as a greedy, womanizing, murdering traitor?"

"Damned lies. I was never a traitor."

"To your country, at any rate."

"Aye, I did kill my best friend."

After a short pause she said, "You never finished telling me how it happened."

He let out a long breath, loath to relive the horrible event. "It was stupid. The whole situation. And all because of an idiotic wager."

"The duel was over a *bet*?"

"It wasn't actually a duel. We'd made a wager to see who could shoot the nose off a stuffed trophy boar over the bar. I was to go first."

"You're kidding me. A boar's nose?"

"No one liked the thing, it was hideous. Preparations took on a dramatic aspect. We pulled out shot and powder to load our pistols, and took our time about it. There were jokes and side wagers all around. Someone ordered more ale."

"There would be drinking involved."

"We were about to leave on our next voyage and had been having a farewell party. For two days."

"Lord, Tyree. What happened?"

"Well…you recall my eye patch?"

She nodded. "I've always wondered about that eye patch. Some of St. James's portraits have it, some don't."

He touched the thin blue scar under his left eye. "I was nicked by a sword during a boarding the previous year. It was basically healed, but…"

"Then why wear the patch?"

He stuck his hands in his jeans pockets. "You really want to know?"

"Sure." Her unsuspecting expression told him she had no idea what was coming. Nothing like the truth to drive the last nail into his own coffin.

"I wore it because the ladies liked it. And I liked the ladies. *That* part of the St. James myth, at least, is true."

She flinched and turned back to the headstones. "Yes, I can believe that. It certainly worked on me."

"Clara—"

"Go on. Please."

"Very well. I was wearing it that night."

"Because the ladies liked it."

She was deliberately goading him. It was working.

"Damn females," he growled, suddenly furious with himself and his eternal weakness. Even after two hundred years he was waging the same battle. "If it hadn't been for that cursed patch…"

"What does the eye patch have to do with killing Sully?" she asked with an edge of impatience.

"Because of the patch on my left eye, I didn't see Elizabeth coming from the left with a tray of drinks. She was distracted and walked in front of me just as I pulled the trigger. I shot her instead of the boar."

"My God."

"I was horrified. Sully'd planned to marry her. She died in his arms and he went mad."

"So you killed him?"

Tyree squeezed his temples between his fingers. "He chased me around the tavern with his sword for half an hour trying to slice me in two. I was growing tired and accidentally cut him when I parried."

"And he ran you through in return."

"That about covers it."

"Is that when he put the curse on you?" Her question caught Tyree by surprise. When he didn't immediately deny it, she said, "I knew it was him."

The woman was like a dog with a bone. He may as well

tell her so she wouldn't be tempted to read the diary to find out. "Aye, it was Sully's dying words."

She shifted the flowers in her arms and contemplated the two headstones. "So he put a two-hundred-year curse on the man who'd killed his beloved. Generous terms, I'd say."

Tyree whipped his gaze to her. "Who said anything about two hundred years?"

"All the Pirate Festival posters say it's the two hundredth anniversary of the duel, and you insist the curse is over on Saturday. It's so obvious I can't believe I didn't see it earlier."

Only if one was looking. Tyree wasn't a secretive man by nature. He'd told Mrs. Yates and his other caretakers everything about himself over the years they lived together. And Rosalind, of course. But no one outside his confidence had ever bothered to add two and two about him and come up with four. No one at the museum, not one of the hundreds of pirate fanatics who'd come to pay tribute to Sullivan Fouquet since Magnolia Cove was put on the map by Maybelle Chadbourn's lurid penny novel of swashbuckling and sex. Not his own father or brothers, who had disowned him at the first whispered rumor of piracy, even before he was killed.

Not until Clara Fergussen. Sully's own great-great-great-great-grandniece. Funny how the universe worked.

He watched as she opened the enclosure gate and deposited her armful of lilies on Sully and Elizabeth's graves, biting back a whiplash of envy. Envy for the love Sully and Elizabeth had shared before their deaths. Envy for Clara's loyalty to her family, however distant. Envy for what might have been between himself and this sensitive, amazing woman, had he been free to pursue her.

"Where is St. James's grave?" she asked as she looked around, snapping him out of the rare bout of self-pity.

He mustered the discipline to point toward the rear fence of the churchyard. "All the way in back. Down the path and to the right."

"Show me?"

He shook his head, avoiding the sight of her empty arms. He'd done what was necessary to distance her, but he didn't have to like it. "I have some errands."

"I'll see you at dinner, then."

Doubtful. He didn't think he had the strength to face her wounded disregard. He pretended he didn't hear.

Well, at least one good thing had come of driving her away, he thought sullenly. He'd managed to avoid visiting his grave. He only wanted to see that weed-infested plot once ever again, and that was on Saturday, when he could finally lie down and sink into its oblivion, leaving this lonely place behind forever.

But before that, there were a few things he needed to tie up. First, he had to check in with Mrs. Yates about her visit to the attorney. Then came the tricky part. Taking the Sea-Doo out in broad daylight. It was risky as hell, but he had no choice.

He wanted to take another look at the Pryce-Simmons House. This time on the inside.

Clara swallowed three times and ignored the stinging behind her eyes as he walked away. Stupid stupid stupid. It wasn't Tyree who was certifiable, it was *her*, for giving a fig about the man.

How did he *do* this to her?

Heading for the back of the churchyard, she upbraided herself for caring.

She couldn't believe she'd actually asked him to go with her on the trip if she won. He was so regretful in declining her offer that if she didn't know better, she'd be convinced of his sincerity.

Ha. That bit about the eye patch had brought her back to reality with a bang. The ladies liked it, indeed. Apparently, she wasn't the only one with a bad-boy pirate fantasy. Small consolation for her heart. He'd already plundered it but good, as skillful in his emotional piracy as his namesake had been on the high seas.

She searched along the fence for St. James's headstone and found it tucked away in a shady spot under an ancient oak tree. Covered by vines and weeds, it was in shocking disrepair.

"My Lord," she muttered, taking in the listing granite stone and drifts of dead leaves nearly obscuring the plot. "This is disgraceful."

Did no one take care of him? She was surprised Tyree didn't pay someone to keep it presentable. Especially if he believed it was his own grave. Or maybe he thought it was too creepy. Tending your own grave might feel a little weird, at that.

Never mind. She'd do it herself.

So for the next hour she kneeled over the mortal remains of the pirate—make that privateer—Tyree St. James and pulled weeds. The whole time making up excuses to herself as to why on earth she'd want to undertake such a thankless, useless task.

Tyree wouldn't appreciate it. St. James himself was certainly beyond caring. Obviously no one else in Magnolia Cove considered him worth braving the mosquitoes and thorny creepers.

But none of that mattered. It was something she just had to do, though God alone knew what compelled her. And when she was finished and sat back on her heels to survey her handiwork, she'd rarely felt as much satisfaction.

She thought about righting the chipped, crooked headstone, but ended up leaving it just as it was. For some reason it looked exactly right in its lopsided ruin.

On her knees, she reached out and ran her fingers slowly over the rough, lichened stone, tracing the weathered letters of his name one by one. She touched the date of his birth and lingered over that of his death, hardly noticing the tear that crested her lashes and slid down her cheek.

With a sigh, she rose to her feet and dusted off her hands, taking one last look at the too-long-abandoned grave.

And realized there was still one thing missing.

* * *

Clara was going to be a very rich woman.

Tyree smiled as he skipped along on the Sea-Doo, dodging sandbars, ducks and thickets of spartina grass in the narrow channels he was using to get to the Pryce-Simmons House.

Boy, was she going to be surprised when she got his lawyer's letter announcing her "inheritance." Maybe then she'd believe Tyree.

Probably not. But it didn't matter. He wasn't giving her the gold bullion so she'd regret not believing him. He was doing it because he wanted to make all her dreams come true, and he wouldn't be around to do it himself. Riches were a poor substitute for love, but it was all he could manage beyond Saturday.

At least...

Nay, he shouldn't think about that. The want of her was too strong in his blood to think about the kind of love he could give her before he left. The physical kind.

But how he craved to take her body in his arms and make her his once more! Make love to her again and again, as they'd done that first night. Quench this overwhelming thirst for the taste of her he'd had from the moment he'd laid eyes on her in Mrs. Yates's kitchen. And rid himself of the heavy aching in his loins so when he left his body behind forever he could do so in a state of sated contentment.

Of course, it would probably take another two hundred years to reach that state with Clara. The only satiety he'd felt when they'd made love was purely temporary. All it would take was one look at her and he'd be needy again.

Too bad he didn't have another two hundred years to spend with her.

Then again, he knew how badly that scenario went. He'd lived it with Rosalind. Loving her so much in the beginning he didn't foresee the harsh reality of their situation. As the years passed and she aged while he remained exactly the same, it had ended up tearing him to pieces inside. She'd taken it philosophically—what choice did she have? When she turned thirty, he'd swallowed his selfish pride and encouraged her to leave him, to find a man of her own age and marry, have children. But she never would, insisting the years they'd spent together as lovers were happiness enough for a lifetime. But by the end of her life, their relationship had devolved into one of platonic affection.

He'd never told Rosalind about the provision in the curse, even then deathly afraid she'd sacrifice her life to release him from his purgatory. Hers was that kind of love. Clara's would be, too, he was sure.

On the other hand, it occurred to him that two factors were very different this time around. In a few days, the curse would be over, regardless of any woman's love or sacrifice. And after that he would be gone for good, so Clara wasting her young life on him was impossible.

Aye, perhaps…perhaps he might risk it.

Just the physical. If she agreed.

She didn't want a relationship. She was worried a relationship would interfere with her plans to win the contest and travel the world. But he wouldn't interfere. He couldn't. And he knew she wanted him. Her body had told him in a thousand different ways. It would be easy to breach her defenses and take what they both wanted.

Aye, tonight he'd do it.

Meanwhile, he wanted to clear up the mystery surrounding the arson case so he could leave knowing there would be no unforeseen complications. The whole thing was probably an uncanny coincidence, but the timing still made him uneasy. He wanted to be sure.

He tied up the Sea-Doo at the Pryce-Simmons dock and made straight for the house. Two young police officers guarded the crime scene from inside their cruiser parked out front. Other than that there was no one about, which was exactly what Tyree had hoped for. He could easily avoid their notice.

He approached the back of the house, climbed in over the lowest spot on the burned outer wall and found himself standing in the remains of the library. Picking his way over the charred beams and piles of debris, he did a quick visual inventory.

Someone had gathered the valuables off the still-damp floor and grouped them on tables according to category. Silver items on one, vases and sculptures on another, books spread out on the largest one to dry. He spotted what he sought, a stack of paintings propped against the wall on top of a sideboard.

He went over and flipped through them, looking for the Thom Bowden paintings listed in the owner's insurance records. There should be three. There were none.

Damn. Usually he liked being right. Not this time.

He glanced around, hoping for some reason the paintings had just been separated from the others. No such luck.

But way back in a corner, almost obscured by a fallen lamp, he saw something that caught his attention. A small book lay sprawled open on a low ottoman, pages akimbo. It looked like a diary. The same kind in which Davey Scraggs wrote.

Leaping over a sodden couch to reach the corner, he snatched it up. As soon as he saw the handwriting inside, damaged as it was by water and flame, he knew it was one of Davey's.

Foreboding licked at Tyree's insides. What was going on here?

Torn, he waffled between taking the diary with him and leaving it for the police. Obviously, whoever had arranged the other things in piles had missed the diary. Tossed into the corner in disarray, it was almost as if it had been thrown there in anger or disgust. But by whom? And why?

He decided to take the diary for now, sliding it into the roomy upper part of his boot.

Suddenly, someone behind him yelled, "Hey, what are you doing there?"

He spun. And nearly fell over.

Sully!

Tyree stood rooted to the spot as the man who'd killed him two hundred years ago climbed over the burned-out wall and strode toward him. Oddly, he was dressed as a modern-day firefighter.

"This is a crime scene and no unauthorized personnel are allowed on the premises!" he said.

Impossible. Tyree didn't believe it. A thousand emotions burst through him. Disbelief, anger, fear.

"Sully?" he managed to squeeze through his paralyzed throat.

Sully came to a stop in front of him, hands on hips and feet spread in the authoritative pose Tyree had seen him strike at least once a day for the last ten years of their lives.

The firefighter narrowed his eyes. "Do I know you?"

God's Teeth.

Chaos flooded Tyree's mind like a tidal wave as he took a deep breath and a closer look at the man. Wearing a denim-blue T-shirt under his yellow firefighter's pants, suspenders and rubber boots, Sully had the same brawny physique, same square jaw and coal-black hair Tyree remembered as though they'd parted just yesterday. And the same piercing look in his brown eyes, which were now regarding him with suspicion.

Tyree swallowed heavily. "You don't recognize me?"

"Should I?"

Only if you're a dead man come to wreak revenge or...

Or what?

"I thought we might have worked together. A long time ago. It's Sully, right?"

The fireman skeptically inspected Tyree. "Captain Andre Sullivan. You a firefighter?"

Andre? So this *wasn't* Fouquet? A whisper of reprieve blew through him. "Na-No. I'm in...antiques. The name's Ty-Tyler. James Tyler." The name on his driver's license.

"Antiques?" Sully asked with a scowl. "Looting is a serious offense, Mr. Tyler. How'd you get past the cops out front?"

But how could it *not* be Sully? He was a dead ringer. Tyree raised his hands, too shell-shocked to deal with anything except getting out of there. Fast.

"I'm not here to loot," he said. "Just checking on the missing paintings. That the ones listed as being stolen are really gone and not hidden somewhere beneath the rubble. For the insurance claim," he added as the fire captain continued to scowl suspiciously. "It's important to be accurate."

"Did you get permission from Inspector Santee?"

"My assistant spoke to him," Tyree said, stretching the truth almost to the breaking point, along with his nerves. "Everything seems to be in order. I'll be going, then."

He slid past Sully, careful not to touch him. He had a terrible feeling if he so much as brushed this doppelganger's hand, something unexpected and unpleasant would happen. Really unpleasant. Like maybe he'd be struck dead on the spot. Truly dead. And never get the chance to say goodbye to Mrs. Yates and Rose Cottage.

Or to Clara.

He hurried back to the Sea-Doo, feeling Sully's eyes boring holes through his back the whole way. He sped his steps.

Because suddenly he realized he wasn't ready to say goodbye. Not to his home, not to his life. And most especially not to Clara.

A sharp, agonizing certainty razored through him.

He didn't want to go. He didn't want to leave her.

He didn't want to die at midnight on Saturday.

Chapter 10

Clara half woke when the mattress dipped and she sensed someone next to her.

"Tyree?" she whispered, sitting up.

"Aye," he said, and she heard the plunk of boots hitting the hardwood floor.

"What are you doing?"

"We need to talk."

"Now?" It was pitch-dark and the middle of the night. She hadn't seen hide nor hair of him since he'd left the graveyard, but suddenly he couldn't wait to chat?

"Now."

She detected the whisper of fabric sliding over flesh.

"Since when do you need to undress to talk?"

"I'm just taking off my T-shirt. It rained earlier and I got caught in it."

She dimly recalled the patter of raindrops on the roof as she fell asleep. "And your pants are wet, too, I suppose," she said caustically.

The mattress dipped again and his hands grasped her shoulders. "Clara. I'm not here to seduce you. Listen to me. You aren't going to believe what happened."

She squelched a slight stab of disappointment. All right, a big stab. Despite everything, she couldn't help herself. She wanted him badly. But she tried to concentrate.

"Okay, tell me. What happened?"

"I saw Sully."

For a moment she just sat there. Stunned.

Oh, God. Just when she didn't think things could get worse, they did.

"Sully?" she asked carefully. "As in Sullivan Fouquet?"

"Aye. Nay. I— It was him. I know it was."

She let out a sigh. "His ghost, you mean?"

His fingers dug into her shoulders, then abruptly they were gone. He swore and dropped onto the bed beside her. "I don't know why I thought you'd believe me about Sully. You don't even believe me about *me*."

She reached for him in the darkness, finding him stretched out, his hands covering his face. Gently, she removed them and laid a palm to his cheek. "Tyree, I believe you're a lost soul. I do. Now, tell me about Sully."

The silence stretched and she let her fingers move over his face, exploring the features she could barely see. His angular cheekbone, the windswept creases at the corner of his eye, the well-defined eyebrow. The rough stubble on his jaw scraped against her palm. She sketched her thumb over his lips and he gave it a tentative kiss.

His hands grasped her shoulders again and started pulling her down, toward him. Only when their lips were almost touching did she resist.

"I thought you didn't come here to seduce me."

"I didn't."

"Then what are you doing?"

"Changing my mind."

She smiled and let him steal a small kiss. "What about Sully?"

"Damn," he said, and pulled her the rest of the way down into his arms. "I saw him today, Clara. I swear I did. I even spoke to him."

She settled onto Tyree's bare chest, trying vainly to ignore how good it felt to be there. "Where? What did he say?"

"It was at the Pryce-Simmons House. He found me there poking through the burned-out library." Tyree rolled and suddenly she was on her back. She could make out the silhouette of his face looking down at her as his body canted over hers. "Clara, he could see me."

She swallowed. "So can I, Tyree. That doesn't mean anything. Did he recognize you?"

Tyree shook his head. "I even asked."

"Then how could it be Sully?"

"It was him. I know it. His name was Sullivan, Captain Andre Sullivan."

"Captain?"

"He's the fire chief at Old Fort Mystic."

"He's working on the arson case?"

"Apparently."

She shifted, but that only brought their bodies into closer contact. His leg was thrown between hers, his broad chest practically blocking the ceiling. Her breath caught when it lowered to within a shadow's width of her breasts.

"Clara, I'm worried."

"Me, too," she choked out.

"What shall I do?"

She could think of a whole bunch of things, unfortunately none of them relevant to the conversation. "Um…"

"What if he's here to lengthen the curse? Or change it somehow?"

His body, half-naked and arousingly masculine, was cool compared to the sleep-warmed sheets beneath her.

"Maybe he came to free you from it," she softly suggested, sliding her arms around Tyree's neck. Could this be his way of telling her he wanted to move on with his life, rid himself of these paralyzing delusions? Her heart tripped with hope.

He didn't move a muscle, but she felt a change in the air around them. Like the crackling of electricity.

"Sweeting," he whispered. "If only that were true."

She buried her fingers in his long, black hair, and urged him closer. Knowing it was the last thing she should be doing. Wanting him too much to care. "Oh, Tyree."

"Don't do this unless you mean it," he murmured, sliding his hand up her thigh, under her sleep shirt.

"I do," she said, and kissed him. "I want you."

He groaned and his mouth covered hers, drinking in her words, plying her with the promise of bliss in return. He deepened the kiss, filling her mouth with the taste of him, his tongue plying her with erotic sensation.

"Are you sure?" he asked, trailing wet kisses across her lips. His hand slid between her thighs, seeking to persuade.

She trembled. "Yes."

"Even knowing this is all it can be? Just a few days of mutual pleasure?"

His brutal honesty brought tears to her eyes. Either that, or the blinding pleasure when he touched and circled her need. She gasped, spread her legs wider and surrendered to the intensity of feeling he invoked.

"Yes," she affirmed. Even knowing that.

He lifted and she felt her sleep shirt swept away. Then he closed the gap between them again, his hard chest and thighs pressing her into the softness of the bedding. She moaned in pleasure at the weight of his body on hers.

He spread her legs with a knee and slid between them. He still wore his jeans, but she could feel his steel-hard length pulsing beneath the denim, barely controlled.

"I wish it could be more," he whispered.

"Do you?"

There was a snap; the nightstand lamp came to life, spreading its dim light across the bed.

"I want to see you," he said, and raked his eyes over her. "So I can remember."

"When I'm gone?" she asked, frustratingly disappointed that he hadn't changed, after all. Angry with herself for still wanting him, at any price, if only for a few days.

She reached down for his waistband.

"Nay," he said, and brushed her away, then his other hand slid back between her thighs.

His fingers circled over her again, making her cry out. Or was it the cruel unfairness of the situation, finding love only to be forced to deny it?

"I'd come with you on the trip if I could. You must believe me," he said, his voice cracking, and she almost did.

He kissed a path down her throat to her breasts, where he lingered, licking and suckling as his fingers brought her right to the trembling edge of forgetfulness.

"Do you believe me?" he whispered, replacing fingers with tongue in his persuasion.

He held her fast, pressing her thighs apart with his powerful hands. With each deliberate stroke of his tongue, she writhed and moaned, aching for him to relieve the need for him exploding inside her.

"Tell me," he demanded softly as she felt the first tinglings spill through her.

"Yes," she whispered, and reached for him. "Yes," she said again as the shudders claimed her, swallowing the lie with their sweet oblivion.

And then he was over her, in her, moving with her, and for the moment, it didn't matter if she believed him or not. He was exactly where she needed him and there wasn't enough heartache in the world to make her want him to stop.

She wrapped her arms and legs around him and held on as he thrust into her over and over. For now, he was hers. She would face tomorrow when it came.

His climax joined hers with a roar. He clung to her, whispering her name as the tremors subsided for both of them.

"I'm sorry," he said softly after a few minutes, holding her close.

She shook her head. She wasn't sure what he was sorry about—making love, being the way he was or leaving. All she knew was she didn't want to think about any of those things right now. She just wanted to enjoy the few, precious moments they had together.

He kissed her and she kissed him back, deep and long.

And prayed for a night without end.

He kept her under him for hours. He made love to her, catered to her, kissed her and cuddled her. But never let her out from under him. Two nights ago, he had encouraged her boldness and delighted in her initiative. Tonight, he seemed afraid to let her stray from the covering protection of his body, determined to be the one to give, not receive.

Clara didn't mind. She basked in his attentions, reveled in the sensation of his body in hers, drowned in the stunning pleasures he gave her. And for a little while, she let her dream pirate sweep her away from the real world to one of just Tyree and Clara. No past, no future. Only now.

It was wonderful.

And when she finally slept, she dreamed of him. He captured her and spirited her away on the *Sea Sprite*, sailing over the endless oceans, never to return to dry land.

Dawn came and she awoke to find him sitting on the edge of the bed, dressed in his pirate clothes, his bucket-top boots in a pile on the floor.

"Leaving?" she asked, hurt blooming that he would desert her so soon. Had regret come with the dawning light?

"Nay, just taking off—" He halted. "I couldn't sleep. Didn't want to wake you."

She sat up, clutching the coverlet to her breasts. "Suffering from insomnia or a guilty conscience?"

"Both."

She sighed. "Well, do me a favor and don't." She had no

regrets about what had happened, but couldn't deal with it if already he was trying to backpedal. "What's done is done."

He regarded her for a moment, then crawled back onto the mattress, grabbed the coverlet and yanked. She gasped.

Suddenly she was under him again, his blue-black eyes gazing down at her.

"Sweeting, who said anything about being done?"

"You're mine now," Tyree whispered in her ear. "Mine."

Clara kept silent and still. Something had changed. Something about Tyree. The way he spoke. The way his muscles rippled under his skin. Something was different.

She pulled away and looked at his face. The man who stared back at her was no dewy-eyed, sated lover. Illuminated by the growing light of morning, he seemed almost…angry.

She smiled uncertainly, but wrapped her arms around him. "Yes, I'm yours. For a few days, anyway."

"I want more than a few days."

"Last night, you were the one who said—"

"That's not good enough," he interrupted. "Not anymore." He set her aside and jumped out of bed. "I have to find Sully."

"Tyree!" she called after him, alarmed as he swiped up his clothes from the floor and stalked out of the bedroom. "Wait!"

She cast about for her sleep shirt and didn't find it, but ran after him anyway. In the living room, he had his clothes on and was sliding his second boot on, hopping toward the door.

"What do you think you're doing?" she demanded.

He turned and ran his eyes over her nakedness. "He's here for a reason. I have to find out what it is."

"How? By barging into the Old Fort Mystic fire station and giving the fire chief the third degree about a two-hundred-year-old curse? They'll think you're nuts."

The scar under his eye twitched. "No one else will see me."

"Oh, that's right," she said as calmly as possible. "You're

invisible. So, they'll all think he's standing there talking to himself. Don't you think that'll raise some questions?"

"So I'll follow him until he's alone."

"That's called stalking. Besides," she argued, "he already denied knowing you. What good will it do, besides drawing attention to yourself?" Something Tyree was always careful to avoid.

He put his hands on his hips and let his gaze drift over her body. She stifled the urge to run back and grab the coverlet; instead, she closed the few steps between them, stopping just short of touching him. His cool breath soughed over her breasts, and she felt her nipples swirl and tighten.

"Forget Sully," she pleaded. "Let's just think about us for the time we have together."

His expression relaxed slightly. "You're right," he said, reaching out to brush his hand over her breast. He pulled her close and kissed her. "You'll have to ask him for me."

"Tyree—"

"Please?"

She couldn't believe he was asking her to do this. But when he looked at her with such…trust, it was impossible to deny him anything at all.

"What am I supposed to ask him? 'Um, excuse me, are you a two-hundred-year-old pirate?'"

He made a face. "You'll think of something. Just find out if it's him."

Of course it wasn't him. But maybe she could use the opportunity to learn more about the fires, something that could conceivably benefit her article.

She checked the mantel clock over his shoulder. Only 7:00 a.m. She snuggled closer. "Come back to bed. We hardly got any sleep last night."

It was so nice just to be in his arms. She didn't want the closeness to end. Not yet.

He tipped up her chin with a finger and smiled. "I have a feeling we still won't get much sleep if we both get back in that bed." He kissed her and turned her toward the bedroom with a light smack on the rear. "You go on. I have a few things to get done this morning."

She swatted at his hand and sent him a pout. "Spoilsport."

"I promise I'll make it up to you later," he said with a wink, and strode out of the bungalow.

She pushed out a breath. Yeah, unless she recovered her lost mind in the meantime. Which she should make every effort to do.

Wandering into the bedroom, she picked up his eye patch from the nightstand. Being with this man was incredibly dumb. Any man would be risky, but this particular one was just plain crazy. She smiled wryly at the unintended but direct hit.

Crazy but marvelous.

Slipping the black leather over her own eye, she gazed at herself in the armoire mirror. How appropriate. Half blinded by a simple scrap of leather. Whether on him or her, the effect was much the same. She couldn't see past it to steer clear of the dangers she was surely heading for.

Ah, well. Now was not the time to fight her feelings. Not with the scent of their lovemaking clinging to her skin and the memory of his tenderness turning her brain to mush. Time enough for that after she'd gotten some sleep. Or, better yet, on Sunday, after he left her for the mysterious appointment that would part them forever.

Crawling onto the bed, she wrapped herself in sheets that smelled of him and told herself that leaving Tyree would not kill her. And for the few seconds it took for her to fall asleep, she actually believed it.

She heard a deep chuckle. "I like it."

"Hmm?"

Clara opened her eyelids, but something was blocking one of them. Tyree leaned over her, an amused look on his face. "You in my eye patch and nothing else. Very sexy."

She reached up and touched the circle of leather. "Oh! I must have fallen asleep wearing it."

"I brought you something. I think they'll go well together." He set a gift bag overflowing with gold tissue on the bed next to her and grinned. He was wearing jeans and a snug T-shirt but he still managed to look like a rogue with mischief on his mind.

She sat up in anticipation and flipped the patch off her eye. "A present? For me?"

He gave her a kiss. "Well, that's open to interpretation, I suppose. Go on. Open it."

Sweet Secrets Lingerie was emblazoned on the outside of the bag in swirly gold letters. She shot him a bemused glance. "Let me guess. A bra?"

"Sort of."

"You are naughty," she said, and dug into the bag, lifting out the treasures it contained. "Oh! They're gorgeous!"

Three of them. All delicate and lacy and incredibly sexy, in different colors and patterns, with matching panties.

"But Tyree, I couldn't possibly accept all these!"

He kissed her again. "Sure you can. Consider them study material for the lessons you're going to give me. I need something to practice on, right?"

She wavered. They were so beautiful. She imagined him peeling each one off her and was about to give in when he whispered into her ear, "There's one for each day left."

That totally spoiled the effect.

Suddenly, the image of him peeling off the bras took on a whole new meaning. For each different one he removed, they'd have one less day together. Until the last one…

She pushed them back at him. "No. I can't."

"This one today, I think," he said as though she hadn't spoken, putting one up to her breasts. It was cream-colored with delicate black embroidered flowers all over. "Aye, definitely this one. Too bad you have to wear something over it."

"No, Tyree."

He regarded her. "I thought you liked them."

"I do. It's just…"

"It's bad enough sleeping with a man you'll be with for less than a week, let alone accepting gifts from him?"

She avoided his gaze. "Something like that."

"Clara, I'm not buying your favors, if that's what you think. I care for you. A lot. And if there were any way—"

She lifted her eyes. "You'd do what? Come with me on the trip? Move with me back to Kansas? We both know the answer to that."

It was his turn to avoid her gaze. "Not necessarily. It would depend."

"On what? No, Tyree. If anything, you'd ask me to stay here, so you wouldn't have to leave the estate. So you wouldn't have to see other people or talk to them. Isn't that right?"

He stroked a thumb back and forth over the satin of the bra cup. "Maybe. It just depends."

"Well, I can't live like a recluse. You know I want to see the world, have adventures, live life to the fullest before settling down. I want to share all that with the man I love, not hide from it."

He looked up. "I'd give anything to be that man, Clara. But you know my situation. Unless it changes…"

"How, Tyree?" she asked, grasping his arms desperately. "How can we change it?"

He shook his head. "It's out of our hands," he said, his expression wretched. "Unless…"

"Unless what?"

"Sully."

Her heart fell. So they were back to fantasyland.

What did she expect? That he had found some miraculous cure in her arms last night? That her budding love was strong enough to make up for whatever terrible hurts had made him like this?

She let out a long sigh. "Okay. I'll talk to him. Find out what I can."

And she would also do her best to shore up her tattered defenses against falling any deeper for Tyree. Defenses he'd nearly managed to obliterate last night. Defenses she badly needed.

"Take these," he whispered, and set the bag on her lap. "Please. I want you to have them."

She nodded, trying to keep the sadness from her smile. "Thank you. No one's ever given me anything so beautiful."

He hugged her close and kissed her temple. "Nothing compared to what you've given me."

"I should get dressed," she said, fighting not to lose it. "The museum will open soon."

"Aye. I'll wait for you in the other room."

She watched him stride out and close the door gently behind him. So straight and tall and commanding. How could a man with such a powerful presence be so loath to venture out in the world?

Today she would find out about Rosalind. Perhaps she was the key to bringing him back to reality. And just maybe the key to Clara's own happiness.

"What's that?" Clara asked.

Tyree looked up as she walked into the main room. She was feeling much calmer, now that she had a plan for the day.

"Another of Davey's journals," he answered, thumbing carefully through the yellowed pages. "It appears to be from 1798."

"Wow. Where did you get that?"

"The Pryce-Simmons House."

Her eyes widened. "You're kidding."

"On the library floor in the corner, hidden behind a table. It looked like it might have been thrown there by someone."

"Thrown? And you just took it?"

"It would have been ruined by the water if I hadn't."

"Tyree, that's evidence! You never thought to turn it over to Chief Sullivan?"

He scowled. "Sully? Surely, you jest."

"There could be fingerprints!"

He shook his head. "I doubt it. They said on the news none were found at the scene. The arsonist evidently wore gloves."

"Have you ever tried leafing through a book with gloves on?"

"Ah." Consternation crossed his face and he looked back at the diary. "Good point."

She fetched a paper bag from the kitchen area. "Put it in here. I'll give it to Sully when I talk to him."

He dropped it in but snatched the bag from her hand. "Not Sully. That arson inspector, what was his name?"

She thought for a second. "Jake Santee."

"Slip it on his desk while no one's looking. That way, they won't connect it to you."

She raised her brows. "Oh, no. They'll catch me for sure. *You're* the invisible one," she challenged, crossing her arms when he tried to hand it to her. "*You* slip it on his desk."

Tyree gave her a grumpy look but to her surprise said, "Fine. I'll leave it in the fire station mailbox."

Progress? She didn't dare hope. She gazed longingly at the diary instead. "I wish I could look through it first."

"Bad idea," he said. "Then *your* fingerprints would be on it."

"True. Maybe Santee will let me see it after the forensics are done."

"Maybe."

"Well, I have to be at the museum, so let's get this over with. Coming?"

"You're going like that?" he asked mildly.

Suddenly, she realized he'd casually blocked her way to the door. She glanced down at her outfit, a pretty lavender cap-sleeved T-shirt with a jean skirt and sandals. She'd also re-lented and put on the bra he'd chosen for today.

"You have a problem with what I'm wearing?"

He gave her an inspection that sent warm shivers through her whole body. "Too sexy," he pronounced.

He sounded like he actually meant it, too. She smiled. "Now you know what it feels like when you walk in wearing those tight pirate pants." Though frankly, the jeans he was wearing hugged him nearly as well and were every bit as appealing.

The corner of his lip curled. "But you're the only one who sees me in them."

"What about Mrs. Yates?"

"Doesn't count."

"Neither does Jake Santee."

"And Sully?"

She splayed her fingers on his broad chest. "Only interests me on paper lately."

Tyree's large hand cupped the side of her face, then slid down her throat to her shoulder. Catching the scooped neck of her T-shirt in a finger, he dragged it partway down her arm, exposing her left breast. His eyes darkened to midnight and she broke out in goose bumps as he deliberately ran his thumb along the satin edge of her bra.

He leaned down, stealing a feathery kiss from her. One that teased more than satisfied. His powerful hand enveloped her breast and the tip quickened instantly.

A soft moan escaped her. That swiftly she wanted him again.

"Just remember you're mine," he whispered in her ear, and pulled up her sleeve. Off balance, she tried to hold on to him as he stepped away, but he slipped from her grasp and said, "Now, let's go see Sully."

Chapter 11

Tyree waited impatiently outside the fire station for Clara.

He'd decided to play it cool. After strolling nonchalantly to the mailbox and depositing the bag containing the journal, he'd taken a seat on a rough stone wall across the street, in full view of the station. So far no one had noticed him. But it had been nearly fifteen minutes since Clara'd disappeared into the old brick building, and his cool was wearing thin.

What was she doing in there? He was tempted to walk in and find out. If it weren't for the fact that Sully could see him, he would. But Clara was right. That scenario would either produce an uproar, or Andre Sullivan would be put on immediate emergency medical leave for acute hallucinations. The first would be disaster, the second unproductive—if tempting.

It seemed like an eternity before she finally came out.

"Let's walk," Tyree said the second she crossed the street, steering her in the direction of the pirate museum. "Tell me what happened."

She gave a soft whistle. "I can see why you thought he was Sully. The resemblance is incredible. Almost as close as you and St. James."

"So I wasn't crazy," Tyree murmured.

Clara smiled wryly. "But he *wasn't* Sully," she said, reading his mind.

"Are you certain?"

"Positive." She bent to touch a rosebud growing along a fence. "I introduced myself as a distant relation of Sullivan Fouquet and said I'd heard he might also be related to him."

"How did he react?"

"With amusement. He assured me he knows his family tree, and there are no Fouquets on any of the branches. And he'd specifically looked."

"Because people have remarked on the resemblance."

"Right." They continued strolling. "I pried a little, and found out his family has been in South Carolina for five or six generations, after coming down from New England."

He glanced over. "Connecticut?"

"Didn't ask. Anyway, about that time Jake Santee walked by and saw me, so the topic switched to the fires."

Tyree wanted to grill her more about Sully. In his gut, he knew Sully's sudden appearance on the scene was no coincidence, but it was obvious she didn't agree and had finished with the subject. So he said, "Anything interesting turn up?"

"You were right about the paintings," she said. "Each house that was targeted by the arsonist contained at least one painting by Thom Bowden that is now missing."

He shook his head, puzzled. "Hard to believe all this is over a few mediocre paintings by an unknown local artist. Doesn't really make sense."

"I agree. But they seem to be following that lead. Santee asked if I know anyone else who owns one. Do you?"

He considered. "Not since they sold my portrait along

with the one of Sully and me that used to hang in the Moon and Palmetto. Guess I could run a computer search on insurance companies' lists and see if I get lucky."

Clara looked at him askance. "You mean hack into their files? You'll be arrested!"

"Unlikely. Besides," he said with a wink, "there's no jail that could hold me."

"Tyree—"

"Hush, now, and give me a kiss."

They'd arrived at the entrance to the museum, and he pulled her into the small niche that framed the front door. She melted into his arms, warm and pliable.

A long moment later, he whispered, "I like the way you obey my commands."

"Obey, nothin'," she murmured. "I just like how you kiss." She gave him a last one and opened the door.

"When will you be home?" he asked, hating to let her go.

She sighed. "Closing time, no doubt. I have a lot to get done."

"Mrs. Yates is volunteering at the desk today. Maybe I'll drop by at lunchtime."

"That would be nice."

He watched her go and fought the impulse to trail after her like a hound dog, making sure she was safe, curling up at her feet as she read.

He grimaced. God's Bones, he had it bad.

What he really wanted to do was go in and throttle Mrs. Yates for bringing Clara to Rose Cottage.

He'd *nearly* made it. With one week left on earth he had been happy as a clam, looking forward to meeting his fate as soon as possible. But now, just four short days later, he was desperate to change the hand of destiny.

The question was, how?

Tyree stretched out on the wooden pier in his favorite spot and stared up at the gray clouds trundling by overhead. It would rain soon, but he didn't care. At sea, he'd been soaked half the time, and had long ago learned not to mind the elements. Besides, in his present state, he didn't feel true cold or heat, wet or dry, just misty shadows of the senses he remembered from life.

First one drop fell, followed by another and another as cloud after cloud rolled past.

What lay beyond the clouds? he wondered. Beyond the sky and the edge of the universe? Heaven?

Was that where he was bound on Saturday night?

He closed his eyes, felt the warm drops trickle down his face and cheeks, and smelled the dark, musty smell of rain hitting the earth.

If not heaven, then where? Ask anyone who'd read Maybelle Chadbourn's penny dreadfuls and the answer would no doubt be...farther south.

But he didn't believe that. True, he'd been hotheaded and hot-blooded when he was alive, but despite his profession he'd never deliberately harmed a person. Certainly never killed anyone other than during wartime. Except for Sully and Elizabeth, and they were both terrible accidents for which he'd already done two centuries of penance.

He raked both hands through his wet hair. Never mind. He'd find out soon enough where he was going. Right now, there were more important things to think about.

Like how he could delay that departure. By about seventy years.

In the beginning, he'd carefully studied books on voodoo, vainly searching for a way to reverse Sully's curse. He'd secretly observed ceremonies in slave quarters, memorized long, mysterious chants. Nothing had worked. All he'd learned was that only the person who cast it could undo a curse. And Sullivan Fouquet was long dead.

There seemed to be only one answer to his dilemma.

Somehow, in some way, he had to bring Sully back. The real Sully.

* * *

"Can I borrow the computer, Mrs. Yates?" Clara asked, walking up to the front desk of the museum. "There's something I'd like to check on the Internet."

She was pleased with her morning's efforts, so she'd decided to take a little break.

"Certainly, dear. Just don't ask me how the thing works. I'm afraid I can't help you there."

The computer set up on an old library table was surprisingly up-to-date. In no time, she was online. Her mission: to find out everything she could about Tyree.

The first thing was to find out if Tyree St. James was his real name. Since he owned Rose Cottage, that should be easy enough to find out in the county land records.

After dismissing a twinge of guilty conscience over invading his privacy, she managed to search her way to the correct county Web site and, after a slight delay tracking down the plat and lot numbers for the estate, was able to access the complete history of the property.

To her shock, Tyree didn't own it as he'd claimed. Mrs. Yates did. And before her, the estate had been held by a series of women, changing ownership every ten to twenty years, all the way back to…

Stunned, Clara stared at the computer screen, certain it had to be wrong. After the original land grant, the first registered private owner of Rose Cottage was a Mr. James S. Tyler, nearly two hundred years ago. But within a year, it had been deeded to one Miss Rosalind Winters, who had retained ownership for over fifty years.

Rosalind!

Could it be…?

No. This was too weird. How could Tyree have known about Rosalind Winters?

He must have done a property search, as well. Perhaps he researched each owner and became obsessed with this Rosalind for some reason.

Or maybe she had a great-great-great-granddaughter of the same name who still lived somewhere in the area. That wouldn't be so strange. Certainly no stranger than Clara herself, a relation of Sully's, turning up out of the blue.

Damn.

Was history repeating itself? If he'd already gone through this before and been hurt in the end, no wonder he was so leery of getting involved with Clara!

How could she fight that?

Did she really want to?

Clara let her forehead drop to the edge of the desk and closed her eyes.

She should leave him alone.

It wasn't fair to make him go through it again. She would also end up hurting him when she left, just as Rosalind had apparently done.

And she *was* going to leave.

Tyree had made his own choice not to go with her. She shouldn't feel guilty. She'd asked him and he'd said no. Period. What more could she do? She wasn't about to spend her life in hiding, and she evidently wasn't important enough to him to change his ways. End of story.

So why did her heart feel like it was being squeezed in a vise?

"What's going on?" Tyree's deep voice behind her sounded concerned.

She jerked her head up and reached for the computer's mouse. "Hi. Nothing much." She quickly logged off and hoped he hadn't seen what she was up to.

"Sure?"

"Yeah." She saw he was holding the handle of a basket. "What's that?"

He lifted it up. "I thought you and Mrs. Yates would enjoy eating lunch alfresco."

"Tyree, that's so sweet! Have you told Mrs. Yates?"

He shook his head. "Wanted you there with me to help catch her when she fainted."

Clara laughed. "Not big on cooking, eh?"

He winked. "Don't tell her, but I faxed the deli and had it delivered."

She grinned. "Your secret's safe with me."

He kissed the end of her nose, smiling. "I know."

She got up and followed him to track down Mrs. Yates, who'd disappeared into the stacks. "Is that how you got the bras, too?"

"Nay. I picked them out myself."

"Really? You went to the store?"

"Before they opened. Don't worry, I left cash and the tags by the register."

She didn't want to know. She really didn't. "Please don't tell me you broke in."

"Okay," he said with another wink. "Ah. Here's Mrs. Yates."

"Oh, no," Mrs. Yates declared when they asked her to join them on the picnic. "I'm in the middle of a small project. You two go on without me."

From the sparkle in the older woman's eyes, Clara figured it was just an excuse to let them be alone.

"At least fill a plate for yourself," she insisted, unsure if she was grateful for Mrs. Yates's thoughtfulness or not. Alone with him, Clara found it impossible to resist Tyree's charms, and she feared she'd just get more tangled up in the web of desire he was spinning around her and be unable to pull herself free when it came time to leave. A time that was getting closer by the minute.

The grass had dried nicely after the morning showers, so Tyree spread the blanket in a sunny spot in the courtyard garden under a magnolia in full bloom.

He nibbled and tried to relax as Clara ate, but couldn't seem to get comfortable. He sensed an uncertainty about her. Her mouth smiled as she chatted, but her eyes, on the rare occasions they met his, contained questions.

What had changed?

Instead of pushing, he decided to give her some breathing room. Leaning on an elbow, he inquired about her morning's research on Sully, prompting her to relate everything she'd uncovered, down to the smallest detail. She'd found nothing new or earth-shattering, but it would all add some nice flavor to her article.

"I also learned something interesting," she offered as she finished up her lunch, "about his name."

"Yeah?"

"Apparently Sullivan was the name of the family that held his parents' indenture."

Tyree stared. "Really. He never told me that."

She put her chin in her hand, and he could tell she was pleased she'd uncovered something about her ancestor he didn't already know.

"Mm-hmm. I guess it was pretty common for servants to give the master's name to a child."

"Aye." That was true enough. But it usually implied a certain degree of respect or liking for the overlord or, in the case of slaves, no choice.

"I wondered, when you said he was Acadian, why he didn't have a French first name. That explains it."

"I suppose it does."

Suddenly, the courtyard door swung open and the man himself stepped through it. Sully halted just inside the garden, hands on hips. Tyree leapt to his feet as adrenaline shot through his veins.

"Sully," he growled, forcing himself to stay calm.

"Captain Sullivan," Clara greeted him cheerfully, also rising. She motioned him over. "Join us. Would you care for some lunch? We have a ton of food left."

"No, thank you, Miss Fergussen. I've already eaten." He glanced suspiciously from her to Tyree. "I didn't realize you two were acquainted. Mr. Tyler, isn't it? In antiques?"

Sully'd always had a phenomenal memory for detail. "Aye.

Miz Fergussen and I met a few days ago. How's the arson investigation going?"

Sully looked around unhurriedly, taking in the cozy picnic. "You from around here, Mr. Tyler?" he asked, ignoring
Tyree's question.

"Virginia. How about you, Captain?"

Sully folded his arms over his chest in that familiar power
stance. Not that it intimidated Tyree in the least. However, he
did have to stop himself from wrapping a protective arm
around Clara. Or maybe a possessive arm.

"You and Miss Fergussen both seem to take an unusual interest in my heritage, Mr. Tyler. Are you a relation of Fouquet's, as well?"

He ground his jaw. "Not in this lifetime."

Sully's black brows arched elegantly. "Or perhaps…
Who's that other pirate? The nasty one who killed Fouquet
and the woman? Blackbeard, that's it. His descendant,
maybe? Here for the festival?"

The bastard hadn't changed a bit in two hundred years; still
irritating as poison ivy. Instinctively, Tyree reached for his
sword to teach him a lesson. Unfortunately, it wasn't there.

Clara stepped between them. "A distant cousin several
times removed, I believe," she fabricated, and swatted at him
behind her back. "Which is also why we're both interested in
the fires. Did you have something you wanted to tell me?"

Sully held Tyree's gaze a moment longer, then his demeanor changed back to professional. "Something to ask." He
pulled the paper bag containing Davey's second diary from
his back pocket. "Either of you recognize this?"

"I may have seen it at the Pryce-Simmons House," Tyree
said evasively. "Can't be sure. There were a lot of old books
lying about."

"Did you handle it?"

He shrugged. "Don't recall."

Before Sully could ask him more questions, Clara moved
in and pretended to study it closer. "Hmm. It looks just like

a journal I'm reading for my research. But it can't be that one. I have it with me in the museum."

Sully appeared genuinely surprised by that information. "A second journal? May I see it?"

"Why, of course." She glanced hesitantly at Tyree.

He nodded and said, "I'll grab the picnic things and be along in a minute."

Sully smiled. "No hurry. Let me help."

Tyree deliberately allowed Sully to take their discarded bags and wrappers to the trash, and pretended not to notice him slip a few into his pocket. For fingerprints, no doubt. Which was fine. Tyree'd been careful to wear gloves at the crime scene, which only left the ones he may have left on the diary. With any luck there'd also be a second set of prints, which would lead the investigators to the right suspect.

As he followed Clara and Sully into the museum and up the stairs to the second floor, he felt a creeping queasiness in his stomach. There was nothing to worry about, he reminded himself. Things were going exactly as planned. The fact that Sully and not the actual arson investigator, Jake Santee, had shown up here told him this visit was more personal than official.

Yet, he was still uneasy. By all appearances, this man was not some incarnation of Sullivan Fouquet. And clearly Andre Sullivan had not expected to find Tyree at the museum. So what was the good captain after?

Suddenly it hit him. The answer was obvious.

Clara.

For the second time, Tyree reached for his sword only to find it wasn't there. Until now he'd always been grateful he'd dropped it before he died. Suddenly, he changed his mind.

He clamped his teeth together. Nay. He didn't mean that. Bloodshed never solved anything—as gratifying as it would feel to run Sully through for everything he'd been put through for the past two centuries.

The other man's voice sliced into his unpleasant thoughts. "You all right, Tyler?"

Forcing the deep scowl from his face, he muttered, "Right as rain. Any progress on the investigation?" instead of allowing his temper to get the better of him. Or his irrational jealousy.

"Your insurance company anxious for an arrest?"

"I'm just the consultant," Tyree reminded him. Luckily he was prepared to prove it. That morning he'd printed up a few business cards in case anyone came calling with questions.

He pulled one from the wallet he always carried in public.

"James Tyler, Antiquarian. Spotswood, Virginia," Sully read, then looked up. "Mind if I keep this?"

"Interested in antiques, Sullivan?"

"My lady friend is. In fact, she's up in northern Virginia right now on business. Wouldn't be surprised if she came back with something old and expensive in her luggage."

Tyree tried to keep the shock from his face. Lady friend? So much for Sully being after Clara.

He gathered himself. "I'll look forward to her call. What's her name?"

Sully tucked the card in his pocket. "Lisa Grosvenor."

And so much for this man being Sully. He figured the real Sully would never betray his Elizabeth with another woman.

"Now, about that journal…." Sully prompted.

Just then Mrs. Yates walked out of one of the small library rooms.

"Oh, my!" she exclaimed, her face going white as a sheet. "Oh, dear!"

Tyree strode over and steadied her as she stumbled. "Mrs. Yates, are you ill?" When she looked up at him, he gave his head a small shake. "Can I get you a glass of water?"

"Perhaps you could help me downstairs to my desk?"

"Of course."

"Ma'am, would you like me to call the paramedics?" Sully interjected, reaching for his cell phone.

"Heavens, no. No need for that. I'm fine, really."

Clara hurried over to her other side. "Are you sure?"

"I'll make certain of it," Tyree said. With that, he took gentle hold of Mrs. Yates's arm and helped her downstairs.

Soon as they'd rounded the corner to the lobby and were out of earshot, she turned to him, eyes anxious. "Is it really him?"

She looked so rattled, he was worried she might expire on the spot. Naturally, she knew all about Sully and, having worked at the museum for years, had recognized him instantly.

"I don't know," Tyree confessed. "He claims his name is Andre Sullivan and he's no relation."

She searched Tyree's face worriedly. "Do you believe him?"

He raked a hand through his hair. "I don't know what to believe."

Suddenly it occurred to him that Mrs. Yates was acting very agitated. Far more agitated than the situation, however complicated, warranted. It was, after all, Tyree who was cursed and stood to bear the brunt of whatever the man was up to.

"Mrs. Yates," he said, narrowing his gaze. "Do you know anything about this?"

She looked stricken. "Me?"

"You."

Closing her eyes, she fanned her face with her handkerchief. "Why, I can't imagine what you could possibly mean, Captain."

"Don't you 'captain' me, Lavinia Yates. What have you been up to?"

"Nothing," she insisted, the portrait of innocence. "Nothing at all. Now, I declare, you better get yourself upstairs and make sure he isn't working his magic on Clara."

He was about to tell her Sullivan was involved with another woman when her words suddenly struck him. *Work his magic.*

Maybe Sully hadn't come back to do mischief to Tyree. Maybe he'd come for Clara. Not to try his masculine wiles on her, but to involve her in Tyree's curse.

The words of the provision came back to him with a roar.

…until you find a love so strong the lady is willing to die in your place…

And they were looking through the diary at this very moment, which contained the full text of the curse.

Muttering a string of oaths he lowered Mrs. Yates into her desk chair, turned and shot up the stairs, taking them two at a time.

Not bloody likely.

Not a chance in hell he'd stand idly by while Sully tricked his woman into giving up her life for him.

He'd do whatever it took to see that didn't happen. Even if it meant spending another two hundred years as a cursed soul. He'd gladly endure two thousand, if it meant keeping Clara safe.

Chapter 12

"*Just what the hell are you doing here?*"

Clara jumped at Tyree's question, growled from the hall doorway behind her. The book she was holding slipped from her fingers as she whirled in surprise.

"What's wrong?"

"Where is he?" he demanded, gaze scanning the room.

"If you're referring to Andre Sullivan," she said, willing her pulse back to normal, "he's gone." And thank goodness for that, judging by the murderous expression on Tyree's face. "Why?"

"Did he look at Davey's journal? The one you have?"

"That's what he was here for, so of course he did."

Tyree's expression grew even blacker. "Did he say anything about it? Ask you anything?"

Where was this going? "He asked me where I'd gotten it."

"Did he read any of it?"

"Not really. Just a line here and there." Why was he so upset? Had something happened downstairs? "Tyree, what's going on?"

"And you? Have you been honoring our agreement regarding the diary?" he asked heatedly.

She eased out the breath she'd been holding ever since he stormed in. "I haven't read the entry from the day St. James died, if that's what you mean." Though for the life of her she couldn't figure out why she was still enabling his mania by going along with that request. Just to annoy him, she added, "Yet."

His answering look was dark and indecipherable. After a long silence, he finally said, "I see I'm fighting a losing battle. Would you like to know what the entry says?"

"Of course," Clara said carefully.

"Very well, I'll tell you."

She couldn't believe it. "Can't I just read the passage?"

"I'd rather tell you myself."

He paced restlessly away from her, then returned to stand directly before her. She didn't dare move away for fear he'd change his mind.

"Davey wrote down the entire text of the curse as it happened. At first, it's a bit jumbled. Something about the devil and flames and hell on earth. Then it gets specific and I am sentenced to haunt the earth for two hundred years, neither living nor dead. But at the last minute, Sully added a provision."

"What sort of provision?"

He hesitated, then said, "If a woman falls in love with me, she may lift the curse by choosing to die in my place."

Clara blinked. At first she didn't understand, then she realized what he was saying. Her jaw dropped.

"Is *that* what you've been worried about? That I'll sacrifice my life for you? So Sully's curse will be lifted?"

A cloud of consternation passed through his eyes. "Granted, it sounds fairly unlikely, but women have always been a great mystery to me. You in particular. I simply didn't want to take the chance. Love does strange things to a person."

He looked so sincerely troubled by the possibility, her heart melted. She reached for him, slid her arms around his neck.

"Oh, Tyree." She kissed and held him close. "How could I ever do anything that would make our time together even shorter than it is?" she whispered.

"Promise you won't?" he softly asked. "Nothing foolish? Swear?"

"I'm not the foolish type. Besides," she reminded him, "what about those beautiful bras you bought for me? I wouldn't want to miss trying them all on."

That earned a roguish smile. "No?"

She shook her head no, feeling a pinch of heat in her cheeks. She still hadn't quite gotten used to their easy intimacy. But she liked it. A lot.

She liked him a lot, too. More than she'd liked any man she'd ever met.

His arms tightened around her. "How 'bout now?" he suggested in a low murmur. She felt a hand stray under her top.

She slapped at it. "Tyree!"

"Sweeting, I'm dead, not a saint."

She chuckled, pulling back. "I still have work to get done this afternoon."

"Now who's the spoilsport?"

"Very funny. What will you do?"

"I believe I'll watch," he said, strolled over and stretched out on the window seat, stacking his hands behind his head. He looked every bit the aristocratic gentleman of leisure from a bygone era. Even the faded jeans didn't detract from his insouciant aura of nobility. The wayward grin on his sculpted lips, the way motes of sunlight danced in his near-black eyes and blacker hair, she found it almost impossible to tear her gaze away and concentrate on her dusty old books. She'd much rather be dancing in those beautiful eyes, too.

Somehow, she managed to make herself sit at the table and take notes on her own ancestor, who was growing less and less interesting for each hour that went by. At least by comparison to the flesh-and-blood man dangling a negligent boot off the window seat. He gazed contentedly, if a bit pensively, out the window at the birds and flowers, watching clouds float by, and she wondered what he was thinking about. Occasionally he turned his eyes to her. When he did that, he looked less content. More like a leopard reclining on a tree branch waiting for the tasty morsel he'd picked out for dinner to wander into his reach. Only the twitch of his tail gave him away—or in Tyree's case, the flick of his boot toe.

Suddenly, Mrs. Yates came tottering into the room in a flurry of lavender and gray. "Captain! Oh, Captain, I thought you'd like to know right away!"

Tyree was off the window seat and by her side in a flash. "What is it? Sully? Has he—"

"No, no. It was—" she gulped a breath and plunked down in the chair next to Clara "—on the news just now. A fire. There's another fire!"

Clara's eyes met Tyree's. "Another fire?" they said in unison and clutched at Mrs. Yates. "Where?"

"Angel Island." She took another breath. "It's arson. They think it's the same person."

Clara looked at Tyree questioningly. "Angel Island?"

"Close. Only about seven miles down the coast. When did it start?" he asked Mrs. Yates.

"A couple of hours ago."

"In broad daylight?"

"Apparently, the owners of the house both work. The report said the fire is still in progress."

Clara let out a light sigh. "Well, I guess that lets us off the hook as suspects. Being with the fire chief is a pretty solid alibi."

Tyree chuckled, but immediately became serious again. "The guy's escalating."

"Huh?"

"The timing of the fires. They're getting closer together.

And now, setting one in the daytime. It's like his sickness is getting worse and he can't contain himself."

"Or he has a deadline," she murmured.

Tyree's head shot up. "What do you mean?"

She glanced down at her hands and shrugged. "I don't know. Probably just projecting." She looked up and pasted on a smile. "I tend to work hardest just before a deadline. Don't you?"

He stared at her for a few moments. "That's not what you meant."

"Well," Mrs. Yates declared, pulling herself out of the chair, "I think I'll go downstairs and make a few phone calls until closing time. Someone in the village must know something."

"That would be very useful," Tyree agreed, and went to help her down the stairs.

Clara took the opportunity to march to the window and scold herself. She shouldn't have said that. She hadn't thought. She didn't want to remind him again of his mythical deadline. Nor did she wish to remind herself of her own all-too-real one.

After a few moments, she felt him glide up behind her. She leaned back into him and he slid his arms around her waist.

"Let's not think about things we cannot control," he murmured. "Or we'll both go crazy."

At the moment, crazy didn't sound so bad. She wished she could just forget about the future, as he was apparently able to do. Live for today. *Que sera sera.* If that's what crazy meant, she wanted some of it.

"Are you finished for the day?" he asked.

"Close enough. I doubt I could concentrate anyway." Especially with his arms around her. He felt so good, she could stay there forever.

"Good. Let's get out of here."

As he stepped away she checked her watch. Only 3:30. "Where to?"

"How about a Sea-Doo ride?"

"As in a seven-mile Sea-Doo ride? Not a good idea."

"Why not? I really want to know if our arsonist took another painting. And what else he was up to. If anything's changed in his pattern."

"We can call Jake Santee later and ask. From home."

Tyree gave a resigned sigh. "I suppose we could check the insurance records on the Internet in the meantime."

"I didn't hear that," she said disapprovingly, and started packing up her books and papers.

He managed a grin. "I'm an insurance consultant. The fire chief said so."

"You also told him you were in antiques. What are you going to do when his Miss Grosvenor calls and wants an eighteenth-century beveled glass vitrine with ball-and-claw feet?"

With hiked brows he took the pile of books from her. "I'm impressed."

"My grandmother has one."

"Ah." His grin faded away. "Well, I doubt I'll have to deal with Miz Grosvenor anyway."

Damn. She'd done it again. Made the future loom ominously over them.

She wished like hell he'd just tell her what was going on Saturday. Surely, knowing couldn't make things any worse.

On their way out, they waved to Mrs. Yates, then opened the front door to the gorgeous afternoon. It was warm with a touch of humidity, and Clara could just catch the salty scent of the nearby sea.

She turned to Tyree as they went around the corner. "Would you like to stop for ice cream or something?" He looked dubious. She rummaged in her tote and pulled out the headset he'd given her at the pub yesterday and dangled it from a finger. "See what I brought? So you don't have to worry about being invisible." Inwardly, she cringed. Had she really said that?

He shook his head and kept walking. "I don't think so."

She jammed the headset over her hair and trotted after him. "Okay, a beer then," she quickly suggested, noticing they were right in front of the Moon and Palmetto. She could go for a beer. And maybe one would loosen him up.

"Clara, I really—"

She reached for his arm. "Please?" She deliberately batted her eyelashes, coaxing a reluctant smile from him.

He looked both ways down the sidewalk, then caught her by the waist, swung, and pressed her up against the pub's window.

She gasped in surprise. "Tyree!"

"Sweeting, we have beer at home, and ice cream. I think Mrs. Yates even keeps some chocolate syrup in the fridge." He leaned in close. His tongue swiped lightly over her bottom lip. "I saw a movie once where they did some very interesting things with chocolate syrup."

Scandalized for being so intimate in a public place, she nevertheless was helpless to prevent her lips from parting, or her tongue from meeting his. She tasted him and closed her eyes. "Mmm. Really?"

His mouth covered hers and she felt the headset slide down to circle her neck.

Perhaps going home wasn't such a bad idea. In fact, it was a darn good one. She hadn't had ice cream with chocolate syrup in ages.

"Shall we?" he murmured, and a coil of heat wound through her at the unspoken promise in the words.

"Okay," she breathed, and opened her eyes.

Suddenly he froze, peering at something just behind her.

"What?" She turned in his arms and saw he was looking at a big poster taped to the inside of the window. It was new since this morning.

He narrowed his eyes, and began to read. "'The Moon and Palmetto announces a Special Celebration of the Two Hundredth Anniversary of the Infamous Duel between Pirates

Sullivan Fouquet and Tyree St. James,'" he quoted. "'High-lighted by the return of "The Pirates" to its Place of Honor over the bar. Saturday, nine p.m. Be there.'"

Tyree looked as though he'd seen a ghost.

An ironic laugh stuck in her throat. He wasn't smiling. "'The Pirates'?" she asked. "Who are they?"

"Not who. What. It's a painting."

An icy tingle of premonition worked its way down her spine. She knew the answer before she asked the question. But she asked anyway. "What kind of painting?"

"The one I told you about that used to hang inside. Of me and Sully. The one by Thom Bowden."

Tyree pulled Clara to his side and stared at the poster. Sure enough, there was the painting, reprinted in all its glory below the announcement. One of Bowden's better efforts. Tyree and Sully stared out from the dual portrait looking particularly bloodthirsty, backdropped by their ships and a couple of palmetto-bedecked islands on the horizon.

Tyree swore an oath he hadn't used in over a century and set his jaw. This was getting ridiculous.

"What's wrong?" Clara asked, eyes wide at his profanity.

"You don't find this an odd coincidence?" he demanded, more harshly than he'd intended.

She shrank away. "Well, I—"

He gathered her back in his arms. "I'm sorry." Clara was the last person he wanted to take out his frustrations on. "I need to get home and think."

He ushered her forward, striding double-time through the village toward Rose Cottage.

"Tyree, slow down!" she said, stumbling in her sandals for the third time. "I can't keep up!"

He didn't miss a step, just swooped her up in his arms and carried her. He should have done it sooner, but he'd been too busy trying to connect the dots in his mind. Unfortunately, they still resembled a jumble of unfamiliar night stars more than any kind of recognizable constellation.

"Tyree, you can't carry me the whole way home."

"Sure I can."

"It's over a mile. I'm too heavy."

He smiled. Truth was, he could barely feel her weight. Another benefit of his condition—an unnatural strength. But he couldn't resist teasing her. "If I get tired I'll just sling you over my shoulder like in the old days."

"Don't you dare!"

"Sling you over my shoulder, take you to my cabin and chain you to my bed so I can ravish you at will."

A tiny frown appeared between her brows. "Did that often in the old days, did you?"

He winked at her. "Heavens, no. Chains were far too noisy."

Her fist hit his biceps and he chuckled. "Sweeting, I told you I was no angel." He adjusted her so he could look into her fire-spitting eyes. "But, Clara, if I'd known you back then, things would have been different."

Her pretty mouth turned down in a moue. "How different?"

He halted on the path, yards from the bungalow. "*Very* different. I'd have been as good as chained to *your* bed."

He leaned in for a kiss. Her face averted.

"How can I believe you?"

"I'll prove it."

He covered the distance to the bungalow in long strides and swept up the steps, paused for a second to gather her against his chest and walked right through the front door.

He felt her eyelashes flutter against his neck. Without waiting for more reaction, he set her down and pressed his lips to hers. She sighed and wrapped her arms around him.

"But first," he murmured, "I want my lesson."

With that, he whisked off her top and reached for her waistband.

She sucked in a surprised breath, blinking at him as he slid her shorts down her thighs. She looked so adorably befuddled, like she had no idea how she'd gotten there wearing only two small scraps of embroidered satin.

She looked good enough to eat.

Perhaps he would.

He crushed her to his chest and fed on her mouth, on her neck, on the sweet nectar of her moans.

It was still all so new and unfamiliar, these feelings of over-powering desire and protectiveness he was experiencing. On the one hand, he wanted to drag her to the floor right there and bury himself deep inside her, never to reemerge; on the other, he wanted to lock her away and keep her so safe even *he* couldn't touch her or hurt her.

He'd never been so confused in his life. *Or* death. Even his sweet, abiding love for Rosalind didn't compare to this…this aching, craving, uncontrollable need he had for Clara Fergussen. As he steered her backwards toward his bedroom, he told himself their affair wouldn't hurt her. She had a good life planned. A life filled with interesting things and places, much as his own had been. She would leave Magnolia Cove and think of him for a little while, then the memory of their love would fade as surely as the stars at dawn.

Nay! That thought was too painful.

He would find a way. A way to stay. To continue the curse if he had to. Somehow he would be with her. He must!

"Show me," he ordered softly when her calves hit the side of his four-poster bed. "Show me how."

Clara's flesh responded instantly to Tyree's low command, sensitized by their nights together, learning the nuances of his every touch, and the days filled with yearning to feel them again. His hands glided over her breasts, sending a shock of pleasure through her. His hard chest and thighs pressed into her yielding curves, making her body hum with desire and her mind empty of everything except the feel of him against her.

"Is it hard?" he asked.

"Oh, yes," she murmured.

He surprised her with a laugh. "You're not concentrating, my love."

"Hmm?"

"On my lesson."

He smiled down at her. His hair had slipped out of its leather binding and cascaded along his angular cheekbones down to his square, black-stubbled jaw. Long lashes framed half-lidded eyes of the darkest blue she'd ever seen. Blue like the sky at midnight. Her knees went liquid at the sight of him watching her, at the knowledge that she belonged to this magnificent man. Only to him.

"I'm of a mind to give you a lesson of my own," he murmured, stroking his thumbs along the front of her bra.

"What kind of lesson?" she asked with a whimper. She was already gone. Lost in the sensual magic her dream pirate spun around her with a single look or soft touch.

"Get on the bed," he directed huskily.

There wasn't an ounce of resistance in her. She wanted him so badly her body trembled. She scrambled up onto the high four-poster, self-conscious in just her lingerie while he was still fully dressed.

"What about your clothes?" she asked.

"All in good time." But he did kick off his boots. "Now, kneel and turn around."

"Why?"

"Do as I say, Clara."

So she did, the power behind the command impossible to defy even if she'd wanted to. Which she didn't. She felt the heated sweep of his gaze on her back and wondered where this fantasy would take them.

The silence lengthened. "What now?"

"Gather your hair and lift it high on your head. Hold it there and don't move."

The mattress dipped, and she felt him edge up behind her where she knelt. His knees slipped between hers and the large frame of his body whispered against her back. Cool breath licked over her fingers where they held her hair up on her head.

"Close your eyes."

She dropped her lids, leaving herself completely open and defenseless.

But not without power. She could hear the harshness of his breathing, could taste the musky scent of male arousal in the charged atmosphere of the room. Could feel the tautness of his body as it pressed harder into her. His arousal was solid and impressive, pulsing to the beat of her heart against the small of her back.

"What would you like me to do to you?" he asked, his voice like smooth southern steel.

"Touch me," she said, wanting to feel his hands on her. "Everywhere."

With a hiss of approval, he obliged, starting from her ankles, which lay alongside his calves on the bed, and working his way up. He used his fingertips, his hands, his palms, his fingernails, torturing her from behind with a slow, thorough exploration of every inch of her body. All except the few inches covered by creamy satin.

She moaned. "Please, Tyree. Please." She tried to lower her hands from holding her hair, wanting to touch him back.

His teeth nipped her shoulder and he held her arms firmly in place. "Too impatient, my sweet. Open your eyes."

His arms went around her as she did so. And she found herself facing the mirrored armoire door. Their eyes met in the reflected image of their embrace.

He fingered her bra. "How do I take it off?"

She licked her lips. "There are hooks in the back. Just undo them."

A light tug in back and she felt the pressure holding her breasts release. She'd never have guessed it was his first time. But then, he had shown talent for a great many things.

"Watch me," he murmured, and his fingers slowly slid the

straps from her shoulders. She followed in fascination as he peeled the cups from her breasts, deliberately, a fraction at a time, until they were bare and free from encumbrance.

He let her move her hands long enough to pull the bra off completely, but afterwards returned her to the task of holding up her hair, and he returned to her breasts. His fingers moved over her, stroking her, kneading her, pinching the aching crowns until she cried out from the pleasure.

"Take off your shirt," she gasped, craving the sight of him, needing to feel her lover's bare skin next to hers.

Before she could blink, his shirt was off and his hands back on her, dipping down to the edge of her panties.

"I want you naked," he whispered, and tugged them off.

She leaned back into him, rubbing up against his chest, savoring the feel of his coarse hair and the hard ridge of him at her back. Unable to resist, she let her hair fall and reached behind to undo the button of his jeans. Then she felt for the zipper tab.

His tongue licked up her neck. "Do you want me?"

"Yes," she breathed, and pulled at the tab. It took a few tries and several low groans from him before she got the zipper down past the unyielding obstruction in its path to set it free.

"Enough!" he growled, and lifted her hands away. He kissed her palms and placed them behind her neck, arrest-style. But she had other ideas. She reached back to grasp his head, burying her fingers in his raven hair.

Strands of black tumbled about her face as she turned her face to meet his lips. His mouth devoured hers, sweet and demanding. She felt him push his jeans down his thighs.

"Keep watching," he commanded, pinning her with the intensity of his hot-blooded gaze, then with shaking fingers turned her back to face the mirror.

He slid between her legs from behind, long and thick, driving her mad with the need for completion.

His fingers searched her out, testing and probing. The breath caught in her lungs. A fingertip slid over the center of her need and she gasped.

"So wet," he murmured, circling over her. "So hot."

Rough, needy moans filled the air and she had no idea if they were his or her own. It didn't matter. She wanted him now.

"Just for you, Tyree. No one else," she whispered.

"Watch," he commanded one last time.

She pried her eyes open as he raised her up and thrust into her.

She came apart in a shuddering, quaking torrent that ripped through her body like a tornado. Around and around it crashed through her, tossing her emotions about like helpless sparrows.

She didn't know when or how, but suddenly she was lying down and he was on her. In her. Pounding in and out, making the tumult jolt to life all over again. She held on to him for dear life, wrapping his waist with her legs, his neck with her arms, wishing she could as easily capture his heart.

One, two, three more tremendous thrusts, and then his guttural roar echoed through the room, blending with her cry of complete surrender.

The pleasure went on forever, her own heart filling to the brim with the achingly sweet emotion of their minds and bodies becoming one, and all she could think was, how would she ever, ever give this man up?

Chapter 13

He felt warm.

Tyree came to that startling realization as he and Clara lay snuggled together in the high four-poster, contemplating the unattractive thought of getting up for supper.

He never felt warm.

He never felt cold, either, for that matter. His body adopted the ambient temperature around him, taking neither comfort nor discomfort in that physiological condition. It simply was.

But there was no mistaking it, a glow of warmth was seeping into him from neck to ankle, wherever Clara's naked body pressed against his.

With a sense of wonderment and a frisson of fear that he had somehow miraculously regained the ability to dream and would wake up the second he moved, he pulled her a tad closer. Which wasn't easy, considering she was already draped over him like a spent sail over a yardarm.

"I don't ever want to leave," she murmured, burrowing closer.

"Me, neither." He would stay here, exactly like this, for all eternity if he could.

She sighed. "Mrs. Yates will be waiting supper, wondering where we are."

"I doubt it." Mrs. Yates wasn't as innocent as she looked. He'd learned that the hard way on many an occasion. "She's probably puttering around in the kitchen rubbing her hands with glee that her plan worked."

Clara lifted her head and peered up at him. "Plan?"

He gave her a wry smile and placed a kiss on her forehead. "I think she set us up."

"Deliberately?"

"Why else would she ask you to stay and install you in my bedroom against strict orders about women on the estate?"

"Because she knew I have a thing for pirates and you have a thing for dressing up like one? Probably figured it was a match made in heaven."

"Hmm."

"Funny how with age comes wisdom."

He barely stopped himself from choking. "Sometimes." He himself was a glaring argument against that theory.

She gazed up at him with all the contentment of a well sated woman. "You don't think we're a match made in heaven?"

Damn. This conversation was veering into dangerous territory. "Sweeting," he said lightly, stroking his hand down her back and over her hip, "I think you're as heavenly as a woman could possibly be."

With that he rolled her under him again and captured her mouth with a long kiss. Hoping she'd forget.

"But you don't think we're a match?" she persisted when he let her up for air.

Damn, damn, *damn*. "Love—"

"What would you do if I said I wanted to stay? With you, at Rose Cottage?"

He swallowed heavily and buried his nose in the softness

of her hair. Breathed in its flowery scent. "You don't mean that."

"But what if I did?"

It was all Tyree could do not to jump up and bellow with rage and smash every piece of furniture in the bungalow to bits. His heart was ready to explode with the unfairness of it all. He thought he'd been living a hell on earth for the past two hundred years, but that hell was nothing, *nothing* like the one he was living through at this moment. Knowing she might be falling in love with him. And having to trample every hope in her heart that he could reciprocate.

He quashed the embers of warmth in his body and soul, and forced himself to say, "I couldn't let you stay."

She went very still under him.

He battled the impulse to crush her to him and tell her he hadn't meant it, that it was all a mistake, that there was nothing on earth he wanted more than for her to stay with him. Instead, he remained silent.

Unless a miracle happened, he'd be disappearing soon. Dead for real, forever. Gone to some unknown destiny in yet another unknown dimension. Hopefully to meet up with Sully once again. So he could beat the living crap out of him.

Clara gave him a peck on the cheek and said unevenly, "I understand."

She didn't. There was not a chance she could even begin to understand. But what could he do? He didn't blame her for not believing in his undead state. No sane living person would. But then how could he possibly explain what was about to happen to him? Why he had to break her heart, and his own, while every fiber of his being screamed in protest?

He could lie.

Or he could simply pretend that all the hideous things she was thinking about him were actually true.

Live up to his reputation. Become the greedy, heartless, womanizing Blackbeard of Magnolia Cove everyone thought him to be. He sighed heavily. He'd tried that once, the afternoon in the cemetery, without much success.

Besides, he probably didn't need to convince her any more than he had just done. And until he was able to break this wretched curse and figure out a way to stay with her, he knew he must not try to redeem himself in her eyes. For her sake. Because there was no guarantee he would succeed. In fact, chances were depressingly slim that in two short days he could find a way to alter the laws of the universe and redirect the hand of fate.

Tyree was once more fairly certain Clara would never speak to him again in this lifetime. Mrs. Yates shot him an inquiring look as the two women prepared supper, referring, he was sure, to Clara's unrelentingly cheerful demeanor while she pointedly ignored him leaning there against the kitchen counter.

Luckily, he was saved by Jake Santee, who phoned just before they were to sit down to eat. The arson inspector asked for Clara, and Tyree wondered briefly how he'd gotten the phone number. But her first words, "I was afraid of that," knocked the question right from his mind.

"You aren't going to believe it," she said after she'd hung up from the five-minute conversation, the whole while Tyree wanting to yank the receiver from her hand and demand to know what was going on. Patience had never been one of his virtues.

"So tell us," he gritted out, the little he possessed having long since fled. He hadn't liked her tone of voice talking to Santee, all soft and feminine and hanging on to his every word. Almost as if she were flirting with the man.

"The house that burned today on Angel Island," she announced. "Our guy got another Thom Bowden painting."

"So our theory's really been proven," he said with satisfaction. "Now someone can contact other painting owners and hopefully prevent any more fires."

"But guess what, that's not all. The people owned a Davey Scraggs diary, too. *And it's missing!*"

That snapped him to full attention. "You're kidding."

"The owner is all upset. It was his prize possession because it mentioned an incident involving one of his ancestors. A rather interesting passage according to Jake."

He swallowed a sneer at her use of the inspector's first name. "Is that so?" he managed.

"Remember the cabin boy? The one on the *Sea Sprite* who fell overboard? Well, he was the ancestor."

"I had no idea he married," Tyree mumbled, flicking imaginary crumbs off the counter as he considered this newest development.

He felt Clara stare at him. "Who? The cabin boy?"

He nodded. "I tried to keep track of everyone." He crossed his arms. "So what did *Jake* want from you?"

"He wanted to know if I've heard about any other Davey Scraggs diaries out there. They're going back to the other fire victims, too, to ask if they had one."

He frowned. "Yeah?"

"What do you think it all means?" asked Mrs. Yates, setting the supper dishes on the table.

"That the arsonist is after more than just the paintings?" Tyree mused. "Or perhaps... What if his real objective is actually Davey's journals?"

Clara looked at him incredulously. "As in, he's not setting the fires to cover up stealing the paintings, he's really taking the paintings to cover up stealing the diaries?"

"Or she."

She snorted. "Right. Isn't that a bit David Mamet for Magnolia Cove?"

"Maybe," he said with a half smile.

"Besides, he didn't take the diary from the Pryce-Simmons house," she reminded him. "You said he threw it in a corner."

"He threw it? Why would he do that?" Mrs. Yates asked.

Tyree pursed his lips. "He was angry."

"Over what?"

They all contemplated the steaming supper dishes, but none made a move to serve up the food.

"Same reason he was angry enough to set the fires," Clara said.

"The book wasn't what he expected to find."

"Right. And if that was the case, what exactly *had* he expected to find?" she asked.

Tyree's eyes met hers. "A different book?"

"Or…a different diary?"

He nodded slowly as things clicked into place. "Aye. That makes sense. The question is, which one? And why?"

"We need to find out how many of those journals there are left and who has them," Tyree said, pacing back and forth while Clara finished up the supper dishes. Mrs. Yates had left for her quilting circle, so they were alone in the kitchen.

"I'm sure Jake and Captain Sullivan are on it," Clara said. After the brief thaw inspired by Santee's phone call, she'd reverted to her earlier cool treatment.

He felt a burst of panic. *He had to get her back.* And he had to figure out what the arsonist was really up to. The problem was, he had no earthly idea how to do either, and each one depended upon the other.

"They don't have our resources," he argued. If he could get her to work on tracking the diaries with him, maybe he could break down her resolve to keep him at arm's length. And at least get back in her good graces.

"*Our* resources?" She wrung out the sponge in the sink with what he considered unnecessary force. "I'm sure you meant *your* resources. I have nothing to do with this, nor do I wish to."

He reached for her. "Clara, love—"

She brandished the wet sponge like a weapon. "Don't. From the first second I saw you, I've been acting like a fool, but this is where it ends."

His chest tightened. Plucking the sponge from her fingers, he tossed it into the sink and grasped her shoulders. "Please, don't say that. I don't want to lose you. Not like this."

"You've made it clear what you want, and it's not the kind of relationship I'm interested in."

He couldn't argue. It wasn't what he wanted, either. But what could he do to convince her? Anything he said would only land him deeper in the mire. Anything he did would simply convince her he only lusted after her body. Which was true enough. But he lusted after *all* of her. Not just the physical part.

"You're wrong," he said, and with effortless ease scooped her up and hoisted her over his shoulder.

For a second she froze, then started kicking the air and pounding his back with her fists. "Put me down you great marauding oaf!" she cried.

"Nay," he answered with equanimity, and headed for the stairs, making a quick detour through the living room to pick up her pile of work. "Right now, I need your mind. And I mean to have it."

"This is so not funny, Tyree! Put me down this instant!"

"Not a chance." If things weren't so serious, he might have grinned. This could be fun under other circumstances.

"Where are you taking me?" she demanded.

He bounded up the stairs. "My office. First we have to find out where Davey's other journals are, and then we're going to go and talk with their owners."

The fists stilled and in an acerbic voice she asked, "How are you going to go talk to them if you're *invisible*?"

This time he did grin. She was mocking him. But he didn't care. "I'm not. *You* are."

"That's what you think," she spat out as he set her down in the middle of the oriental rug in his office.

He turned the old-fashioned skeleton key in the lock and deposited it in his jeans pocket—the front one—and dared her with a look.

She glared back. "This is kidnapping, you know."

"And your point is?"

"You're unbelievable," she muttered, flinging her hands out.

"Don't forget obnoxious and impossible."

"What do you want from me?"

Now, there was a trick question if ever he heard one. And the bravely veiled hurt in her voice was enough to bring him back to reality.

"Just relax and work on your article," he said. "I brought your stuff." He handed her the pile of books and papers from the living room. "Or, you could read through the rest of our diary and see if there's anything that might be relevant."

She looked at him uncertainly. "Really?"

He hiked a shoulder. "But only if you want to help."

He could tell she didn't want to be curious, but she couldn't help it. It was her nature. "All right, fine," she grudgingly relented. "I'll do it. But only because it could help my article."

Play it cool, he told himself. Don't give her a big hug. Not even a kiss on the forehead.

"Good," he said. "Let me know if you find anything." And in a supreme effort at self-control he took his seat at the computer and for the next two hours pretended to ignore her.

All in a good cause.

Clara tried to concentrate. Honestly. But it was rough going when *he* was sitting in the same room. Tyree was working the keyboard like a man possessed, leaning in to examine the screen, letting out little sounds of impatience, occasionally grunting in satisfaction as he punched the Print button and the printer spit out some hard-earned bit of information.

She didn't want to be involved with any more of Tyree's schemes. She didn't want to be involved with *Tyree*. He'd hurt her so badly she could hardly stand to be in the same room with him.

Her own fault. She'd known all along he was a heartache waiting to happen. The worst part was she couldn't blame him. He'd always told her he wasn't in the market for a relationship. Next time, she'd listen to herself. And follow the rules.

Rule Number One: Stay away from handsome men in eye patches.

She just wished she didn't still want him so much. Or *like* him so much. No question, he was an insufferable Neanderthal. But every time he did something stupid, it always seemed to be in order to get close to her. How could a woman fault a man for desiring her that much?

However, bed was as far as he wanted to go. And for Clara, that simply wasn't enough.

The pain of his rejection swept over her again. Her mother had always said nothing good came of throwing yourself at a man. Boy, was she right. Tyree was the first man she'd ever done that with, and you could be damn sure it would be the last time she'd ever, ever make that mistake. Far too humiliating.

It did have one good effect, though. Her determination to win the *Adventure Magazine* writing contest doubled. A year-long trip around the world would go a long way to making her forget her hurt and embarrassment, and hopefully put an end to these impossible feelings that had crept into her heart while she wasn't looking.

With a renewed sense of purpose, she opened the diary and began to read. It didn't take very long to reach the part where Scraggs recorded what had happened at the Moon and Palmetto on that fateful night when Fouquet and St. James took each other's lives. She followed the action with fascinated interest, noting that Davey's version agreed even down to the smallest details with what Tyree had told her.

Tyree had obviously read the diary the night she'd found him sitting in the kitchen at the bungalow. And to think it had all sounded so real that she'd almost believed he was the ghost of St. James. She chuckled at her own naiveté.

"What?" he asked, looking up from the computer.

She came back to the present with an awkward awareness. She'd managed to avoid his searching looks or speaking to him, but she didn't like being outright rude.

"Just reading about the night of the duel."

His forehead pleated. "You find it amusing?"

"No." She shifted the book in her lap and sighed. "No. I was just— Anyway, I wondered about this bit of the curse." She turned the page back.

"Which bit?"

"The part where St. James says that thing about the fire."

Tyree leaned back in his seat. "Ah. You mean when Sully said, 'The only fortune I seek now is your soul cursed to eternal hell on earth,' and then I said, 'If so, I'll see you when the flames burn hottest, my friend.'"

She fiddled with the edge of the diary's thick parchment without looking at him. "Do you think the arsonist may know about the curse and is setting the fires because of it?"

He was silent for a moment. "I can't imagine why," he finally said. "Seems a stretch."

"Yeah," she agreed. "It was just a thought. Although…it is kind of strange that Sully's look-alike showed up at this particular time as the fire chief."

That made him smile. One of those sexy crooked ones. "Add it to the list of weird coincidences lately. It's getting pretty long."

"Hmm."

In case Tyree mistakenly thought she had started speaking to him again, she turned back to her reading.

It was interesting to learn what had happened in the aftermath of the duel. Apparently, each captain had left fairly specific instructions as to what would happen to his ship and crew in the event of his death. The fact that they both died simultaneously complicated matters, but in true pirate fashion new leaders were elected and took over with little dispute, carrying on the trade. Although there was some discussion over whether they should still consider themselves privateers or if they reverted to outlaw status, since the letters of marque were made out to the captains, not to the ships.

"I wonder whatever became of the *Sea Sprite*," she remarked without thinking.

"She went down in a gale off Barbados," he said. "1814, I believe." There was a melancholy in his voice that made her look up. "About a quarter of the crew perished. Davey Scraggs was among them."

"Oh! That's awful."

"Indeed."

It was uncanny how he knew everything about local history. "How did you learn all these things?"

He just gave her a sad smile. She shivered. It was almost as though… .

Stop it.

There were no such things as ghosts. Or cursed spirits. He was as alive as she was. Just a little more…complicated.

She blew out a breath and went determinedly back to her reading. But almost immediately she ran across something that made her sit bolt upright in the leather sofa.

"Omigod!"

Her face must have reflected her excitement because he came to his feet immediately. "What have you found?"

"The treasure!" she exclaimed. "Remember the missing chest?"

He looked from her to the diary. "*Davey took it?* Not possible. He would never have—"

"No, no! Not Davey. A man named— Wait, let me read it instead." She lifted the book and read the spidery scrawl aloud.

"'T'night at the M&P John Peel come up all cherry merry and talking nonesuch about how he'd be a rich man soon. I pressed him and got a fantastical tale about how John follered the old Cap'ns one night to the place where they buried ther loot and he were goin' back to get it.'"

She looked up eagerly. "John Peel. Have you heard of him?"

"Aye, I remember him. He sailed with Sully. Older guy, with a passel of kids. He wasn't like the other men. He enjoyed the family life so he'd only go out with us every two or three years, just when he needed coin."

"Well, that would certainly give him motive."

Tyree looked somewhat baffled. "I suppose it does. Well, in that case, I don't begrudge him taking the chest. It's not like I needed it."

She smiled at his spirit of generosity to a beneficiary who had died generations ago. Had Tyree really recovered the rest of the treasure himself? He claimed he had. Of course, he also claimed he'd done it nearly two hundred years ago.

"I still wonder why Peel didn't go back for the other chests," she remarked.

She didn't doubt that whoever had recovered the bulk of the treasure, there'd been a chest missing. So far, every bit of historical detail Tyree had offered had proven correct. Lord knew where he'd learned it all, but it was always dead-on.

"Maybe he thought one chest of gold was enough?" Tyree tapped a finger on his chin. "Or he might have died before he could come back, as you suggested the other day."

"Is there any way to find out?"

"Clara," he said gently, "this doesn't really have anything to do with the fires."

"Tell me again why we care so much about who's setting the fires? I'm sure Jake Santee is making good progress with the arson investigation."

For a split second Tyree looked distinctly annoyed. Then he said, "You're right. And I guess it would be interesting to know if Peel did find the treasure. Does Davey say anything else about it in the diary?"

She pursed her lips. "I don't know. I haven't read beyond that entry."

"Why don't you skim through the rest and see if anything pops out at you about the treasure or…anything else."

"What will you do?"

He sat back down at the computer. "I want to check something out. There was a big lumber outfit called Peel Timber Mills that started in the early 1800s. If John Peel actually found the treasure, he may have used it to start the company."

She'd barely gotten into her task when Tyree slapped the desk in triumph. "I'll be damned. John Peel did found Peel Timber Mills! And he died less than a year later."

"Let's see," she said, and went to stand next to him.

"I remembered the mills went bankrupt just a few years ago. This is a newspaper article that was run at the time on the history of the company."

She read over his shoulder. "Wow. Quite a colorful account. And it explains why he didn't go back for the other chests."

"Thank goodness, otherwise I'd— Well, I'll be double-damned," he said, pointing to a paragraph she hadn't reached yet. "Look who's a direct descendant of John Peel."

"Maybelle Chadbourn!"

"Our favorite penny dreadful author and founder of the Magnolia Cove Pirate Museum."

Clara stared at the screen, nonplussed. "That's interesting. But I'm not sure what it means."

"Probably nothing." He leaned back in his chair and turned to face her. "There was no doubt a family legend about their money coming from pirating and she got caught up in it." He gazed up at her sardonically. "Much as you did."

She bristled. "I only collected a few swords and ships-in-a-bottle, not a whole museum."

"Yet, here you are," he said mildly, and caught her around the hips. "Thank God." He tugged her close, into the V of his legs.

"Tyree—" She put her hands on his shoulders to keep him from dragging her closer still, but to no use. It was like trying to stop the continental plates from shifting.

He buried his face against her midriff, a motion that

brought back a flood of sensual memories. Memories she didn't need right now.

"Please. Don't do this," she pleaded hoarsely.

"I can't let you go, Clara," he said, and pressed a kiss to her abdomen. "I understand you're angry and disappointed. I even understand if you don't want to sleep with me again, though Lord knows I'll try to change your mind." He gazed up at her. "But don't ask me to give up our closeness. I'll go mad if I can't hold you. Just hold you."

She squeezed her eyes shut against the desperation, against the tears that threatened to break through her crumbling strength of will.

Could she do it? Let him back into her arms and therefore her heart? If she did, what would become of her after he was gone? What would happen to her if she didn't? If she let these last two days slip away, without the touch of his hand, the sound of his voice, the comfort of his embrace?

Either way, she would lose.

He said he was destined to die on Saturday, but she was beginning to think he had it all wrong.

She was the one who'd surely perish come Saturday.

Of a broken heart.

Chapter 14

"I never meant to hurt you," Tyree whispered. "I need you to believe that."

Clara didn't know if it really was anger or if it was her bitter disappointment that metamorphosed into self-preservation, but suddenly she was fuming.

"Why?" she asked. "So you can feel less guilty as you go off into outer space, or wherever the heck you're going? Or maybe you're not going anywhere, maybe you just—"

"Clara!" he said, giving her hips a firm but gentle shake. "Don't do this."

She pressed her lips together. The truth was, she was being unreasonable. A petulant child throwing a tantrum when her favorite toy was taken away. A toy she'd known from the beginning wasn't hers to keep.

Her anger deflated, but not the hurt. "I'm sorry. I can't help it." Tyree was so much more important to her than any plaything. Too bad he saw this all as some kind of game.

"I'd give anything for things to be different, but they aren't," he said.

"I get it," she assured him. She also had hopes and dreams for her life and they didn't include his fantasy world. "Please, let go of me."

He did, slowly, reluctantly, his expression filled with an emotion she couldn't name and didn't want to think about.

"I'm going to bed," she stated. "Alone. And I'm locking the door. Please don't use the secret passage," she added, certain there must be one in the bungalow since locks hadn't stopped him before.

He didn't say anything. Just watched her gather her things and hold out her hand for the key to his office door. He looked at her open palm, then up into her eyes.

They stared at each other, a silent battle of wills.

Oh, God, she thought.

He wasn't going to let her go.

There was something about having a woman captive that brought out the worst in a man.

Tyree had witnessed the phenomenon on several occasions during his career, but thankfully had never himself felt the primitive urge to dominate. The closest he'd come was with that Irish wench, but it had been *she* who'd had the urge, not him.

Until now.

He was oh-so-tempted to keep the key in his pocket and make Clara stay with him. Make her slip out of her clothes and lie back on his oversized, butter-soft, brown leather sofa. So he could feast his eyes and memorize every inch of her, every smooth, beautiful part of her body.

So he could remember exactly what she looked like and, when he got to where he was going, bring out that memory and savor how she had been his for a few precious days.

And long for her. And kick himself for not finding a way to be with her forever.

Inwardly, he swore fiercely. God's Teeth, this was worse than being tied to a stake at low tide to drown when it came up.

He jammed his hand into his pocket and fished out the key, slapping it onto her palm. "I promise nothing," he said by way of salving his frustration.

Her eyes widened, but she didn't give him an argument. She just whirled and fumbled to get the key in the lock, finally succeeded and fled down the stairs.

He strode out onto the back gallery and watched by the rail as her shadow scurried from the house and down the path to the bungalow, hearing the firm smack of the door shutting behind her. Then everything was quiet.

The orchestra of cicadas and other insects gradually took up their instruments and began a lullaby of soft night music. But there would be no sleep for him. Suddenly, he felt the weariness of two hundred years of being awake. Saturday's conclusion beckoned, holding out the prospect of eternal peace and slumber. An end to this unnatural purgatory.

Nay!

This was no way to think. He still had two days to find a means to turn the tides.

Shaking off his lassitude, he stalked back into his office, furious at his brief impulse to give up. Tyree St. James *never* gave up! He always got what he wanted, come hellfire or brimstone. Which, in this case, were both distinct possibilities.

He swept over to the floor-to-ceiling bookcases where he kept his special collection of books on curses and spells. He'd carefully studied every one of the hundreds of volumes, trying over the decades every possible spell and counterspell that might counteract Sully's curse. Nothing had worked. But maybe he'd missed something.

Starting with the top shelf, he methodically went through each of the books, praying for some new bit of voodoo to show up in their pages that he'd somehow overlooked in the past. But the only thing he discovered was that he must have been very distracted last time he'd gone through them. Some of the books were out of order, and one was missing from its usual spot. At least, he thought it was missing. But in his present state of mind, who knew.

He made himself stop about an hour before dawn. By then, he'd tried reciting half a dozen incantations and had gathered a pile of about five books, which contained cryptic spells that required a second person to perform them over him. He'd ask Mrs. Yates to do the honors later today, just as in the past he'd asked his other caretakers. In his heart, he despaired of any of the spells working this time, either, but he couldn't give up. He'd try them again, and pray something would be different now. Something that would awaken the magic in the words and allow him to remain on earth.

With Clara.

His soul gladdened at the thought.

But what would happen then?

Would he go on for the rest of eternity as a restless spirit, doomed to walk the twilight path between life and death, unseen to all but a few, condemned to watch everyone he loved grow old and die before his eyes? The very state he'd longed for an end to, with every fiber of his being, for nearly as long as he could remember?

Could he really continue like that?

He thought of Rosalind; young, beautiful, vivacious Rosalind, who had been so faithful a companion for so many years. His heart wept at the sacrifices she'd made to remain with him.

Could he do the same to Clara?

Rosalind had been a woman of her time, raised to marry and make her husband's life her own. But Clara was different. She had no intention of becoming an appendage to a man, any man, husband or no. It would kill her soul and spirit to bury herself here at Rose Cottage for her whole life. There were too many things she had yet to see, to experience. And what would she do when she realized he would never age, would always appear a man in his prime, whereas she would lose her youthful outer beauty, her smooth skin and lively step?

Tyree ground his eyes shut, stifling a groan of anguish.

He couldn't do it to her. He'd been dreaming to think he could stay with her. It would be too cruel and selfish.

Nay, *he* must make the sacrifice this time. And free his love to live the life she deserved, even if it be without him.

But he'd be damned if he'd waste a single minute of the time they had left together.

Determinedly, he rose from his chair and made a beeline for the bungalow. At least he could hold her as she slept. Give her comfort in her dreams. Ease the prospect of his own bleak destiny, if only for the few hours until dawn.

And maybe, just maybe, she would find it in her heart to forgive him when he left her.

Clara knew she was in trouble the second she awoke in Tyree's arms. Or more accurately, plastered over his chest, her face buried in the crook of his neck, holding on to him as if there were no tomorrow.

He was awake, stroking her back with long fingers that felt arousingly male and sensually in command.

"I thought I told you not to use the secret passage," she muttered testily. This was ridiculous. She didn't want to feel aroused or sensual. She wanted to feel furious.

"I didn't," he said.

Oh, that's right. The man walked through doors. How could she have forgotten?

"And I made no promises," he added.

She gasped when he rolled her under him. Back in his pirate clothes, white shirt billowing, dun breeches clinging like a second skin, he was handsome and exotic, irresistibly compelling as he scraped stray strands of hair from her face and drew those powerful fingers along her cheekbones.

"What are you doing?" she asked breathlessly. Excited by the blatant desire shining in his eyes. Appalled at how easily he was able to break down her firmest resolve not to have anything more to do with him.

He leaned down and pressed a kiss under her ear. "Don't worry. I'm not seducing you."

"Oh, really?" She didn't know whether to be happy or mad. Or even to believe him…

He kissed the spot right next to the corner of her mouth. "Unless you've changed your mind?"

"Not likely."

"But possible."

"No," she made herself say.

He sighed but didn't move other than to settle his body more comfortably over hers, stretching out far past her toes. His strong arms bracketed her head and shoulders, supporting his weight so he didn't crush her.

She closed her eyes and willed herself not to enjoy the feel of him quite so much. But it was no use.

This was so unfair. He played dirty.

"What do you want?" she whispered.

He brushed a kiss into her hair and inhaled deeply. "Just to hold you while we plan our day."

Uh-huh. "What kind of plans did you have in mind?"

He lifted up and met her gaze for a moment, to her surprise visibly focusing.

"I never got around to mentioning it last night," he said, "because we got distracted tracking down John Peel, but I managed to find the whereabouts of three more of Davey Scraggs's diaries. I think we—that is, you—should talk to the people who own them."

She made a feeble attempt to refocus also. "And ask what?"

He shook his head. "I wish I knew. If they were local, I'd say ask them if you could skim through the journals, but they're spread out around the state and we don't have that kind of time. Any ideas?"

Other than the ones inspired by his body pressing eroti-cally into hers?

"Um…well…"

"Trouble concentrating?"

"Not at all," she lied. Clearing her inappropriate thoughts, she reasoned, "Obviously we should ask where they got the diaries. Maybe a descendant of Davey Scraggs sold them and is still in the area."

He nodded. "And possibly kept some. In which case, he or she might be in real danger."

She shifted under him, instantly regretting the movement. His thigh dropped between hers, bringing their bodies into even closer contact.

He stifled a soft groan. "Sweeting, I believe this is where I try and get you to change your mind about making love again."

An unwilling smile curved her lips. As much as she wished she could hate him, it was impossible. He was obviously doing his best to be a gentleman—as far as that went with a pirate. He hadn't even made an attempt to remove her sleep shirt. His chivalrous behavior was almost enough to make her soften. But not quite.

She exhaled slowly, and her smile faded. "I don't think so, Tyree. It'll just make it harder when we part ways. And there doesn't seem to be any way around that."

He bent down, his face coming so close all she saw was his eyes. Mysterious, sultry as midnight. His long, black lashes lowered and he moved closer still, brushing his nose and cheek over hers.

"I'd like you to imagine," he said, "just for a moment, that everything I've told you is true."

She began to protest, but he hushed her. "Just pretend. Pretend it's true that I am dead, that I am indeed Tyree St. James—the original one—and that your infernal ancestor put a two-hundred-year hex on me."

Again, she opened her mouth to speak and this time he met

it with a gentle kiss. "Use your ample imagination, Clara. Put yourself in my place."

That was far too great a leap. But he seemed so intent on her cooperation that she allowed her mind to try and wrap itself around the outrageous idea.

"All right. Now what?"

"Now imagine, despite all precautions, you fell in love with a wonderful mortal woman, someone you long to spend the rest of your life with. Except your life, such as it is, will end in less than two days."

Her eyes sprang open but his stayed stubbornly closed so she couldn't look into them.

"What would you do, Clara?" he asked.

But she was still stuck back at the part where he fell in love. A stinging started behind her eyelids. Could it be true? Could it really be true? Or was this simply part of his elaborate, out-of-control delusions?

Either way, the smartest answer for both of them had to be…

"I would let her go," she answered unsteadily. Whatever was to happen Saturday night, whether his trapped soul finally flew up to heaven, or he left on a long business trip, or he voluntarily checked himself into the nearest mental institution, there was one thing she was sure of. She couldn't be with him.

"You have to let me go," she whispered.

His body tightened around her, rebelling against her words. "I can't do that," he said. "Not until I have no choice."

She didn't fight him, and he didn't stir, not for a long time. They lay there cleaved together like lovers, yet irretrievably separate.

She didn't want to think about what he'd said. About being in love with her. If he really was in love with her, he would find a way to be with her. As she had twice tried. The only situation that was unsolvable would be if he really was a ghost. And she refused to believe that.

There were no such things as walking spirits.

She was not that gullible.

She had not fallen in love with a dead man.

Not a ghost of a chance.

He was simply a guy who had been through a lot of heartache and as a result had some problems, chief of which was the inability to commit.

Which was fine. Really. Because she honestly wasn't ready for this.

Any of this.

Especially the part where she was beginning to doubt her own sanity, due to the niggling feeling that he just *might* be telling the truth.

Oh, God. If he would just let her go, she'd finish up the few items of research she had left, enjoy herself at the Pirate Festival tomorrow, head back to Kansas bright and early Sunday morning, and hopefully forget she'd ever met a pirate named Tyree St. James.

As if reading her mind, he rolled off her and lay by her side, holding his head between his hands. "This is madness," he muttered, then bounded out of bed. "Meet me in the kitchen," he ordered, and then he was gone.

She lay there, cold and aching, wondering what the hell had happened to her good sense over the past few days. Wondering how the hell she'd get through the next two.

Concentrate on your goals, she told herself as she rose and got ready to face the morning. That had always worked before. One day at a time. One step at a time, if necessary.

Today, she wanted to double-check some information on Sully's sister, her own great-great-great-great-great grandmother, Theresa Fouquet, which was the last thing she needed in order to complete her article. She was glad she'd decided to do the actual writing back home in Kansas. She'd need that—to pour herself into an activity that took all her attention and energy. So she couldn't think about—

"Tyree!" she gasped, startled at his unexpected reappearance in the open frame of the doorway.

He stared at her, his face turning a peculiar shade she'd never quite seen before. She looked down at her attire—a short skirt and his second bra, sky blue, of the sheerest lace. Her top was still clutched in her hands, ready to be pulled over her head.

Her traitorous body reacted instantly. Her nipples hardened and reached toward him, the rest of her turned to malleable clay, eager for his hands to mold her into whatever shape his passion willed.

Frozen to the spot, she was unable to flee, unwilling to surrender. "What is it?" she asked, fighting a tremor in her voice. Uncertain she could deny him if he decided to claim another lesson.

"There's a phone call for you," he said, his expression indecipherable. "It's Jake Santee."

Clara took perverse pleasure in seeing Tyree squirm as she talked to Santee. He didn't like it when she flirted with the other man. Not that she was interested in the inspector. Despite his handsome features and ripped body, the guy was far too rigid and forbidding to be attractive. To her, anyway. But Tyree didn't have to know that. Besides, Jake was undoubtedly completely clueless to the innuendo. He was always one hundred percent business.

"It seems the first two victims did own diaries," Jake stated after apologizing for calling so early.

"We were afraid that would be the case."

"We?"

"The insurance consultant, um, James Tyler. Didn't Chief Sullivan mention him?" She raised a brow at Tyree as he scowled, leaning against the kitchen counter with his arms banded across his chest.

"Tyler? You're working with him?"

She tipped her head. "Well, we've exchanged a few theories. As a matter of fact, he was able to track down three more diaries for you last night."

Tyree's scowl deepened.

"Excellent. Can you fax me the information?"

She smiled. "Why don't I just bring it on over to you at the station? Say, in about an hour?"

Tyree jerked off the counter and stalked over to her, hands on hips. She showed him her back. She was being petulant again, but Lord knew she needed this. To give him a taste of his own medicine. Torment ran both ways.

"Sure, that's fine. I've got a couple more things to tell you but they'll wait."

She could feel Tyree standing behind her. Close. If she leaned even a fraction of an inch backward, she was sure she'd hit his solid chest.

"I'll look forward to it," she told Santee in a throaty voice. "See you soon."

Tyree's fingers gripped her shoulders and pulled her back against him. Cool and rock hard.

Before Santee hung up, the inspector asked, "Can you also bring the diary you have? I'd like to take a quick look at it."

"It would be my pleasure," she said, and reached out to return the phone to its hook.

Tyree grabbed it and banged it down for her, trapping her between the counter and his immovable body. "What do you think you're doing?"

"You heard. Dropping off those names to Jake," she said, attempting to slip past him.

He caught her by the waist. "Who said I planned to give them up?"

"Don't be absurd. You want this case solved even more than Santee does. Though God knows why."

His arm tightened around her. "I don't want you going to the station."

"Why not?"

"Fax him the information. Or e-mail it."

She turned around to face Tyree. "Why?" she demanded, pushing against his grip.

A muscle bunched in his cheek. "I don't want you talking to him."

"By what right do you—"

"You're mine," he growled with a finality that was deafening, silencing her in shock. *"Mine.* Until Saturday night when I have to go, you're *mine.* Even on Sunday when you leave this place without me, you'll be *mine.* Every time you meet a new man, maybe even marry one, you'll still be mine. *Mine, for the rest of your life.* Do you hear me?"

He wrapped his hand around her jaw and his mouth came down on hers, claiming her, putting an end to any protest she might have mustered even before it formed in her mind. Dizzying her with the intensity of his kiss. Of his feelings.

She whimpered, giving herself up to it, to him, to the whole impossibility of the situation.

"Yes. I'm yours, Tyree," she whispered, clinging to him like a lost child, knowing this was inevitable. "Only yours."

On and on the kiss went, deeper and deeper, mixed with his moans and her sobs, ending only when Mrs. Yates walked into the kitchen and exclaimed, "Oh! I beg your pardon!" Mrs. Yates immediately backed out of the room again, but the spell had been shattered.

Tyree held her until her thundering heart had slowed and her sobs had turned to hiccups. Lifting her face, he drew his thumbs across her cheeks, gathering the tears. "Don't cry," he said softly. "Damnation. Please don't cry."

His eyes glistened when she looked up at him. "Oh, God, what are we going to do?"

"There's nothing we *can* do," he said hoarsely. "Except go on. Accept what is to be."

"How can I?"

"Win that contest and follow your dreams. You'll do fine."

"I don't want to. Not without you."

"You must. Clara, I didn't mean what I said about—" He swallowed. "Sweeting, someday you'll find a good man. I want you to marry him, have his children, be his heart and soul. Just know that—" His voice broke and he suddenly set her away, striding from the room. "Forget about me, Clara. I can't give you what you want."

Chapter 15

"**I**'m so sorry I interrupted," Mrs. Yates apologized a while later as she came bustling back into the kitchen. Clara peeked up from where she'd sunk onto one of the age-worn kitchen chairs and Mrs. Yates hurried over. "Oh! My dear! Whatever is wrong?"

Clara lifted her head from the table, swiped at her eyes, and gave a weak chuckle. "You name it." It was either that or dissolve into another gush of tears.

"Did he hurt you?" Mrs. Yates demanded.

"Define hurt."

"Why, that old scallywag! I should have stopped that kiss when I came in. I thought I heard a muffled sob, but, well—" she turned scarlet "—then I thought…oh, my…"

This time, Clara's laugh was genuine, if half-hearted. "No, Mrs. Yates, Tyree wasn't hurting me with his kissing."

"Then why are you crying? Did he—"

"No, he didn't. It's just—" She laid her forehead back down on the table. What was the use of hiding it? Her problem had to be obvious to anyone with eyes. "It's just, I'm in love with Tyree, and the whole thing is so hopelessly impossible."

"Oh." Mrs. Yates sat down with a thunk. "Oh, dear me."

Clara sighed. "Yeah. That pretty much sums it up."

"This is all my fault."

"No, of course it's not."

"If I had just minded my own business—"

"I am an adult."

"—and not interfered—"

"I have to accept the consequences of my own actions."

"—and not tried experimenting with those spells—"

Clara blinked. "What?" She sat up straight. "What did you say? Spells?"

Mrs. Yates had a guilty look on her face. A *very* guilty look. "Well. The thing is…I may have done something…just a wee bit…imprudent. That is to say, without thinking it through. All the way."

Clara rubbed the tears from her cheeks and frowned. "What are you talking about, Mrs. Yates?"

The old woman fiddled with the lace hankie from her apron pocket, plucking at one of the threads. "Indeed, I'm afraid it is all my fault." She yanked on the thread and half the hankie unraveled into pieces in her lap.

Mrs. Yates looked from it to Clara in dismay. "You see, one of the spells I cast was to make you fall in love with him."

Ho-boy. Ho-boy, oh boy, oh boy.

Clara marched down the oyster-shell path toward Magnolia Cove telling herself to be calm.

If there were no such things as ghosts, how could there possibly be such things as curses and love spells?

There couldn't. So she had nothing to worry about. Mrs. Yates was just a well-meaning old lady with bats in the belfry.

Bats and potions.

And a big, bubbling cauldron.

Clara halted and fisted her hands, bonking herself on the forehead. No. No. No. *No.* She took a deep breath and kept marching.

Maybe she wasn't cut out for this adventure stuff. Her imagination was obviously far too spirited to take the strain. Maybe she should forget about the article and the contest, and just stay home in Kansas and try to appreciate her pleasant, unexciting copy editor's job. Find herself a nice steady guy with a farm and a tractor and have herself a bunch of kids and—

Oh, God, who was she kidding?

Mrs. Yates had confessed to putting a love spell on her so she'd fulfill the part of Sully's curse where a woman in love could lift it by dying in his place. She also admitted she'd done it Clara's first night at Rose Cottage, hadn't thought about the actual consequences, and would never forgive herself if Clara really did—

Well, there was no risk of that. She might be feeling a lot of things at the moment, but suicidal wasn't one of them. *Homicidal,* maybe…

Especially since Mrs. Yates had also confessed to working several other spells, as well, but adamantly refused to go into any more details.

Clara arrived at the station and dropped off the names and the diary for Jake, saying she'd pick it up again on her way home. Telling herself all the weird things that had happened this week had nothing to do with Mrs. Yates's hocus-pocus, she went to the museum and finished up her Fouquet research.

It didn't take long. It felt strange to pack up all her notes when she was done and put away the heavy, musty books for the last time, clearing the window seat and big wooden table so they looked as though she'd never been there.

She wanted to take some photos of the museum and the village for her article, so she'd brought along her camera today.

After snapping several of the library and the courtyard, she wandered down Fouquet Street and took pictures of the places she wanted to remember. She got several of the Moon and Palmetto, outside and in, especially the spot where the duel had taken place. The magazine would like that. Very atmospheric.

Her next stop was the graveyard. Sully and Elizabeth's ostentatious headstones had been spruced up and draped with flowers for the festival tomorrow. They looked sweet, even with their dopey rhymes. After taking pictures from several angles, she turned her gaze back toward St. James's grave.

Of course, she'd have to get photos of that, too. And she wanted to see how the Noisette rose she'd planted on it was doing. After she'd cleaned it up the other day, she'd known something was missing. Life and color. The world's memory of St. James had been tainted by the one dark moment in his life. He deserved some lightness and beauty, even if it only adorned him in death.

She heard Tyree's footsteps as she bent to sniff one of the fragrant red rosebuds. She recognized the measure and strength of his stride. The muted scrape of his leather boots on the pathway. The resoluteness of each footfall as they grew closer.

Except there was a slight hesitation as they came around the final bend. And then to an abrupt halt behind her.

"Did you do this?" he asked.

She turned to him, unprepared for the disbelief in his expression. As if he doubted his own eyes, which were now raised to hers.

"Yes," she said, "after you left the other day."

Following a long silence, he asked, "Why?"

There were a thousand reasons she could give, but ultimately none of them mattered. Because every reason sprang from her love for the man standing before her. But he didn't want that love.

"Just because," she said, trying to keep the defensiveness from her tone. "I felt like it."

He smiled. "Thank you. It looks very nice. I like roses."

She raised her chin. "But did he?"

"Who?"

"St. James. Did he like roses?"

A strand of Tyree's hair danced around his face, lifting in the breeze as rose petals fluttered. "Aye. He liked roses. Red best of all."

She refused to ask. "Excellent."

"Red like your lips," he murmured.

"Tyree."

"Red like the blood of your heart."

"Tyree."

"Red like the tips of your—"

"Tyree!"

His smile went roguish. "—cheeks when you blush."

She felt herself do so furiously. "Oh! You are—"

He raised his hands. "I know. I know. Far too witty for this tedious setting. Come on. I have something to show you."

Without thinking, she snapped a picture of him as he glanced one last time at the rose and gravestone.

He darted her an appalled look. "Did you just take my photograph?"

"There's a certain irony in that image, don't you think?"

He grimaced. "Whatever. It doesn't matter. The photo won't come out anyway."

"Why not?"

"They never do."

That shut her up, Tyree thought with satisfaction, taking her by the hand and leading her away from the disquieting graveyard. She was hard-pressed to keep up with him, but he didn't slow his pace. They had too much to accomplish before tonight. And he didn't want her thinking about their earlier conversation at the cottage. Or freaking about why he couldn't be captured on film.

"So, does this mean you're a vampire, too?" she asked when they stopped at the main thoroughfare to let traffic pass.

"Don't be absurd," he muttered. *So much for not freaking.* "Vampires don't exist."

"Neither do ghosts."

"I told you, I'm not—" He snapped his mouth into a thin line. Ah. She was baiting him again. Anger was good. Anything was better than more tears.

He gripped her hand and tugged her through a break in the traffic. Since their bodies were linked, he could probably just have towed her through the cars with no ill effect, but he didn't want to upset her. Or take any chances. He'd never experimented with just how much of a connection there needed to be for another body to take on all his unnatural physical powers.

"Here we are," he said, then stopped in surprise when he saw a notice of demolition taped to a front door on the building he wanted to show her. "I don't believe it."

"What is this place?" she asked, peering up at the narrow, timbered row house. "It looks ancient."

"It is. It's where I used to live. In my privateering days."

Her interest rose. "The place that's supposed to be haunted?"

He rolled his eyes. "What can I say. I needed somewhere to live while I was looking for the treasure."

"Makes perfect sense to me," she muttered.

He pointed to the adjoining row house. "Sully lived next door." He glanced up and down the street. "Looks like they're tearing down the whole block. Guess damage from the last hurricane was worse than I thought."

"What a shame. Haunted or no, it's an awfully pretty building." She lifted her camera and started shooting. "Better take some pictures while it's still standing."

"Wait here. I'll be right back."

Tyree wanted to see the inside one last time. He'd spent some good times here. And if they really were demolishing the house, there was something he definitely needed to do.

Making his way around the alley, he glided through the

back entry and went down the hall. Cracking open the front door, he motioned to Clara. "Hurry. Come in."

"How did you—"

He pulled her in and shut the door. "I always kept a spare key under the flower pot."

"Sure you did." She looked around warily. "What are we doing in here?"

He grinned. "Looking for treasure."

She puffed out a breath. "Again? Hope we have better luck this time."

"Something tells me we will."

They meandered through the empty, darkened rooms, dank with disuse and sadly neglected. The house had never been light and bright, but it had once been cheerful, filled with an abundance of glowing candles and cozy furniture, silken throws and warm grog. An eighteenth-century bachelor pad, designed for comfort and indulgence on every level.

How he wished he had known Clara then. She wouldn't have stood a chance against his seduction. And once he'd gotten her in his bed, he would never have let her go. Life would have been very different. He would have been a family man like Peel, with a wife to come home to at the end of a long voyage, and a waiting crew of his own un-ruly offspring, all towheads with bright Caribbean-blue eyes. And he would never have been in the pub that night....

Upstairs she turned to him, her blue eyes sparkling. "Any sign of the treasure?"

He gazed at her, wishing like hell... "Standing right in front of me. I'd trade all the treasure in the world for one more day with you."

"Tyree, please don't," she said, the spark dimming. She slid away from him, running her finger along the paneled wall, leaving a track in the dust. "I'm trying very hard to keep my sanity here." She shot him a look. "Sorry."

He smiled wryly. "No apology necessary."

He wanted to laugh. She thought he was crazy. He wished to heaven he were. Crazy could be cured.

"The treasure's in my bedroom," he said.

Her brows hiked charily.

Lord, she was cute.

He resisted sweeping her into a kiss and turned instead to the room on their left, pushing open the dark wooden door. The bedroom was small, made even smaller by the late addition of a walk-in closet where the bed niche had been in his day. Rich paneling had also been installed throughout, covering the original rough tongue-and-groove wallboards.

"Here," he said, opening the door to the closet. "This is where my bed used to be."

"In the closet?" she asked, peering curiously into the dark space.

"Nay, that's new. Originally it was one of those built-in beds."

"That looks like a cupboard, you mean? With curtains?"

"Aye." He rapped his knuckles against the closet's wood paneling. "Sully's bedroom was on the other side of this wall."

"I can't see a thing in here."

"Scared?"

"Of what? That I'll run into a ghost?"

He chuckled. "Don't suppose you brought a flashlight?"

"Nope."

He rapped again where the head of the bed used to be, and heard the hollow sound he was searching for. "Aha. Here it is. Stand back."

With that he swung his boot up in his best imitation of a Bruce Lee kick. If Tyree'd been alive, no doubt he'd have fractured his leg in three places from the blow, but again his preternatural physical strength came in handy. The wood splintered.

"What on earth are you doing?" Clara squeaked. "You can't do that!"

With a few tugs, he had it down to the original wallboards. "Why not? It's my bedroom. And my treasure. Mine and Sully's."

"What are you talking about?"

She bumped into him just as he found by feel the hidden lever embedded in a timber joint. He yanked it and pulled her aside as the mechanism clicked. The secret door didn't budge.

"Damnation."

He gave the door a bang with his fist and it swung free with a whoosh, hitting him in the shoulder.

"What's that?" she gasped, clinging to him in the pitch darkness.

"This," he said, reaching into the yawning blackness of the small square space, trying not to think what manner of crawling creatures he might encounter inside, "is Sully's and my old hidey-hole. And this," he said, pulling out a long-absent but familiar solid weight, "is my box of personal treasures. Here, take it." He shoved the modest wooden chest into her arms.

"I don't— Omigod. It's a strongbox."

"Aye. And here—" he shoved his hand far back into the hole, back to Sully's side of the secret cupboard, and grasped the other box he'd known would be there— "is Sully's treasure chest."

"You've got to be kidding me. Tyree, we can't take these, they don't belong to us!"

"Sure they do." Suddenly, his hand brushed against something that felt like a rolled up parchment. "Wait. There's something else. That's odd..." Gingerly, he extracted the two-foot-long, tubular object. "Let's find some light."

Bringing both chests and the mysterious tube, they exited the closet and went over to the window. The glass was covered with a thick layer of brown grime, but still let in a fair amount of light.

"What is it?" Clara asked, juggling his box in her arms.

He took it from her and set it on the floor along with Sully's. "I'm not sure. Let's take a look."

Gingerly setting the rolled object in a patch of sunlight, they knelt down and examined it closely.

"It looks like some kind of fabric."

"Canvas," he supplied. "It's a roll of painter's canvas."

"Maybe we've discovered some unknown masterpiece," she suggested eagerly. "Wouldn't that be cool."

"I can't imagine what Sully would be doing with an unknown masterpiece."

"How do you know it was Sully's?"

"It wasn't mine, and we were the only two who knew about the hidey-hole. We constructed it ourselves so it could be opened from either side."

"And nobody found it in all these years?" she asked skeptically. "That seems too incredible."

"I always meant to go back for the boxes," he mused. "I even sent Rosalind after them once. A wealthy solicitor bought the block after Sully and I were killed and leased out the flats. Rosalind pretended to be interested in renting one. But he'd put fancy paneling on all the walls, hoping to fetch higher rates, so she was unable to get to the secret cupboard from either room. When he passed on, I bought the building from his estate. So I knew our treasures would be safe enough until I went to fetch them." He sighed. "For some reason, I never got around to it."

"Until now."

"Aye." He smiled into her doubting eyes, anticipating her change of expression when he opened the chests. "Nothing like waiting until the last minute."

"And you own the building?"

"One of my holding companies does." For another few days, at any rate.

"I thought you said you weren't a millionaire."

"I thought you said you weren't interested in me for my money."

"I'm not."

"Then what does it matter? Let's go home. I need my keys

to open the chest. And Mrs. Yates's advice as to how to un-roll this canvas without destroying it."

"Okay. But first I have to stop by the station to pick up the diary from Jake Santee," Clara said, jerking Tyree back to everything he didn't want to think about.

Should he be a selfish bastard and forbid her? Or should he practice reining in his new and uncomely tendency to jealousy…

"Nay," he ground out. "Do it tomorrow." Or better yet, never.

"Tyree—" But something in his expression must have warned her off, for after a second's hesitation, she said, "All right. I guess it'll keep for a day."

Picking up the two chests, he said, "Good. You carry the canvas."

"Well, that's interesting," Clara said, drawing the words out.

Pencil drawings. That's what was on the canvas.

Tyree stared down at the top half of the painting-sized rectangle which Mrs. Yates had managed to unfurl by suspending over a couple of pots of boiling water. Probably not the best method for preserving the integrity of the brittle fabric, but at this point he didn't care. He wanted to know what was on it.

"We'll need more steam to see the rest," he said, wondering what the hell the misshapen pencil drawings depicted. To him they looked rather like blood spatter, but he'd probably just been watching too many reruns of *The New Detectives*.

"Islands," Clara said, standing back. "It looks like a map of a bunch of islands."

He furrowed his brow. "I'll be damned. It does kind of— *Christ's Bones!*" he exclaimed, suddenly recognizing the configuration. "It's a map to the treasure cache! Quick, unroll the rest!"

Steaming was not a process that could be hurried. Tyree

paced a rut into the kitchen floor as Clara and Mrs. Yates endeavored to relax the bottom half of the rectangle, which had been rolled much tighter than the top.

"Didn't you say it took Sully and you both to find the island cache?" Clara asked, wiping condensation from her brow as they delicately spread the remaining inches of canvas open. A larger perspective drawing of an island was revealed, the very familiar lines of which left its identity unmistakable.

"Aye."

"Then how could Sully have a map to it?"

Good question. He was loath to believe what he was thinking. Not of the man whom he had loved as a brother for half a lifetime, in spite of the unhappy ending to their friendship and resulting ignoble curse. But...

"There is only one explanation that I can think of," he answered with a heavy heart.

"What would that be?" Clara asked, glancing up at his bitter tone.

"I suppose," he said slowly, "my good friend and partner, Sullivan Fouquet, had made plans to betray me."

Chapter 16

"**I** don't believe it," Clara stated categorically as she and Tyree walked through the flower garden toward the bungalow.

She could tell he was hurting. Trying not to believe the hard evidence they'd left drying on Mrs. Yates's kitchen table. She knew there had to be another explanation.

"Sully would never betray you."

"And you know this how?" His voice was eerily quiet.

"Through my research. I know him better than anyone. His blood flows in my veins, for Pete's sake. He loved you, Tyree."

"His *sister's* blood flows in your veins," Tyree corrected. "And *I* knew him better than anyone. How could you possibly fathom whether he loved me?"

She gazed up into his cheerless eyes. *Because I love you.*

"How could he not?" she replied. "He was your best friend and would follow you to the ends of the earth. He wouldn't betray you. Especially not for money."

Tyree opened the bungalow door then turned to her. "But would he betray me for love?"

"Love? I don't understand."

They went inside and he paced to the table where earlier they had dropped off the two chests. "I know the legend, that Sully and Elizabeth were the ideal couple, loving and true, their perfect romance cruelly and prematurely ended by a dastardly villain. Yours truly," he said with a little bow.

"Are you saying they weren't?"

"Sully was madly in love with her, that much is true. But toward the end, he'd started suspecting…"

"What?"

"That she was not as enamored as she pretended to be. He suspected she was seeing someone else."

Clara stared at him, and suddenly it dawned on her what he was implying. *"You?"*

"It *wasn't* me. I didn't like Elizabeth in that way, and even if I had, I would never— Sully was my friend."

Unreasonably relieved, she pulled out a chair and dropped into it. "But you're saying he might have thought you had?"

"It's possible. Something he said during the duel. He accused me of wanting her for myself. I thought he was just mad with grief. But perhaps…"

Clara took Tyree's hand and pulled him into the chair next to hers. "No," she said resolutely. "I still don't buy it. He would have confronted you, not gone behind your back."

He gave her a searching look. "I guess we'll never know." He leaned a little closer. "But I like how you're finally saying 'you' and not 'St. James.'"

She blanched. "Did I? I didn't mean to."

"You've done it before. When you were worried about me. Or my feelings."

She shook her head in denial. "Don't be silly. Why would I worry about you?"

All at once she realized she'd never let his hand go, because he started reeling her in by it. Pulling her closer, sliding her farther and farther off her chair so pretty soon she'd have no choice but to stand or end up on his knees.

"Because you're in love with me," he said, and with one firm tug she was in his lap.

"I'm not," she said, but even she could hear the lie.

His hand slipped under her top and she wriggled in protest.

"You're wearing one of my bras," he murmured. "Let me see."

"Ty—" but before she could utter his name her top was off and across the room on the floor "—ree!"

And then he touched her, caressing her breast with a loving reverence that choked off the objection that rose to her lips.

"The jade-colored one. Beautiful."

She gazed into the depths of his soulful indigo eyes and knew she was lost to reason.

No use. Saying no to Tyree was impossible. It didn't matter that she would be terribly hurt. She was already in enough pain over this man to last a lifetime. This way, at least she'd have another night with him to remember.

"I suppose you want another lesson?" she whispered.

He brushed his fingers over the swell of her breasts. "Nay."

"What then?"

"I want to unlock my box of treasures. There's something in it I'd like you to have."

"How do you know what's inside?" she asked, though she knew he wouldn't answer.

He pulled a small ring of keys from his jeans pocket, all ornately old-fashioned, suspended from a silver watch chain she'd seen clipped to his pirate breeches. With a sense of unreality, she watched him select a squat key and insert it into the lock of the dusty, cobweb-covered chest he claimed had belonged to him two hundred years before. She wasn't even surprised when the catch snapped open.

He lifted the lid.

What did a man like him consider personal treasures, worthy of being secreted away, safe from prying eyes and the long arm of the law?

First came a letter. "From my mother, when she was ill and I was sent to stay with a friend," he said, a tortured expression briefly flashing through his eyes. "This was her."

He passed Clara a small, oval portrait painting of an elegantly fragile lady dressed in the style popular around the time of the American Revolution.

"She's lovely," Clara said, noting the close resemblance between them. "You look like her."

"So my father often reminded me."

She glanced up but he'd moved on, extracting a cracked leather pouch spilling gold coins. There had to be at least fifty of them. "Oh, my God! They must be worth a fortune!"

"No doubt."

Her jaw dropped when he set them aside as though they had no more significance than a bag of popcorn, then plucked out a bundle of papers.

"Ho. Receipts for the spoils of our last voyage." He leafed through them. "From the department of war for their share, and several from private parties who bought the bulk of the goods. It was a Spanish spice trader, as I recall." He tossed the packet of receipts at her. "Here. They'll help your case for proving we were privateers and not pirates."

Her jaw fell even farther. "Tyree, do you have any idea— Do you realize— I couldn't—"

"Sure you could. I have no use for them…."

Where I'm going. He didn't say the words aloud, but they reverberated through her head as though he'd shouted them.

No, she wanted to shout back. *It isn't true.* It couldn't be. It was simply too preposterous to be true.

"Ah. Here it is. Put those down and turn toward me. Close your eyes."

She realized she was trembling as she did so. She sucked in a breath as he placed something cool and slippery around her neck and clasped it in place. It dangled across her chest and tumbled down her breasts. "Can I look now?"

When he didn't answer, she cracked open an eyelid. He was staring at her breasts again. Hungrily. As if he were the Big Bad Wolf contemplating the possibilities when Red walked through the door at Grandma's wearing nothing but a jade lace bra.

She shivered and looked down. Her breath caught deep in her lungs. Resplendent against her pale skin was a necklace of sparkling blue-green gems so beautiful she'd never seen anything like it. Not in a museum, not even in her imagination.

"I knew they'd match," he said huskily.

"Match what?" she asked, too stunned to think.

"Your eyes. I was saving this necklace for a woman. A special woman whose eyes would be the exact color of the stones. I knew I'd find her someday. And now I have."

She looked up at him, her heart at once swelling with love and aching with regret. "I can't accept this, Tyree. I'm not that woman."

If she were, he'd stay with her. He wouldn't leave her with a handful of cold stones rather than his own warm body.

"Wear it while we make love," he murmured, dragging his lips across her temple and down her cheek, seeking her mouth. He found it and her will deserted her. Not that she'd ever had any willpower when it came to this man. He'd been a pirate from the first and would be till the last, sweeping into her life to plunder and take everything she had to offer.

But she'd given it all willingly. And knew she would do so all over again if given the chance. For how could one deny one's own deepest fantasy?

His mouth claimed hers and she moaned in pleasure.

He must have sensed the change in her, for he scooped her up and carried her to the bed, leaving a trail of her clothes along the way. All but the necklace.

He lay her on the mattress, gazing down at her as he tossed away his own clothes.

As always, he was gorgeous naked. Hard-muscled and broad-chested, slim-hipped and magnificently aroused. His long pirate hair lay across his shoulders, freed from the band that kept it civilized.

Good. She didn't want civilized. She wanted wild and savage and something to remember for the rest of her life.

Her breasts tightened deliciously at the scrape of the necklace across them. She opened her thighs, slowly, deliberately exposing herself to his view.

Never in her life had she acted so wantonly. But she intended to live out every fantasy daydream she'd ever harbored about this man, before and after she'd actually met him, for as long as she possibly could.

Until he left her tomorrow.

Please don't let him leave me, she begged in silent prayer as he lowered his weight onto her. *Not tomorrow. Not ever.*

How could heaven possibly be better than this?

Tyree lay spread-eagled on his back in the bed being tortured by Clara's lush lips and cunning teeth as they grazed over his flesh seeking his body's most sensitive spots.

He tried not to groan too loudly when she found yet another, in a hollow just beside his hip bone. Who would have thought a hip could be so vulnerable to a woman's touch?

No doubt it was anticipation. He knew in which direction she was headed.

She found her mark, and he dissolved into a blinding white mass of pleasure.

"Clara," he moaned. "Sweeting, you must stop."

"Why?" she asked. She used her tongue and he lost the answer to her question. In fact, he nearly lost consciousness.

He gathered his wits enough to roll them over as one, pinning her beneath him. "Because it's late afternoon already and we have much left to do today."

Her answering smile was worthy of the most seasoned Cyprian. "Yes, we do."

How could he resist a smile like that? He couldn't, so he gave up and slid into her, joining their bodies as he would join their souls if he could but find a way. He covered her smile with his own, finding a taste of himself on her lips, a singular and reassuring confirmation of his continued existence.

For the time being.

So for the time being, he immersed himself in her warm flesh, drowned himself in her eagerness, surrounded himself with her love. And forbade himself from thinking about what would happen tomorrow.

Eventually, the fires of their passion burned down to a warm glow, and they collapsed in each other's arms and Clara fell into a light slumber. Tyree held his lover close to his heart and finally couldn't stop the unwelcome thoughts from invading his contentedness.

Unless he could figure out some means to prevent it, tomorrow he would be dead and gone. Dead for good. Only it wasn't good. How would he ever find the courage to look her in the eyes and say goodbye?

But what could he do?

He'd tried the voodoo, and it hadn't worked.

Sully? Captain Sullivan stubbornly refused to admit being Fouquet despite the uncanny resemblance and repeated attempts to prod him out into the open. Maybe it really wasn't him.

Then there were the tangled mysteries of the fires and the treasure. And now the new information about Sully's betrayal. What did it all mean? Were these things related, or just a bundle of unlikely coincidences? More importantly, did they have any consequence for tomorrow? How could he find out?

He must unravel them. That was his only chance.

Clara stirred and opened her eyes. She smiled up at him, so warm and adoring. "What are you doing?" she murmured.

"Holding my woman and thinking."

She reached up and kissed his jaw. "About what?"

He gave her a squeeze. "How amazing you are."

"Uh, no. You're the one who's amazing." She sighed. "Where do you get the stamina?"

He winked. "My supernatural powers."

She didn't laugh as he expected, just canted over him and propped her chin on her fist on his chest. "Hmm."

Not a good sign. "I was also thinking about our various investigations."

"Figure anything out?"

"I think we've got the treasure thing solved. Don't we?"

"Well, let's see. The missing chest was taken by John Peel, who followed you to the island. Then he started a lumber mill with the gold, but died shortly thereafter."

"And his descendant was Maybelle Chadbourn, penny dreadful novelist and founder of the Magnolia Cove Pirate Museum."

"Don't forget insipid gravestone poet."

He smirked. "Right. And malicious despoiler of my own reputation."

She cupped his cheek. "All lies."

"Thank you, my love." He gave her a kiss. "Are we forgetting anything?"

Her pretty lips pursed, distracting him. "The drawing."

"Hmm? What drawing?"

"Of the island, from the hidey-hole."

"Ah. What of it?"

"John Peel must have drawn it."

He shook his head. "Nay, it's Thom Bowdon's work. I recognize the style."

"Thom Bowdon? You mean—"

"Aye," he said. "Same as the paintings. Sully must have had Thom follow us earlier and draw him a map to the island."

"So he could find it without you."

"Aye."

"But wouldn't he have been worried Thom would go after the treasure himself? Didn't you say the artist was always broke?"

"That he was," Tyree admitted thoughtfully. He reached around and smacked her lightly on the bottom. "Time to get up. Put that necklace somewhere safe. We've got work to do."

Half an hour later, they were in his office, sitting together in front of the computer.

"It doesn't make sense," she said, reading over the short bio of Thom Bowdon they'd found on the Internet. "He lived for another ten years but never showed any signs of having money. Why wouldn't he have gone after the treasure? And don't tell me about some old dead man's superstition. If your children are hungry, you don't worry about that kind of thing."

Tyree drummed his fingers on the desk. "All I can think is he must not have known what he was drawing. He wasn't told the treasure was buried on that island."

"Which proves he couldn't have been in cahoots with Sully," she said triumphantly. "I knew it."

"It proves nothing," Tyree said grumpily, "except that Sully was extremely clever."

"Runs in the family," she said, deliberately bumping him with an arm. "And don't forget it."

He sensed it was time to change the subject. Besides, they seemed to have hit a dead end with the drawing.

"All right, Miz Clever, tell me who's setting the fires."

She leaned back and steepled her fingers. "We should be able to figure it out. We have all the clues."

"Do we?"

"Okay, let's work with what we have. First, his pattern. His victims are old historic houses with local pirate collections, specifically Thom Bowdon paintings and Davey Scraggs diaries. Our guy is stealing all the paintings, but seems to be looking for a specific diary. In both cases, why?"

"Obviously, one of the diaries contains information he wants or needs for some reason."

"But what?"

"Maybe he's looking for the lost treasure and thinks Davey wrote down the directions in one of them."

"But again, if Davey knew where the treasure was, he'd have gone after it himself."

Tyree sighed. "True enough. Davey was never one for silly superstitions."

Just then, they heard the phone ring downstairs, and a moment later Mrs. Yates called up, "Clara dear! That nice Inspector Santee would like to speak with you!"

"Phone?" Clara asked, casting around the desk for one.

He resisted the urge to growl. "In the hall," he said as politely as his gritted teeth would allow.

He didn't know why the inspector ticked him off so badly. He knew Clara wasn't really attracted to the guy; she had only flirted with him to get Tyree's goat after he'd been a jerk. But he still didn't like the man. Probably because the bastard'd still be around on Sunday and he wouldn't. Too many possibilities. Tyree knew Clara would end up with another man one day, but he'd be damned if he wanted to know who it was. And he'd be double-damned if it was someone in his own backyard. Let her go back to Kansas to find her future husband. Or better yet, Alaska.

"Guess what!" she cried, bursting back into the office a moment later.

"What?" he snapped, then caught himself and sent her a smile. "Good news?"

"They know who set the fires!"

"Really? Who?"

"You are not going to believe it. His name is Wesley Peel, and—"

"Don't tell me. He's John Peel's descendant."

"Exactly!"

"Why does Santee think it's him?"

"It was the diaries that led to him. That's why Jake called, to thank us for pointing him in that direction. Peel had apparently put out inquiries to a bunch of antique book dealers and even a few Internet auction sites, asking about more journals. And this is the weirdest part."

"What's that?"

"You'll never guess which one he was looking for."

Tyree chuckled at the little-girl excitement on her face. "Let's take a wild stab. Yours? From the year of my death?"

Her mouth opened. "How did you know?"

He winked. "Cleverness runs in *my* family, too."

"Hrumph. Well, now you've spoiled it. Mrs. Yates wants us downstairs for supper at once. She said she made all your favorites."

And there it was. Suddenly, his whole desperate situation came crashing back on him. He forced a laugh. "The last supper for the condemned man, eh?"

All the color drained from Clara's face. "Don't say that, Tyree. It's not funny."

He rose from the chair and opened his arms, folding them around her when she ran to him. "Hush, sweeting. It'll be okay."

"No, it won't. Please, Tyree. Wherever you're going tomorrow, don't go. If it's a business trip you can cancel—"

"It's not a business trip. You know where I'm going, Clara. And you know there's nothing to be done."

He wasn't sure exactly when it had happened, but sometime in the past day or so her disbelief had begun to crack. He didn't know whether to be relieved by this development or tell her it was all a big crazy lie. Thinking the man you love is insane was hard enough; believing him to be a walking dead man was unimaginable.

"No," she said fiercely, grabbing his shirt in her fists. "It's not true. It's *not*. It can't be."

Gently, he pulled her away from his chest and kissed her quavering lips. Obviously, she hadn't come completely to terms with it, if that was even possible. Best to let it alone for now.

"Come. Mrs. Yates is waiting for us. Last supper or no, she'll have my hide if it gets cold."

"I thought you didn't eat," she said, adorably stubborn to the end. God's Bones, how he would miss her!

"I think I'll make an exception tonight. Come now." He wiped the single tear that wet her lashes and kissed her eyes. "We must both be brave, for Mrs. Yates's sake."

All three did an admirable job of maintaining good cheer throughout the meal, much due to several bottles of wine and champagne that Mrs. Yates carried up from the cellar. She had outdone herself on the menu, as well, preparing every one of the dishes Tyree had mentioned being fond of during his life or occasionally lamented missing. He made himself eat a hearty portion of each and, indeed, it was no hardship to drink the wine, though he passed on the champagne after he realized Clara was partial to it and witnessed the mellow mood it put her in.

There was never any doubt they'd wind up back in bed at evening's end. Together.

"Tell me where you would most like to sail on your trip," he urged much later, as they snuggled after making long, sweet love. "What faraway lands and sights do you want to see?"

She'd drunk just enough champagne to make her think only of her dreams and not remember her nightmares, so he listened contentedly as she told him of all the exotic places she longed to visit and the articles she would write for *Adventure Magazine*, and how her friends and family would read them and finally understand her insatiable wanderlust and approve of her choices. He didn't correct her when she unconsciously began including him in her plans and ruminations, just murmured his approval and gave her kisses of support. Tomorrow, reality might dim the light shining in her eyes, but tonight he didn't have the heart.

They made love again, achingly sweet and tender. And when it was over and they lay in each other's arms again, he had to squeeze his eyes shut with all his might against the overwhelming emotions that welled up inside him. Fury, helplessness, misery, love. Most of all love. His heart broke with it, shattered into a million pieces over the life they would not share, the children she would not bear him, the years they could not spend together working and fighting and laughing and growing old together.

It was not fair. *It was not fair.*

But he had to resign himself. There was no way to stop what was coming. No way to regain that which would be lost.

He had tried, and failed.

Peel and the fires had nothing to do with the curse. Andre Sullivan was not Sully and therefore could not help him. Voodoo spells had had no success.

His fate was sealed. He may as well accept it.

Tyree held his sleeping love in a close embrace by his side and spent the rest of the night gazing up at the deep black moon shadows that crept slowly across the bungalow ceiling. Rather than going mad thinking of what would be denied him, he forced himself to remember all he had done in the generous years he'd been granted on earth. All the good.

One last time, he went over in his mind the final arrangements he'd made for his fortune. For a brief moment, he considered canceling them all and giving everything to Clara.

But nay. She'd have plenty with the gold bullion and the sapphire necklace. In the end, she'd have no choice but to accept his gifts, unwilling though she was.

The rest would go as planned to the orphanages, women's shelters, soup kitchens and other charities he'd founded and maintained over the many years. Rose Cottage, with everything in it, would go to Mrs. Yates for her loyal service. On Monday morning, he'd have nothing left.

Because he'd need nothing.

Once more, all would be as it should with the universe.

With one small exception. Clara. He'd be leaving her behind with a broken heart.

The only living legacy of Tyree St. James would be pain.

And as the last black shadow crept down the far wall and softened to gray, the most extraordinary thing happened.

For the first time in two hundred years, he wept.

Chapter 17

Clara's eyes jerked open to blinding sunshine.

Instantly she knew what day it was.

Instantly she began to tremble.

A solid, cool weight burrowed into her from behind, tugging her back against it when she tried to move away.

"Let's stay in bed all day," Tyree murmured, holding on to her tightly. As if he guessed she was planning to flee.

The tingly chill of his body had always been welcome before, a delightful contrast to the sultry South Carolina heat, soothing her inner fires, tempering the white-hot passions that constantly arced between them. This morning, it made her shiver.

"I can't," she said, wriggling to get away. "I promised Jake I'd drop by the fire station."

"When did you make that promise?" Tyree's voice was icier than his body.

"Last night. On the phone."

She scrambled from the bed, stopping in her tracks when

she caught sight of him. Leaning against the headboard, hands linked behind his neck, he was dressed in full pirate regalia, bucket-top boots, eye patch and all. The very image of the first time she saw him.

She swallowed heavily, suddenly aware of her nakedness. "Already dressed for the festival?" she asked. "I thought you wanted to stay in bed."

Slowly, he crossed one booted ankle over the other. "Not too many hours ago, wearing these clothes would ensure I did. Along with your company."

Her cheeks warmed, along with her memory. She swallowed again. "Yes, well…"

"What has changed, sweeting?"

Pain lanced through her, sharp and agonizing. "You're leaving today."

"That is not anything new."

She crossed her arms over her abdomen and hugged herself. "I'm sorry. I can't pretend it's a day like any other. I can't just lie next to you, make love with you, knowing any minute you'll stand up and walk out of my life forever." She glanced away, out the window to the garden where two bluebirds twittered. "Don't ask me to do that. I can't."

"Fair enough," he said, sliding his boots off the bed and rising to his full, impressive height. "But don't ask me to spend my last day sharing you with Jake Santee."

He walked around the furniture toward her and her breath caught. God, he was handsome. Handsome, dauntless and everything she'd ever wanted.

She stepped backward. "I promised. To get the diary." He tossed away his eye patch and kept coming. She kept moving back. "Maybe we can find it—what Wesley Peel was looking for, I mean." She gasped as he caught her around the waist.

"Don't think you can avoid me, Clara Fergussen."

"Please," she pleaded, desperately gripping his arms. "Please, Tyree. If I touch you…if you kiss me…I'll fall apart."

He studied her for a moment. The tiny scar under his eye twitched. Then he let his hands drop to his sides. "Go then. Because I can't look at you and not want to hold you."

He turned on her and stalked to the window, grasping the frame with white-knuckled fingers.

And she fled.

The village was packed.

Tourists had invaded Magnolia Cove in droves for the Pirate Festival and jammed Fouquet Street, which had been blocked off to traffic and was now filled with scores of bunting-festooned booths selling pirate souvenirs, Lowcountry arts and crafts, Southern culinary delicacies and tons more. They jostled for space on the narrow sidewalks and filled every inch of the village restaurants, boutiques and the pirate museum, where Mrs. Yates was spending the day helping as a volunteer. The Moon and Palmetto was standing room only.

Even the fire station was a crush, as firefighters showed off their new ladder engine and various other equipment in a display for crowds of curious children.

Clara didn't know why she had ever thought this would be fun.

She found Jake Santee hiding upstairs, hunched over a desk in the station common room.

"There you are," he said, closing her diary with an annoyed grimace. "I was just going through all the journals again, trying to figure out why Peel is so interested in them."

"Why don't you just ask him?" she suggested, taking a seat on the arm of a beat-up sofa next to the desk.

"I would—" his grimace turned even grimmer "—but we haven't caught him yet."

"What?" she asked, surprised. "I thought you arrested him last night."

"He wasn't at his apartment when the police got there. They've had it under surveillance ever since, but he hasn't turned up. You didn't happen to mention our conversation to anyone, did you?"

She blinked. "Well, I did tell Mr. um, Tyler. But he wouldn't have—"

"Where is he now?"

"Trust me, he didn't talk to anyone after that."

Santee's brow arched knowingly. "Okay, I'll take your word for it." He handed her the diary and picked up three similar volumes from the desk. "Don't suppose you'd be interested in going through these? I could use your expert eye. You might spot something I missed."

"Well, I'm actually leaving for Kansas in the morning." She was amazed she could say it out loud so calmly. Without screaming or dissolving in a torrent of tears.

"And you want to see the festival. I understand."

"Not really. Too crowded." She shrugged. "Okay, I'll try to take a look at the diaries. But you'll have to pick them up at Rose Cottage tomorrow. I doubt I'll have time to bring them back."

"No problem. I appreciate the help."

Tucking the books carefully into her tote, she made her way back through the throng. She paused in front of the Moon and Palmetto and found herself staring at the poster advertising tonight's unveiling of Tyree and Sully's portrait. By Thom Bowdon.

Hmm.

Surely, Wesley Peel wouldn't attempt to steal that one? Not in front of a thousand witnesses and knowing he was being hunted by the police?

No. He wouldn't be that stupid.

Santee wasn't stupid, either. She was sure he'd have the cops watching the pub, just in case.

She'd be there, too. She wanted to see the portrait, and this would be her only chance. Besides, it would be a way to avoid watching the clock tick down toward midnight....

She drifted along, letting the jostling and bumping of the

crowd direct her footsteps, getting lost in the anonymity of faces and limbs. She wanted nothing more than to be back at Rose Cottage with Tyree, but was scared to death to face him. What would they talk about? How would she keep the tears from falling? How could she stop herself from wondering what would happen when the clock struck twelve?

The mass of humanity closed in on her tighter and tighter, and finally she couldn't stand it any longer. Elbowing her way through the tourists, she practically ran through the village until she reached the oyster-shell path home.

Tyree met her halfway. "What happened?" His worried expression betrayed how stressed out she must look.

"Too many people," she said with a shaky laugh. "I got claustrophobic."

"You're sure that's all?"

"Yeah," she lied.

He put his arm around her and led her toward the shore of the inlet. "Let's go sit on the dock."

Puffy clouds wafted overhead, insects buzzed lazily and the sea grass bent back and forth to the caress of the breeze as they strolled along. The occasional rumble of loudspeakers from the village drifted over the water, disturbing the usual serenity. The waterway also hummed with the motors of folks going by boat to the festival.

Stopping halfway down the pier at the fishing platform where they could have more privacy, they stretched out side by side on the windblown wooden planks.

Neither of them spoke. Clara desperately wanted to relax, to let the warm sunshine melt away her pain and her fear, but it was impossible. She was on pins and needles, expecting him to reach out to hold her. And if he did, she'd lose it completely.

"What did Santee have to say?" he asked, making her jump.

Grateful for the fairly neutral topic, she answered, "They didn't arrest Wesley Peel last night," and related the rest of her conversation with Jake. She also mentioned her concern about the portrait unveiling at the Moon and Palmetto.

"The man would have to be out of his mind to try it," Tyree agreed. "But I hope he does. That way, they're sure to get him."

"True." After a moment she said, "I'd like go see the painting." She turned to him. "Will you take me?"

He continued to stare up at the sky. "Mrs. Yates said something about wanting to attend the ceremony. Go with her. I don't want either of you alone in the village tonight."

Issuing orders to the end. If she'd been able to, she would have smiled. "Aye, aye, Captain."

"Clara—"

She gave her head a shake, warning him off, and heard him sigh. After another long silence she couldn't take it anymore. She rose to her feet.

"I have packing to do," she announced. "Oh. Here," she said, remembering the diaries in her tote bag and digging for them. "Why don't you skim through these for Jake? You'll probably… Hmm. That's odd." She stopped talking to concentrate on searching more thoroughly.

"What is it?"

With growing panic, she knelt down and dumped the contents of her bag on the dock. In disbelief, she stared at the scattering of items, seeing everything but what she was looking for.

"Omigod!" she exclaimed. "The diaries. They're gone!"

Clara berated herself over and over for her carelessness, but as Tyree pointed out, there was nothing she could do about it now.

Jake Santee was less than thrilled when she called to tell him the news.

"At least we know Peel's still in Magnolia Cove," he muttered.

She hadn't thought of it that way and was glad for the small positive crumb gleaned from her colossal blunder.

Tyree agreed. "It also tells us he has unfinished business here, or he would be long gone."

"The portrait?"

Tyree shook his head. "I can't believe he'd be that foolish. There must be something else we're overlooking."

"Back to square one," she muttered.

A moment later, Mrs. Yates called from the museum and asked Clara if she'd meet her there when it closed. The poor woman was trying so hard to be brave, but her voice wavered when, after making their plans, Clara asked if she wanted to speak to Tyree.

"Better not, dear. We knew I'd be gone all day, so we said our goodbyes last night. Give him a big hug and a kiss for me, and tell him I love him dearly."

The last words were spoken with a tremor that broke Clara's heart. She wasn't the only one who was going through hell today.

"I will," she assured her. "I'll see you at six."

"So that's it, then," Tyree said when she'd hung up. "Six o'clock."

"Yeah." She wiped her hands on her shorts. "I better get packing. I have an early flight in the morning."

"Aye."

They gazed at each other for a moment; then she turned and walked to the bungalow, Tyree following behind. He planted himself in the middle of the bed, stiff against the hard wooden headboard, arms crossed, morosely watching her pack her things into her pink tapestry suitcases.

When she finished it was already 5:30 p.m. She'd have to go soon.

Oh, God.

She sat down on the bed. She could feel his eyes on her back.

"Come with me to the village," she said softly. "It's hours till midnight."

"Stay," he countered. "Make love with me instead. Mrs. Yates will understand."

She bowed her head, knowing if she went to him now the devil himself couldn't tear her from his arms come midnight.

She gnawed on her lower lip. Maybe that's what the curse meant by being willing to die in his place. She glanced around at him, searching his face. What would happen if she clung to him like Super Glue at the stroke of twelve, refusing to let go? Would the powers that be take her instead and let him continue on with his interrupted mortal life? Or would it be his walking death that would go on? Or would she just vanish with him?

"Clara!" he said, loudly, as though it wasn't the first time he'd called her name. He leaned forward and grasped her shoulders. "Whatever you're thinking, forget it."

"But—"

"Nay, Clara." The words were gritted out, brooking no dissent. He cursed under his breath. "This is exactly what I feared."

Or perhaps she would find the midnight minute passed just like any other, leaving her in its wake to choose between a lovable neurotic and her life's dreams....

"Enough!" He leapt from the bed, taking her with him. "You must go. *Now.* Meet Mrs. Yates, and don't come back here until after midnight. Swear to me you won't."

"Tyree—"

"Swear!"

"All right," she said, fighting to stay composed. *This was it.* Whatever happened, he would be gone when she returned. And she would never know what might have been. "I swear."

Tyree had done a lot of difficult things in his days on earth. As a child, he'd endured his father's beatings with nary a sound; he'd toiled his way up from cabin boy, subsisting for months at a time on maggoty hardtack and stale brown ale, until he'd made full sailor and, in record time, become captain of his own vessel; he'd brought down fully loaded merchantmen with no shots fired. He'd killed and been killed by his best friend; he'd stood by helpless as his dearest loved ones grew old and passed away before his own still-youthful eyes.

But nothing, nothing, compared to having to watch Clara Fergussen walk down that oyster-shell path toward a future without him.

When she'd gone, he stalked around the estate blindly, unable to see anything save her pale, heartbroken face as she'd said her last goodbye and turned away from him, never to look back.

He wanted to shout and curse and rage about like a madman, breaking anything and everything in his way. But what was the use? None of that would change his miserable fate.

Why couldn't it happen *now*?

For the next hours, he felt on the verge of insanity, rattling around the house unable to sit, unable to concentrate on anything. The only constructive thing he managed to do was hide the necklace in Clara's suitcase and the bag of gold coins in a box with her name on it.

Finally, after eleven o'clock, he went out onto the second-floor gallery and forced himself to take a seat on the porch swing, gazing out in the direction of the village.

Not long now.

What was she doing?

Between a packed evening schedule of festival events, ending with a spectacular display of fireworks at midnight, Clara would have had plenty to occupy the hours. Maybe she was sitting with Mrs. Yates now at the Moon and Palmetto toasting his newly unveiled portrait?

Christ's Tears, how he missed her!

He would give anything for one last look at her.

Just one look…

He took a deep breath.

Then vaulted to his feet, checking his pocket watch. 11:42 p.m.

There was still time.

Tyree paid no regard as to who could see him and who couldn't; this was the one day of the year being dressed as a pirate made him blend in. He darted back and forth between people, and occasionally simply strode through the body blocking his path.

Where was she?

Three times he'd searched the crowd gathered to watch the fireworks and had spotted neither Clara nor Mrs. Yates. He checked his watch for the dozenth time. 11:54 p.m.

Desperation crawled through his soul.

Where were they?

He prayed they were together and that nothing was wrong.

He'd already sprinted to the Moon and Palmetto and found it buttoned up tight; a note on the door stated the pub would reopen after the fireworks display. The place had been dark with no one about but a uniformed cop posted to guard the place.

Tyree swept his gaze back in that direction, hoping to see Clara and Mrs. Yates walking arm in arm along the cobblestones.

Instead, his blood froze at what he saw.

Smoke!

"Clara!" he roared, and flew down the jammed street, shouting, "Fire! Fire!" in case someone, anyone, could hear him.

But no one did. They only obscured his view and blocked his way as he struggled to move faster. It took every ounce of strength he had to concentrate on dematerializing through so many solid objects in a row. Finally, he broke through and turned the corner a block from the Moon and Palmetto.

His heart stalled.

Flames were everywhere, shooting out of the windows of the pub, leaping over the alley next to it and twisting up the wall of the neighboring boutique. The cop lay prone on the street, unconscious.

Tyree cursed violently, sprinted to the cop and grabbed his walkie-talkie, punching the signal button several times along with every other button as the thing squawked to life. That should bring the cavalry. Tossing it aside, he looked up.

And his world lurched violently. Mrs. Yates stood at the mouth of the alley gesturing frantically as Clara disappeared into it at a run.

"Clara!" he yelled, and took off after her.

"Captain Tyree, thank God! Hurry!" Mrs. Yates called out.

"What the *hell* is she doing?"

"Someone's stolen the painting!"

Dammit, dammit, *dammit*! Where the blazes was Santee? He'd *known* this might happen! Tyree heard the sound of sirens in the distance. Thank God!

Tyree charged for all he was worth down the alley after Clara. Would he have time to reach her before midnight?

The sirens grew louder. *How many minutes did he have left?*

The alley was fast becoming an inferno. Fire consumed the buildings on both sides; inside he could already hear timbers crashing from the upper floors.

"Clara, stop!"

She didn't slow, but he was gaining on her. He saw the man she was chasing. A large canvas was tucked under his arm.

"Hey, you!" Tyree shouted.

To his utter shock, the man stopped and whirled. There was a gun in his hand aimed at Clara.

She slid to a halt, face ashen.

Pure panic flooded Tyree. "Give it up, Peel!" he shouted, waving his arms as he closed the gap between them, his mind desperately scrambling for some way to protect her.

Suddenly, the aim of the gun shifted. To him.

Peel could see him!

Behind them, a fire truck air horn blasted.

Tyree almost fainted with relief. "Throw down your weapon, Peel! They know who you are."

"They'll never catch me! I have the secret!" Peel croaked, coughing from the smoke pouring everywhere. The gun tipped down. "Not even you can stop me!" Jerking it up, he took aim again, right at Tyree's heart.

From far away Tyree heard the deep ring of a steeple bell.
Bong.

Please, not yet! Not enough time!

Peel's finger moved on the trigger. Clara screamed. And suddenly she was in front of him, arms spread.

Bong, the bell rang again.

The gun exploded and Clara's body jerked sickeningly.
"Naaaay!"

He caught her as she collapsed, blood blooming over her shoulder.

Bong.

He clutched her frantically around the waist and struck out with his fist at the gun that was still aimed at her. It sailed onto the cobblestones with a clatter.

Bong.

Suddenly there was a knife in Peel's hand. The long, deadly blade gleamed red, reflecting the flames all around them.

The air was stifling hot. Overhead, Tyree heard a loud crack.
Bong.

Peel lashed out, and a searing pain pierced Tyree's abdomen. He staggered briefly under Clara's weight. *Strange,* he thought. In disbelief, he looked down. Thick blood poured from a wound at the side of his stomach. He almost laughed. Blood? What madness was this?

Bong.

He staggered again, falling to his knees. Clara's head lolled against the crimson pool engulfing her chest. He panted in desperation, the edges of his vision blurring. His fingers went numb and he felt Clara slipping from his grasp.

Bong.

Just ahead, a door crashed open in the side of the building and a fireman leapt through the flames and ran toward them. Though dressed head to toe in soot-smudged yellow firemen's gear, his arrogant stride and powerful frame were unmistakable.

Bong.

Sully!

Tyree's own fateful words came back to him, bitter and haunting. *I'll see you when the flames burn hottest, my friend.*

Bong.

This time, Tyree did laugh. A desperate, ironic bark of defeat.

Damn his hide. *Damn his bastard hide.*

He'd done it.

Sully had gotten his ultimate revenge.

Bong.

His best friend and worst enemy bent over him, and Tyree howled with anguish as Clara's limp body was pried from his fingers. "Don't take her from me. For God's sake don't take her!"

"Let her go, man. It's over."

Bong.

Struggling to draw his last breath on earth, Tyree rasped, "Damn you, Sullivan Fouquet! Damn you for cursing me. Damn you for killing the only woman I ever loved! And damn you to live with a loved one's betrayal as wretched as that you dealt me."

There was a muffled shout and a huge crash, but without Clara in his arms, Tyree felt nothing.

Bong.

And so, with the final toll of the midnight bell, he closed his eyes and let the blackness roll over him forever.

Chapter 18

Flames licked at her shoulder, burning like acid. She whimpered. Where was he? She tried to remember who she was looking for. But couldn't...

Clara woke with a start and clawed her way out of her nightmare, taking big gulps of air. She looked around and realized she wasn't at Rose Cottage. She was in a hospital room. And her arm was in a sling.

What had happened?

Slowly it all came trickling back: the never-ending Pirate Festival, chancing upon that man sneaking out of the Moon and Palmetto with the stolen painting, the terrifying fire blazing all around, Tyree coming to her rescue. Jumping in front of the gun to save him...

She groaned. Oh, great. Tyree would never forgive her for—

Tyree!

Suddenly, she remembered.

Oh-God-oh-God-oh-God.

She bolted upright but was immediately engulfed in an avalanche of pain. She collapsed back on the bed, terror pushing aside the physical hurt.

That's who she'd been looking for.

"Mrs. Yates?" she called out, but could barely get the sound past her parched throat. Mrs. Yates would know what had become of him. She'd been there. She had to have seen.

"Back in the world of the living, I hear," said a chipper voice from the other side of a partition curtain. A second later, a steely gray head popped into view, followed by the rest of a stout, matronly nurse. "Don't try to move, it'll— Ah. I see I'm too late."

"Where's Mrs. Yates?" she asked. "I need to—"

"She's fine and dandy, don't you worry none. Kept her overnight, but she went home yesterday."

Yesterday? That meant— "Tyree," Clara whispered, tears filling her eyes.

"What's that?" the nurse asked. "Your family? They were called and are on their way in from Kansas. I don't mind saying your mother is *very* worried about you. Dr. Anderson tried to reassure her—"

The nurse droned on, fiddling with her IV and fussing with her pillows and blanket. But Clara didn't have the energy to listen. Even to news of her family. All she could think of was Tyree, and how she would never see him again.

Dr. Anderson came in and Clara stoically endured being poked, prodded and pronounced well on the road to recovery.

Right.

What did doctors know anyway?

"Do you feel like seeing a visitor?" the nurse asked when the doctor whisked out again. "From the fire department."

"Sully?" she asked, perking up. She had a vague memory of him being there, too. Though she couldn't quite place him...

"You mean Captain Sullivan? Oh, no, the poor man. I'm

afraid he's quite beyond visiting at the moment. He was crushed by a falling wooden beam while pulling you out of that alley."

Clara gasped, horrified. "Pulling *me* out? Oh, my God is he…?"

The nurse tsked. "A pure miracle he survived. Broke half a dozen bones in a score of places, but no, he'll pull through. Physically, at least."

Dismay washed over Clara. "There was brain damage?"

"No apparent head injury, but he's surely been muttering some mighty odd things." The nurse tapped her graying temple. "Hallucinating. About being a *pirate*."

Clara stared in disbelief. *Oh, no.* "You're kidding."

The other woman leaned in conspiratorially. "Must have mixed up the festival with reality in his rattled brain. Thinks he's Sullivan Fouquet of all people." She chuckled heartily. "Must be the similar name. But not to worry. Doctor says the captain should snap out of it when he regains full consciousness."

Clara's stomach sank. For some reason, she had her doubts about that.

"Anyway, your visitor is Inspector Santee. He's being quite…persistent. So if you feel up to it, you'd be doing us all a big favor, if you know what I mean." The nurse gave her pillow a final fluff. "What do you say?"

The last thing Clara wanted was visitors. But at least Santee could tell her what happened at the fire.

"Why not."

Jake entered the room with a red face and a large bouquet of yellow daisies. "Hope you're feeling better, Miz Fergussen. The, uh, guys sent some flowers." He deposited the vase on the nightstand like it was a burning hot coal, wiping his hands on his jeans afterwards.

She managed a sincere smile. "How sweet. Thank them for me."

"Sure." He cleared his throat. "Anyway, I just wanted to come and apologize in person for getting you into this mess."

"What?" She changed gears and took a good look at him. Self-recrimination was written all over his face.

"If I hadn't involved you—"

She cut him off. "Please don't say that." She recognized the guilt trip because she was feeling exactly the same way about Captain Sullivan. "It was my own choice to go into that alley," she assured him. "If I hadn't, maybe Captain Sullivan wouldn't be fighting for his life right now."

"The chief was doing his job," Santee countered emphatically. "You were doing mine. *I* should have been chasing Peel, not you."

She pushed out a breath. "Let's call it a wash, then, okay? At least we got him."

Santee looked at the floor. "I guess. Although that's one needless death in my book."

"Peel died in the fire?"

"We assume so. Haven't found the body yet, but there was no way he could have gotten through that inferno. He's in there somewhere."

"And the diaries?"

"I assume they're gone, too."

"What a shame. Why do you think he did them? The fires I mean."

Santee shrugged. "His family says he hasn't been the same since the mill went bankrupt. He's been obsessed with finding money to reopen it. Apparently, he ran across some old papers clearing out the mill office that made reference to pirate treasure and some kind of clue contained in one of the Scraggs diaries."

"If that is true, it really is too bad they were burned."

"Yeah. In any case, at least it's all over." His mouth thinned. "Well, I better get going. Just wanted to drop those flowers off."

He took his leave and she let out a heartfelt sigh. Poor man. He'd taken a heavy burden upon himself. She hoped he had someone who'd help him through it.

She wished she did, too.

But the only person in the universe who would understand what she was going through couldn't help her now. Could never help her again.

She might as well face up to it. Tyree was gone from her life. And somehow, she'd have to find the strength to go on.

Exhausted, she lay back on the bed and stopped fighting the overwhelming hurt, inside and out. She let it wash over her, sweeping her away in a sea of misery—heart and soul and body.

Tyree was gone.

How would she ever live without him?

Everything was muzzy. Muzzy and white.

White room. Bright white lights. White-clad people gliding noiselessly past.

No wings, he noted.

And his belly hurt like hell.

Which probably eliminated heaven as his present abode.

Not that it mattered. *Nothing mattered any longer.*

The distinctive smell of cleaning solution scrubbed the lingering cobwebs from Tyree's brain. He cracked an eyelid and peeked at the instruments beeping to one side of the bed. He'd never been in a hospital before, but he recognized his surroundings from countless daytime soap operas.

What the hell was going on?

He closed his eye again and lay there for a moment getting his bearings. A maneuver that had saved his life on many an occasion in his privateering days.

He started. He wasn't wearing his pirate togs! His upper chest was bare and some flimsy cloth covered his lower body. His abdomen was bound up in a bandage tight as a drum. Which probably accounted for the throbbing pain.

"Oh, Mr. Ty-ler!" a young feminine voice sang out, shocking him further. "Come on now, I can see you're awake."

Tyler? Could she be talking to *him*? Nay. He squeezed them tighter.

A duo of giggles sounded from a nearby doorway. "Maybe he's shy," one of them suggested to another round of giggles.

That's when he realized someone was running a warm, wet sponge over his naked chest. He froze. A second later, the sponge made another pass.

That's it.

He grabbed the young woman's wrist. "I'll thank you to stop that," he said in his most authoritative voice, opening his eyes into a ferocious scowl.

She gasped, along with the other candy-stripe-clad young ladies at the door.

He hadn't intended to scare them, but he was a bit rattled. He'd been expecting angels with harps or possibly imps with pitchforks. But giggling candy canes with sponges…nay. Not on his list of possible afterlife scenarios.

"Kindly tell me where I am," he commanded ill-temperedly. He didn't like surprises. Not one bit.

"W-why, the Old Fort Mystic Medical Center, Mr. Tyler. Is there a p-problem?" she stammered.

Old Fort Mystic— Impossible. That was the big city near Magnolia Cove. Not heaven or hell.

And why did she keep calling him Mr. Tyler?

"Why am I here?" he demanded in confusion, releasing her.

"The fire, Mr. Tyler. Don't you remember? You were stabbed." She pointed to the bandage on his belly.

He ground his jaw. Of course he remembered. Grotesque images had danced in his mind like a macabre light show behind his every waking thought. The fire, finding Clara, the helpless agony of holding her in his arms as she died. He would never forget those ghastly, horrific minutes as long as he—

Sweet Jesus!

"God's Bones," he breathed, "I'm alive!"

The girl with the sponge let out a soft chuckle and looked at him with sympathetic amusement. "As you see, Mr. Tyler, you are very much alive and kicking. Now, about your sponge bath…"

He didn't know whether to laugh hysterically or find a knife and finish the job Peel had started.

"Nay," he choked out, warding her off. "No bath." He slapped a hand over his eyes so she wouldn't see the sudden despair in them.

He was alive.

And Clara was dead.

His worst nightmare had come to pass. She had sacrificed her life for him, putting herself in the path of a bullet that would have sailed right through his ghostly body with no ill effect.

Ah, Clara, Clara! Why did she do it?

As Sully promised, the curse had been lifted; miraculously, he'd been granted a new chance at a real life.

But now he had no reason to live.

"We'll let you rest, then, Mr. Tyler," the girl said, and quietly gathered her bowl and sponge.

He couldn't bear to ask about Clara's funeral, but when she reached the door, he pulled himself together enough to ask, "Mrs. Yates, the old lady at the fire. Is she all right?"

"She's good," the girl said, turning. "Released yesterday. Oh, and your Miss Fergussen, she'll be fine, too."

For a second he couldn't breathe.

"Miss Fergussen?" Paralyzed, he stared at the girl. "Clara…she's alive?" he burst out.

The girl nodded, smiling. "Inspector Santee said you'd be asking about her." She turned out the light and said, "Get some rest now."

But Tyree barely heard her.

Clara was alive! *Alive!*

Insensible to the pain that gouged his midsection, he leapt out of bed. Or tried to leap. It ended up more like a desperate crawl. Which resulted in a hopeless tangle of wires and tubes that held him prisoner to a bank of beeping devices, a tall pole and bag of liquid.

He ripped off the taped wires and yanked the plastic tube from his forearm. Oblivious to the resulting bloody runnel on his arm, he lurched to the door, grabbing at the pole for support and dragging it along with him as a wheeled walking stick. Once outside his room, he spotted the sponge girl at a circular desk along with a group of nurses.

"Where is she?" he croaked, absurdly light-headed, panting with the simple effort of standing. His lungs stung from dragging in air; his eyes smarted from the bright lights. Smells assaulted him from every direction. *But he had to get to her.* "Clara, tell me where she is!"

"Mr. Tyler! You need to get back to—"

"Tell me or I'll look through every damned room in this whole place!" he boomed.

For a second, there was absolute silence. Then the girl indicated the hall to his left. "Four twenty-one. Right down the—"

He didn't wait for her to finish, but staggered down the corridor as fast as he could hobble, snarling at anyone who got in the way. Nothing was going to keep him from reaching Clara.

He was seeing spots by the time he found room 421. Somehow, his free hand found the door lever and jerked it down. With his last ounce of strength he pushed, and the door opened wide.

There, lying on the bed, was the most beautiful sight in the world.

"Clara," he sighed, his heart taking wing. "Sweeting, I'm here."

Clara looked up at the commotion at her door. "What's go—"

And all at once, time stood still.

She gazed at the man standing in the doorway and couldn't believe her eyes. Was she dreaming again? Or had she wished so hard she'd conjured up Tyree's beloved image even while awake?

She swallowed, not wanting to speak, not wanting to move, in case he vanished.

"Clara, it's me," he said, his voice weak and raspy. His lips were cracked and trembling.

The rest of him looked terrible, too. His broad chest was livid with a violently purple bruise and his stomach was wrapped in a huge white bandage. Blood oozed down his arm. His feet were bare, and he clung to an IV pole as if he'd fall over in a heap without its tenuous support.

Her heart stalled. "Tyree?" she whispered. "Is it really you?"

A broad smile broke out across his pallid face. "Aye. Back to haunt you."

A laugh escaped her throat. She'd take it. She'd take him any way she could have him. Dead or alive, spirit or Looney Tune. She'd follow him to the ends of the earth or stay at Rose Cottage until the end of her days. Whatever would keep her with him.

Her eyes widened as the doctor marched up and grasped his arm. "Mr. Tyler, I don't know what you think you're doing, but you'd better get horizontal and double-quick!"

"Nay, I—"

Nurses bustled in to do the doctor's bidding.

"Wait!" Clara cried. "Don't take him away. Here." She scooted to the edge of her bed. "Let him stay with me. Please?"

The doctor looked from one to the other and pursed her lips to hide a smile. "Very well. *Five* minutes. But if he pulls out his IV again, there will be serious consequences."

Tyree limped over to the bed and eased in beside her, reaching for her hand. She squeezed it tight as the doctor replaced his IV, felt his forehead and inspected his bandage.

When the others finally left and they were alone, she whispered, "You look terrible. Are you all right?"

He raised her fingers to his lips. "Just don't make me laugh."

She smiled. If he could crack jokes, he was okay. "The doctor, the nurses, they can all see you," she ventured carefully.

"Aye," he said, kissing each knuckle in turn. "That they can."

With each kiss her heart soared higher and higher. "That means…you must be…" Did she dare say it? Did she even dare hope?

He turned his head and met her gaze. The glow of happiness in his eyes told her without words it was true.

"No longer a lost soul," he confirmed softly. "Thanks to you, the curse is lifted."

"But how? I'm still alive."

"I don't quite understand it myself," he said, shaking his head. "When I realized I was really alive I was frantic, knowing what must have happened to you. And yet, here you are." He gave her a long kiss.

She sighed happily. "Thank God."

"It must have been the wording of the curse. 'Until you find a woman *willing* to die in your place.' Willing to die. Not actually die. I'd never thought about the distinction before." He glanced at her patched-up shoulder and a frown darkened his joyful expression. "But what *possessed* you to step in front of that gun?"

She smiled weakly. "I couldn't help it. I love you."

Tenderly, he reached over and put his arms around her. "Oh, Clara. I love you, too, sweeting. More than you'll ever know. But if you ever put yourself in danger like that again, I'll…I'll…"

"Make me walk the plank?"

He chuckled and brushed his lips over hers. "I'd like to think I could get a little more creative than that."

She snuggled in a little closer, mindful of his injury. "In that case, no promises."

"I knew you were a troublemaker the first time I saw you."

"You ain't seen nothin' yet."

"Bring it on, darlin'." He tipped her chin up with his fingers. "Everything you've got. I want it all."

Her heart filled with joy. "Good. Because I like it in Magnolia Cove. I think I'll stay for a while."

"What about your trip around the world?"

"I've decided not to enter the contest. There's more adventure than I can handle right here with you."

"Hmm," he said, giving her a lazy smile. "That's unfortunate. Because I'm leaving."

Her pulse stalled. "You're what?"

"That's right, I'm booking a berth on that yacht trip."

She gaped at him. "You are?"

"Aye. You know I've wanted to go sailing for a long, long time." He winked. "Besides, I thought you'd need me to hold you up. Remember?"

She remembered. And there was nothing she'd like better. "I can't believe you'd do this for me."

"You've given me back my life, Clara. In so many ways. Write your article. Win the contest. We'll sail away together."

"You really want to?"

"Try and stop me. From now on, there'll be no more talk of pirates or spirits or curses, and most of all no more hiding away from life."

She didn't think it was possible to be so happy. Well, except for one small detail. She sent him a moue. "No more pirates?"

He tilted his head and sent her a roguish grin. "I suppose we could strike a bargain on that point."

"Oh no, you don't." She shook her head in warm anticipation. "I know all about your bargains."

"What can I say." He waggled his eyebrows. "I am a pirate."

"Has anyone ever told you you're—"

He held up a hand. "I know, I know. Impossible, unbelievable, incorrigible, unmanageable, obnoxious… Have I left anything out?"

She touched his cheek with a fingertip, tracing over every dear part of his face. "Well, I was thinking more along the lines of wonderful, handsome, intelligent, sexy…"

"Mmm," he purred low in his throat like a contented lion, "Those are much better." He kissed her, long and tender, just the way she liked. "But I'd like to add one more to the list."

"And what would that be?"

He kissed her again and looked deep into her eyes. "Married."

She blinked and her lips parted in surprise. "Married?"

"If you'll have me, Clara my love. Could you find it in your heart to marry a crazy pirate, if he promises to reform?"

Joy exploded through her. "Oh, Tyree! Being Mrs. Tyree St. James would be the very best adventure of all."

A flicker of consternation flashed over his face. "Ah. Unfortunately, there might just be one tiny problem with that."

Her heart stalled. "Oh?" She held her breath.

"The part about being Mrs. Tyree St. James. All my current papers—driver's license, passport, everything—says my name is James Tyler. I'm afraid you'll have to be Mrs. James Tyler."

With a relieved whoosh of air from her lungs, she pretended to consider. "Well, it's not nearly as romantic as Tyree St. James. But I suppose if I have no choice…"

"I'll change it back," he said. "It'll just take a month or two."

"Not necessary," she quickly said. She didn't want to wait a month. She didn't want to wait a minute.

"I also should mention, much of my fortune is gone. I gave it away, thinking I would no longer need it."

As if that mattered. "You know I don't care about your money, Tyree. It's *you* I love. Even poor as a church mouse and called James Tyler."

"In that case, will you marry me, Clara? Will you be my wife?"

"Yes, oh, yes I'll marry you. Of course I'll marry you!"

He gave her another slow, thorough kiss to seal the bargain.

"Strange how things work out," he murmured. "I thought

Sully's curse was the worst thing ever to befall a man. But instead it has ended up giving me the greatest gift a man could receive—a bright future with the love of my heart."

"Oh, Tyree. I do love you," she whispered, knowing there was not a chance she'd ever, ever let this wonderful, amazing man go.

"I love you, too, sweeting. With all my heart."

Not a ghost of a chance.

* * * * *

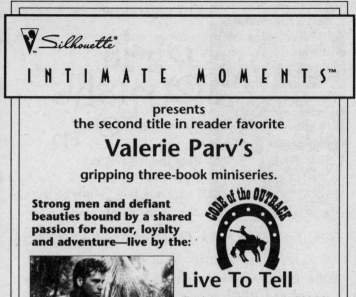

If you enjoyed what you just read,
then we've got an offer you can't resist!

Take 2 bestselling love stories FREE!
Plus get a FREE surprise gift!

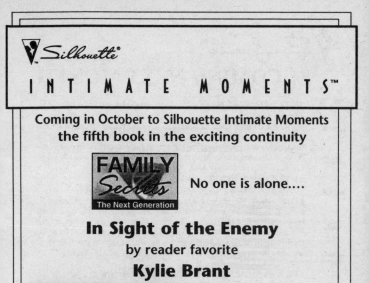

COMING NEXT MONTH

#1321 NOTHING TO LOSE—RaeAnne Thayne
The Searchers

Taylor Bradshaw was determined to save her brother from death row. Bestselling author Wyatt McKinnon intended only to write about the case, but ended up joining Taylor's fight for justice. As time ticked down their mutual attraction rose, and with everything already on the line, they had nothing to lose....

#1322 LIVE TO TELL—Valerie Parv
Code of the Outback

Blake Stirton recognized a city girl when he saw one, but leaving Jo Francis stranded in the bush wasn't an option. She had information he needed to find his family's diamond mine before a greedy neighbor foreclosed on their ranch. When his feelings for her distract him, it puts them both in danger. And the explosive secrets they uncover as they work together up the stakes—for their relationship…and his family's fortune—exponentially.

#1323 IN SIGHT OF THE ENEMY—Kylie Brant
Family Secrets: The Next Generation

Cassie Donovan's ability to forecast the future had driven a wedge into her relationship with Shane Farhold, until, finally, his skepticism had torn them apart. But when a madman saw her ability as a gift worth killing for, Shane took her and their unborn child on the run. And not even Cassie could predict when the danger would end....

#1324 HER MAN TO REMEMBER—Suzanne McMinn
Roman Bradshaw thought his wife was dead—until he found her again eighteen months later. But Leah didn't remember him—or the divorce papers she'd been carrying the night of her accident. Now Roman has a chance to seduce her all over again. But could he win her love a second time before the past caught up with them?

#1325 RACING AGAINST THE CLOCK—Lori Wilde
Scientist Hannah Zachary was on the brink of a breakthrough that dangerous men would kill to possess. After an escape from certain death sent her to the hospital, she felt an instant connection to her sexy surgeon, Dr. Tyler Fresno. But with a madman stalking her, how could she ask Tyler to risk his life—and heart—for her?

#1326 SAFE PASSAGE—Loreth Anne White
Agent Scott Armstrong was used to hunting enemies of the state, not warding off imaginary threats to beautiful, enigmatic scientists like Dr. Skye Van Rijn. Then a terrorist turned his safe mission into a deadly battle to keep her out of the wrong hands. Would Skye's secrets jeopardize not only their feelings for each other but their lives, as well?

"You never cease to amaze me."

Elizabeth sighed happily. "Imagine driving all the way into New York just to have lunch. Anyone would think this was a special occasion."

But it is a special occasion, Nick thought nervously now that they were back out on the street. He leaned forward to look for a carriage. *This is probably the second most special occasion in my life, with the first yet to come.*

"Once around the park, please," he told the driver when they were finally settled.

"You know, Nick," Elizabeth said, feeling like royalty, "you're spoiling me, darling, and I love you for it!"

"It's easy to spoil you, Elizabeth," he assured her, checking his suit pocket for the tenth time just to see if the package was still there. He sat back abruptly, fumbling in his pockets. "Damn, I must have dropped it."

"Dropped what?" Elizabeth asked as if on cue, already leaning forward to search the floor area of the cab. "I don't see anything—oh, heavens, what's this?"

She sat up slowly, holding the small square box gingerly with both hands, eyeing it warily as if it were alive.

This was it; this was the moment he had been waiting for, working toward, plotting out so meticulously....

KASEY MICHAELS is the *New York Times* and *USA TODAY* bestselling author of more than sixty books. She has won the Romance Writers of America RITA® Award and the *Romantic Times* Career Achievement Award for her historical romances set in the Regency era, and also writes contemporary romances for Silhouette and Harlequin Books.